"Reed, there is something I need to talk to you about…"

He smiled. "I hope it's an answer to my asking you for a date."

"Well…"

"Because in case you haven't noticed, I kinda, sorta like you, Camryn. I'm finding myself thinking about you an awful lot." He reached for her hand and stepped closer. "I've especially been thinking about that kiss, and when I saw you just now, I had a strong urge to see if it was as great as I remember."

She smiled. "Are you asking for permission…?"

"No, ma'am." He moved his hands to cup her face and threaded his fingers into her hair. "I'm just giving you fair warning that I'm determined to find out."

His face lowered. She blinked an instant before his lips settled on hers. And then she let her eyelids flutter closed and her mouth melt into his.

Dear Reader,

Starting over can be a scary time in anyone's life. And it can also be exhilarating, full of possibilities. I should know. After forty years in south Florida, I am moving all the way to north-central Florida! Not a big deal, you say? It is for me. I'm a widow. I live with my adorable pup, Willie, and together we are moving into a fifty-five-plus community.

I feel a special kinship with the twin who stars in the first book of my latest trilogy, *Baby Makes Four*. Camryn is recently divorced, a single mom and coping with major disappointments in her life. But she makes a move from the city to a small farm near the coast of South Carolina. She leaves behind her family and her sister, who is her best friend, and begins a new adventure.

Thanks to a few stalls she has in her barn, and a stray dog who shows up on her porch, Camryn meets her new neighbor, a vet who is embarking on his start-over, as well. I hope you enjoy the journeys these characters make to find peace, family togetherness and love.

Look for the other twin's story next.

Cynthia Thomason

cynthoma@aol.com

HEARTWARMING

Baby Makes Four

—

Cynthia Thomason

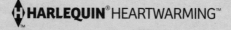

Recycling programs
for this product may
not exist in your area.

ISBN-13: 978-1-335-51069-3

Baby Makes Four

Printed in U.S.A.

Cynthia Thomason inherited her love of writing from her ancestors. Her father and grandmother both loved to write, and she aspired to continue the legacy. Cynthia studied English and journalism in college, and after a career as a high school English teacher, she began writing novels. She discovered ideas for stories while searching through antiques stores and flea markets and as an auctioneer and estate buyer. Cynthia says every cast-off item from someone's life can ignite the idea for a plot. She writes about small towns, big hearts and happy endings that are earned and not taken for granted. And as far as the legacy is concerned, just ask her son, the magazine journalist, if he believes. Please contact Cynthia at cynthoma@aol.com and cynthiathomason.net.

Books by Cynthia Thomason

Harlequin Heartwarming

The Cahills of North Carolina

High Country Christmas
Dad in Training
High Country Cop

The Daughters of Dancing Falls

Rescued by Mr. Wrong
The Bridesmaid Wore Sneakers
A Boy to Remember

Firefly Nights
This Hero for Hire
A Soldier's Promise
Blue Ridge Autumn
Marriage for Keeps
Dilemma at Bayberry Cove

Visit the Author Profile page
at Harlequin.com for more titles.

This book is dedicated to all those who have experienced start-overs, especially my strong and inspired stepdaughter, Lisa Beaumont. I hope I do half as well as you have, darling.

CHAPTER ONE

SALTY'S FEED AND GRAIN was busier than usual this Monday morning. Trucks were lined up against the loading dock. Camryn recognized about half the drivers. Not bad considering she'd only lived in the area for two months. Bufflehead Creek, South Carolina, was filled with friendly people, cotton fields and lots of animals.

Camryn found a narrow spot and backed her truck into the space. She stepped out of the cab and marveled again at the wonder of a beautiful day. October was a prime month in the low country. Warm days, cool nights, promising harvests and hopefully no more hurricanes like the Category 1 storm that had blown through two weeks ago.

Becky Johnson, one of the feedstore's friendliest clerks, came to the edge of the dock. "Hey, Cam. How are you? Nice day, isn't it?"

"Sure is."

"I've got your order right here. Let me finish up with this other customer, and I'll get to you in a minute."

"No hurry," Camryn said. "I'm not in a rush. Still got a few more errands to run in town, including delivering one hundred copies of *Alphabet Days* to the elementary school."

"One hundred?" Becky said. "That's more than your publishing company has ever sent. Enough for all first and second graders, I'd say."

It was true. Camryn had worked a deal with Southern Square Press, publisher of elementary school magazines for Charleston schools. She'd been designing the covers for the magazines for several years, and had gotten the idea to have extra copies sent to her in Bufflehead Creek in exchange for giving up a small raise in pay. Well worth it, she thought. Just because Baycomb County didn't have as much money to spend on activity books as Charleston schools, it didn't mean local schools shouldn't introduce their kids to the wonder of words.

"Can I see a copy?" Becky asked.

"Sure." Cam went to her truck and pulled

half a dozen issues from the cab. "This month's title is *Ollie the October Owl*," she said. "Give them away to kids that come in the store."

Becky scanned the cover quickly. "That's adorable, Cam. I wish I could draw like that."

"I get quite a bit of help from a computer program," Camryn said. "But this job does feed my creative spirit and keeps Esther's Barbie doll in the latest fashions."

"How is your daughter? Is she still happy at the grade school?"

"She's making friends," Cam said. "That was my biggest worry after leaving Charleston."

Checking off a supply list on her clipboard, Becky asked, "And how are you feeling?"

"Great," Camryn said.

Becky was the only person in town who knew about Camryn's pregnancy and the only one besides Camryn's family and the baby's father. Cam had just about reached the first trimester mark, and maybe she could relax a bit. Though after two miscarriages in recent years, she didn't think she'd be fully free of anxiety until she was holding a healthy baby in her arms. But buying a small farm and moving to Bufflehead Creek had been a step in the right direction.

She leaned against the hood of her truck, feeling the warmth of the engine seep into her back. She almost felt like moaning with pleasure, but figured she'd get odd looks from the farmers and ranchers around her. The 2003 Ford truck was another good investment she'd made recently. She and her daughter, Esther, had named the truck Energizer Bunny, which seemed to suit its personality and coordinated well with the sign on the front of her property, Cottontail Farm.

"Okay, darlin', I'm ready," Becky called out to her. Becky was only about ten years older than Camryn's thirty-two years, but she had such a store of down-home sentiments that Cam had gotten used to being called "darlin'," "sweet pea" and "sugar bear."

"Your order's right here," Becky added. "I'll load it up for you."

"I can help," Camryn said.

"No way," Becky insisted. She lowered her voice, respecting Cam's privacy. "After four kids I remember what I could and couldn't do when I was in your condition. And we're not taking any chances with that precious little bean growing inside you."

Becky called out the sacks as she dropped them in the truck bed. "Ten pounds of chicken feed, twenty pounds of goat pellets and ten pounds of kibble for Rooster."

An image of her lumbering forty-pound mutt popped into Camryn's head. The dripping wet dog had shown up at her house one rainy night, and after an exhaustive search to find his owner, Cam and Esther had just decided to keep him. When he started chasing the chickens around the barnyard, Camryn had joked, "He must think he's a rooster and he needs a girlfriend," she'd said.

Giggling like a typical nine-year-old, Esther had firmly declared that Rooster would be the dog's name. Unfortunately for Rooster, he had to learn right away that chicken hunting was not an acceptable practice at Cottontail Farm. Not when the owner made part of her living selling free-range eggs. But Rooster learned quickly and gave up pestering the chickens for a cozy spot in the house.

Once she was loaded, Camryn drove her truck around to the front of the feedstore where she would pay her bill. Becky met her at the cash register. "Are you using a card, honey?" she asked.

Camryn longed for the day she could pay everything by cash, but operating a small farm did not lend itself to a cash budget right now. She slipped her credit card into the reader and waited for her receipt. Good thing Mark had sent Esther's child support payment on time.

"Have you met your new neighbor?" Becky suddenly asked her.

Taken aback a moment, Camryn said, "Do you mean the Boldens? I sold them ten of my hundred acres a month ago. Did you forget?"

"I don't mean the elder Boldens. I mean their son."

"Their son? What are you talking about?"

"Haven't you seen activity on that parcel? The son—Reed's his name—is having a modular home built. There should have been trucks coming onto the property."

Yes, of course Camryn had seen the commotion. And heard it. Hammers pounding, saws screeching. She'd just figured the Boldens had decided to give up their luxury motor home life and build a more permanent structure. But she'd been so busy she hadn't even gone over to see what was going on. "I had no idea their son was building there. It's awfully close to my property line."

When she'd sold ten acres of her land to the Boldens, she'd needed the fifteen thousand dollars to make improvements on her farm and to set up a nursery for the baby. She hadn't put any stipulations on the sale that would have prevented the Boldens from selling part of their purchase or even giving it away. She wondered now what she had gotten herself into. What if this new neighbor didn't like the sounds of chickens clucking and a dog barking?

Then he shouldn't have moved to South Carolina, she thought with a smile.

"I wouldn't worry about how close the man's house is to yours," Becky said. "He's only been in the area about a week and obviously you haven't seen him."

No, she hadn't. In fact, Camryn hadn't even come to town in the last seven days. Her routine was now the new normal in her life. Up at six to feed the chickens. Fix breakfast for Esther, braid her hair and make sure she was ready for the school bus when it stopped in front of the house. The rest of her day was spent working on graphic designs for Southern Square Press and on planting and fertilizing the organic gardens that added a bit of income when she sold the healthy produce.

Right now, aside from her regular paycheck from Southern Square, most of Camryn's money came from eggs and what she sold at the Saturday farmers market in Bufflehead Creek. But as soon as she persuaded a few leading hotels in Beaufort and Charleston to buy vegetables from her regularly, the money squeeze would ease up.

Becky fanned her face. "Let me tell you, Cam, if I wasn't married, I'd set my sights on that fella."

"Who?" Camryn asked, bringing her mind back from her money situation.

"Reed Bolden," Becky said. "I was just talking about him."

Camryn laughed. "Sure you'd set your sights on another man, Beck. I can just see you leaving Judd for the latest man du jour."

Becky sucked in a quick breath and adjusted her posture. "Don't look now, sweetie, but Mr. Hunkystuff just walked in."

Camryn switched her attention to the door of the feedstore, where a tall man in a cowboy hat seemed to fill the entrance. Rugged-looking in jeans and boots, he appeared to belong in the country, as if he was born to it, actually. Not like Camryn, who'd been raised in classic comfort in historic downtown Charleston.

"Hi, there, Reed," Becky called. "Come on over here, hon, and meet your new neighbor."

Camryn felt her face flush—the same face that probably still had hay stuck to a cheek and smudges of dirt everywhere else. "Becky, what are you doing?"

"No time like the present." Becky's smile was a mile wide.

The new neighbor ambled over. The closer he got, the more Camryn realized he wasn't all country. His hat didn't have any of the customary sweat stains on the brim. His skin showed signs of a new, and probably painful, sunburn, different from the "farmer's tans" so many of the guys around Bufflehead sported. When he took his hat off and brushed hair off his forehead, Cam noticed a neat style and no oily strands. Obviously, this guy put grooming at the top of his list of priorities. When he settled the hat back on his brow, he returned to Mr. Meltaway Country Cool.

"Reed, this is Camryn Montgomery," Becky said. "She's the gal who sold the property to your parents."

Reed extended his hand. His fingers were surprisingly clean. Cam felt like hiding her own hand behind her back. "Hi. Nice to meet you," she said.

"I've been meaning to drop by and introduce myself to you," he said. "That piece of property you sold my parents is great. They're letting me settle on five acres of it."

"Look at this," Becky said, handing him the latest issue of *Alphabet Days*. "Camryn designed this cover. Isn't it cute?"

Camryn wanted to find a counter to crawl behind. But her new neighbor handled the obvious flattery with grace. "Yeah, very cute. Who doesn't like an owl?" he said.

Becky handed him two copies of the magazine. "Give these to your boys, compliments of Camryn."

He smiled. "Thanks. I'll do that."

After an awkward moment of silence, Camryn said, "I saw building materials being unloaded a couple of days ago. Becky tells me you're building a house?"

"Just a modular for now. Need a place for myself and my two sons. If everything works out, I'll think about a bigger structure down the line."

"Sounds like you're here to stay," Camryn said.

"Hope so. Trying to get a few details straightened out so I can move my family out of my parents' motor home. It's a big RV, but space is still tight."

His family… Becky hadn't mentioned a wife. Maybe that little detail had stayed off Becky's radar. Oh, well, Cam was just recently divorced. The last thing she needed was another man, another complication in her life. She had enough going on just managing her farm.

Becky handed Camryn her receipt. "You're all set, darlin'. What can I do for you, Reed?"

"I'm hoping that colic medicine I ordered

is in," he said. "My horse and pony should be here soon, and I don't want to be without emergency medications."

Cam should have moved on, but she stayed near the cash register to hear as much of the conversation as she could. After all, this man only lived a short distance from her, and she'd no doubt be running into him.

"Got it right here," Becky said, producing a package from under the counter. "You use our address as long as you need to, hon. Happy to oblige."

He took the package and leaned toward Becky. "Thanks, Becky. Maybe you can help me with something else."

"Sure, I'll try."

"It'll probably be a few months before my paddock and barn are constructed."

Paddock and barn? This man was building more than a house and keeping horses on his property? Camryn appreciated her solitude and didn't know how she'd feel about so much activity next to her property.

"I need a home for my horses in the meantime," Reed said. "They're ready to be hauled up from Atlanta as soon as I say the word. I'd

like to find a place close to where I'm building the house, if possible."

Cam started to walk away. She sensed
Becky's enthusiasm aimed directly at her,
and she didn't want Becky getting any ideas.
Oh, well. Too late.

"Hold on, Cam. You've got an old barn
and fenced area just sitting empty, don't
you?"

Ah, yes, she did. When she'd bought her
real estate, the land had come with a small
farmhouse and a few outbuildings. None of
the structures were fancy, but they were definitely serviceable.

"This is truly an act of fate," Becky said.
"If Camryn agrees, you can lease her barn.
Heck, you can walk over there in just a few
minutes."

"I don't know anything about taking care
of horses," Camryn said. "My livestock is
limited to chickens and a couple of goats."

"You wouldn't have to do a thing," Reed
said. "I'd come over every day to feed, clean
and exercise my animals. All I really need
is a place to keep them out of the elements.
I'll pay you rent, of course."

No doubt she could use the money. But

did she really want this man coming over on a regular basis? Camryn was establishing a comfortable, worry-free zone for herself and Esther. Her main priority was ensuring an anxiety-free pregnancy for herself, delivering a healthy baby, keeping Esther safe and working to expand her organic gardens and hen farm. Did she need strangers coming on the land whenever they wanted to?

"I don't know, Mr. Bol—"

"Reed," he said.

"I don't know, Reed. I'm planting organic vegetables. I'm also allowing my chickens to run range free. I couldn't risk having horses trample over any of the land right now."

"They wouldn't," he said. "If you've got a fenced area, I'll take them there for outside time. And I can ride them on my property. They shouldn't interfere with what you're doing." He smiled. "Are you married, Camryn?" he asked.

"Ah, no. What does that have to do with anything?"

"Just curious," he said. "I'd be happy to lend you a hand from time to time."

Camryn wasn't used to asking for help she didn't pay for. Was this man suggesting that he had handyman skills he could offer for a price?

"I don't need help," she said. "I can do pretty much everything on my own."

"That must make things simpler. I was just offering. I'll need to come over and check out the barn of course," Reed said, "but assuming it meets my needs, how does four hundred a month sound? I'll supply whatever my horses need, so there wouldn't be any expense for you."

Four hundred a month sounded like manna from heaven. "I should be home in a couple of hours," she said. "Come on over if you like." Good grief, she'd just practically committed to this deal. And an ongoing relationship with this man's family, however many there were!

"Great. I'll see you later." He tucked the package of medicine in his pocket and left the store.

"What did I just get myself into?" Camryn said to Becky. "For all I know, this guy has a wife and several kids, and all of them might soon be swarming over my new cultivation."

"In the first place," Becky said, "he's only got two kids. And no wife. As far as I'm concerned, that's the best news." She grinned at Camryn. "Really, darlin', you should try to keep up with neighborhood gossip. You never know when opportunity is going to come knockin'."

Camryn thought about Becky's words as she drove to the elementary school. She hoped Reed Bolden hadn't noticed how not-a-bit-subtle Becky had been. "Look at Camryn's drawing… Camryn has a barn…" Good grief, Becky had done everything but said, "Camryn is a lonely divorcée who could appreciate a neighbor like you, Reed." Wasn't true. Camryn wasn't lonely. She was actually happier than she'd been in a long time. Well, maybe not happy, but definitely content. And who would argue with content?

FEELING SOMEWHAT OPTIMISTIC about his chance meeting with his neighbor a few minutes ago, Reed headed out to the highway, where he would find the stores he needed to fill his mother's shopping list. Especially since he and his boys were currently living in her motor home, he hadn't the heart to deny his parents any reasonable request, including running errands. So he checked the list on the passenger seat of his SUV.

Bed Bath & Beyond for a copper griddle. Walgreens to pick up a prescription. And the supermarket for all the items that would keep his mom and four males sufficiently fed for a couple more days until the modular home was finished. Then, Reed reasoned, he'd have to learn to cook in a minimalist kitchen far different from the gourmet one he'd enjoyed in Georgia—not that he'd ever used it much.

In Atlanta he and his ex-wife had had a Sub-Zero double door monstrosity of a re-frigerator. The unit in the modular was going to be eighteen cubic feet. Reed stepped on the accelerator and let the powerful engine in his Escalade chew up the miles. As long as the fridge had room for all the snacks his sons liked and a couple of beers for himself, he'd survive.

With any luck the horse problem would be solved by this afternoon. Camryn Mont-gomery seemed like a nice lady, willing to help a newcomer to South Carolina in need. She had "good neighbor" written all over her, and his mother had said only positive things about her. He'd have to make her barn work for his horses. Come hell or high water, those four-legged beasts would be here soon.

Finished with his errands, he swung by the elementary school and got in line to wait for dismissal time. He figured he might as well pick up his sons and save the bus driver the headache of having to deal with the Bolden boys.

He knew his sons had problems with discipline, and he supposed it was as much his fault as it was his ex's, but he didn't like to think it was. Being too busy supporting a family to be a superdad was better than being a neglectful mother, right? Anyway, he was definitely going to up his daddy game here in Bufflehead Creek. Maybe soon someone in authority might refer to the Bolden boys with something other than cringing disdain.

When he saw his sons exit the school, Reed got out of his vehicle and hollered. "Over here, boys. Don't get on the bus." Phillip, with an eleven-year-old's bravado, pretended to trip the kid walking next to him. Justin laughed at his big brother's antics.

They were both still laughing when they got in the car. "Why are you picking us up, Dad?" Phillip asked.

"We're going somewhere this afternoon," he said. "After I drop off the groceries at Gran's, we're going to see our closest neighbor."

"I don't want to go," Justin said. "I'll stay with Gran."

Totally bad idea. "No, you won't." Reed knew his mother loved the boys and she tried to bond with them. Truly she did. But it was only a matter of time before she called out to her son, "Reed, get in here and talk to these boys!"

"Why can't I?" Justin asked.

Short of admitting that his youngest was about to drive his Gran crazy, Reed said, "You need some time outside without video games. When we get where we're going, you can run around, let off some steam."

"What does that mean?" the nine-year-old asked. "It's not even hot today."

Reed smiled. "It's an expression. I'll let

you know when I see steam coming out of your ears."

"What?"

Of his two sons, Justin took everything literally, which made teasing him so easy.

Reed pulled into the manicured drive that led to his parents' elegant black-and-tan motor home. His father had done some landscaping to the spot, but kept the low country oak trees lining the drive. Maybe not quite as impressive as the two-story, three-thousand-square-foot home his parents had owned in upstate New York, but it looked darn nice anyway.

And his parents never stopped bragging about their decision to minimize responsibility and live the life of wanderers of the open road. True campers. Right. How many motor homes had dishwashers and washing machines and dryers? All in all, Reed was happy for his mom and dad. They had raised two kids, helped put him and his sister, Penelope, through college, and they deserved a posh, carefree lifestyle if they wanted it.

"All right, boys," Reed said to his sons. "Let's get these packages inside for Gran, and we'll head over to our neighbor's place."

Justin made one last attempt to stay in the motor home instead of going "somewhere so boring," but one glance from his mother told Reed she wasn't up for the idea. "It's not a good time, Justin," Bertie Bolden said. "Your grandfather and I are just settling down to watch our shows."

The prospect of spending an hour with the cooking channel convinced Justin that he was better off with his father. So away they went, the three Bolden men, on a quest to find a barn.

Reed stopped outside a simple wrought iron gate with a bunny medallion in the center of the swinging arms. The words "Cottontail Farm" made him smile. The woman he'd met this morning seemed like just the type to pick a quaint, cutesy name like Cottontail for her patch of paradise.

He soon realized that paradise wasn't really an apt description. The split-rail fencing around the front of the property looked new, and the porch itself appeared to have been freshly painted a gleaming white. However, the rest of the modest structure seemed to have suffered years of low country perils, salt water breezes and high humidity. The clapboard siding had faded to a sickly gray.

But the twin front windows were large and airy, and the gray metal roof provided adequate protection from the sun and rain. A screened-in side porch gave the small house a homey look, and a single dormer window indicated the dwelling at least had an attic.

Camryn came out of the house to meet him. She was followed by a medium-size, unpedigreed, shaggy dog with a friendly face, though Reed had never met a dog he didn't like. When the dog saw him, his ears perked up, and a low growl came from his throat. Camryn put her hand in front of the dog's face and said, "No." After that, the animal was content to sniff Reed's pant legs.

As for Camryn, she looked different yet the same—natural and unadorned. But gone was the sweatshirt she'd had on at Salty's, replaced by a solid yellow T-shirt tucked into well-fitting jeans. Her face was clean, and her hair, which had been stuffed into a careless bun this morning, was now gathered into a neat blond ponytail. In short,

Camryn Montgomery looked darned good considering his first impression of her was only that she would be a good neighbor.

CHAPTER TWO

CAMRYN FELT SLIGHTLY RIDICULOUS. Short of showering and applying a full application of makeup, she'd at least changed clothes and primped a bit for the arrival of Reed Bolden. So why did she feel ridiculous? Because she had no intention of flirting with Reed or any man so soon after her divorce, and she hadn't worn makeup since leaving Charleston. Also, when she'd met her daughter at the bus drop at the end of her drive, Esther had looked at her and said, "You look pretty, Mom. Are we going somewhere?"

She "looked pretty" in jeans and a T-shirt? What did that say about the way she normally looked when she met Essie at the bus drop? She supposed she could blame her twin sister, Brooke, for the fussing—though minimal— she'd done today. Her sister's motto: "It's not *just the grocery store*. At least apply blush and mascara."

"No, we're not going anywhere," she'd

said to her daughter. "But someone might stop by to see about renting our barn."

Unimpressed, Esther had simply mumbled, "Oh," and chased Rooster up the drive to the house. Now Reed had arrived, and Camryn wasn't at all sure how she felt about him showing up. Did she want to rent him barn space or not? Did she want him having access to her land whenever he wanted it, or did she not? Did she need the money? An extra four hundred a month would be nice.

Camryn had only been divorced two months. But her marriage had been over for more than three years, starting when Mark had begun staying out late and "forgetting" to check in. He'd been unhappy with her, feeling she hadn't jumped into the role of the power broker wife that he'd wanted her to play, and hadn't done a good job of hiding his disappointment. And Camryn had suffered increased panic attacks whenever she tried to fulfill the role. Camryn had never been comfortable in social situations that required more charm and smile power than she believed she had, and the greater Mark's expectations became, the more her anxiety level rose.

The day she and Mark decided to call it quits was the day she realized she'd been lonely for a long time. And neglected and unhappy. She attributed her two miscarriages to the pressures of living up to Mark's fast-lane society goals, and she blamed herself for the two failures. No corporate ladder was worth jeopardizing a pregnancy.

Before agreeing that they were over, they'd tried counseling, thinking perhaps a bit more effort might save the marriage. The result was a relationship that still had no hope and a fourth pregnancy, which had become the ultimate priority in Camryn's life. She would change her life by seeking a calmer, saner environment, and she would have a healthy baby. Bufflehead Creek, South Carolina, had so far proved to be the place to accomplish these goals.

Now she was meeting the first man who'd caused any sort of stir in her for years and chastising herself for being juvenile. Becky had said that Reed Bolden wasn't married. But even if he were available, the last thing she needed as she struggled to put her life back together was another demand on her time and damaged emotional resources.

But goodness, he looked fine getting out of his expensive SUV. He'd traded his jacket for a button-down blue denim shirt with the sleeves rolled up to his elbows. The cowboy hat was still in place, partially hiding that medium-brown hair, the color of the Spanish moss dripping from the trees in Camryn's yard.

Two boys scrambled out of the back seat. "Come over here, boys," Reed called. "I want you to meet Miss Montgomery."

The kids looked like they'd rather eat raw snails, but they ambled over anyway. The older one said, "Hi." The younger didn't say anything. Camryn smiled and welcomed them. Reed reminded them that Camryn had been responsible for the two magazines he'd given them. "Miss Montgomery designed the cover," he said. Neither responded, which didn't surprise Camryn. The issue was aimed at younger children. She was appreciative that Esther managed to do the simple dot-to-dots just to please her mother.

"What are we supposed to do?" the one Reed had called Phillip asked.

Reed glanced around the property. Surely he noticed the open areas where Camryn had recently scattered grass seed with hopes of producing a soft carpet of green. If he did, he ignored her future lawn and suggested the boys play tag without warning them to stay off the new growth. "But stay out of trouble," he said. "Don't go near the road."

"And try to stay off the new grass," she called out, not knowing if the boys heard or not.

"Nice place you've got here," Reed said to Camryn. "Looks like a good, fertile patch of land."

"So far it's proving to be. I finally harvested enough to set up at the local farmers market last Saturday and I hope for more produce when the November harvest season sets in."

Looking over her fields, he nodded. "Shall we take a look at the barn?"

"Of course."

"Hey, Mom, is this the man you were waiting for?"

Camryn turned at the sound of Esther's voice. "Yes, honey. I'll just be a minute. You can come or sit on the porch if you want to."

"Cute kid," Reed said. "She your daughter?"

Camryn nodded.

"Mommy, I know those two boys," Esther said after staring at Reed's sons. "They go to my school."

Reed rubbed his jaw. "Oh, that isn't necessarily good news."

"What do you mean by that?" Camryn asked.

"Lately I'm not sure what comment is going to come after your daughter's last one. As long as she isn't in one of their classes, we should be okay."

Finding Reed's comment confusing and strange, Camryn brushed aside her curiosity. "The barn's this way."

They passed the chicken coop where Camryn's three dozen laying hens were currently roaming free in a large screened enclosure. She was proud of the coop, a purchase she'd made on Craigslist. A local handyman had helped her reassemble it on the property. It had come complete with nesting boxes, enough for her entire brood.

"Good-looking hens you've got," Reed said. "Mostly pullets?"

"Yes. Leghorns and Rhode Island Reds. They're the most promising layers, and they're docile. I generally get five eggs a week from each of my girls. But I'm hoping to branch into different varieties."

"If you're interested in egg production, I might be able to help you. I can make suggestions on which hens to purchase. I have a few contacts in animal husbandry."

Camryn glanced up into his eyes, which she couldn't help noticing were the same color as his brown hair. "Really?"

"Yeah. In my other life I was a vet." He smiled. "That sounded weird because actually I still am a vet. I just sold my practice in Bucks County, Georgia, a couple of months ago."

"You sold your practice?" Camryn repeated. So they'd both recently started new lives. She couldn't imagine why any successful veterinarian who lived in upscale Bucks County would make such a decision.

He shrugged. "I'd been at it for over fifteen years. And when it suddenly occurred to me that my boys, growing up without a mother, were turning into miniature nightmares, I decided a change was necessary. Right now I'm concentrating on improving my career as a dad."

His boys didn't have a mother. Camryn wondered what had happened to her.

She led the way into the barn. "Sorry, but you'll have to use sunlight to see. I doubt there has been electricity in here for quite some time."

Reed squinted into the slanted rays of sunlight coming through cracks in the barn's exterior walls. "You wouldn't mind if I hired an electrician to hook it up, would you? Days are getting shorter now, and I'll probably be over here after dark."

"Suit yourself," Camryn said. "I don't have the money to put into it right now." She swatted at a huge cobweb. "And the barn isn't a big priority at this point. The only time I was in here was when I looked at the property with a Realtor." She kicked a few clods of dirt with the toe of her boot. "It's kind of embarrassing how dirty it is."

"That's not a big deal," Reed said. "I can hire a couple of guys to clean it up." He smiled. "And I've got two willing helpers running around your yard right now."

She chuckled, wiping her hand on her jeans. "Willing?"

"That might be an optimistic statement."

She led him to the area where four stalls stood empty. "Do you think these are big enough for your purpose?"

"Sure. I'd say they're twelve by twelve. As long as my horses can use some outside territory once a day, this is fine."

"You can let them loose on the acre behind the barn. I'm not farming there yet. You might have to cut the growth out there."

"No problem. I bought a riding mower." Reed stuck his hand out toward her. "So, do we have a deal? Four hundred a month, and I pay all expenses for my animals?"

"Don't you want to sleep on it at least one night?"

"Don't see what difference that would make. I can have the horses here tomorrow afternoon. You're my closest neighbor. The barn's within walking distance. Stalls are big enough. Our kids go to the same school, which could be a plus if we ever need to carpool. Once I spruce the place up…"

He stopped talking when loud voices came from the yard by the house. Camryn ran out of the barn first. Esther, her fists on her hips, was standing a few yards from the house. "It's not an old lady's name!" she shouted at the boys.

"Is so!" Phillip taunted. "I'll bet you're not a kid at all. You're really a little old lady in a short body."

"Am not!" Esther was trying to hold her own, but her voice started to quiver.

Camryn ran to her daughter's side. Reed hollered at his boys. "Stop teasing her right now."

"She can prove she's not an old lady," Justin said. "She can climb the fence with us and jump off."

"Is that what you kids have been doing?" Camryn said. "Climbing on my new fence?"

"There's nothing else to do," Phillip pointed out.

Esther wrenched free of her mother's arm and ran toward the boys. "I'll show you I'm not an old lady. I'll climb the fence and jump even farther than you did!"

"Old lady, old lady!" Phillip taunted.

Camryn quickly caught up to her daughter. "No one is jumping off the fence again," she said. "Find something to do on solid ground."

"I can do it, Mommy," Esther pleaded.

"They'll tell everyone at school that I'm an old lady."

Reed caught his oldest son by the scruff of his collar. "No, they won't," he said in a voice that should make any kid quake in his shoes. "Tell her you won't, Phillip."

The boy looked up into his father's determined face. "I won't…maybe."

"Go inside the house," Camryn told Esther. "I'll be in as soon as I finish my business with Mr. Bolden."

Esther tugged on Camryn's T-shirt. "But Mommy, I really want to jump off the fence."

Wonderful. Camryn shook her head. *Just what I need*, she thought. *A daughter with a broken leg.* "Go inside now, Esther. We'll talk about this later."

Reed ordered his boys into the SUV and told them to stay there. When the adults were alone, he tried to make light of what had just happened. "I know. They're horrid."

Camryn's mouth dropped open. "That's how you refer to your children…as *horrid*?"

"Well, when you hear it enough…"

She remembered Reed saying he was upping his attempt to be a good father. That goal required some determined training and attitude adjustment on everyone's part. And the first thing he needed to do was to stop thinking of his kids in such negative terms.

"I'll tell them not to come over here," he said.

All at once Camryn felt bad for Reed's sons. "They're children, Reed. Show me a kid who's never teased anyone else. I'm sure they didn't mean any harm."

"Sure. Thanks for understanding, but I have a ways to go to undo years of discipline neglect. Look, it's milk and cookies time for Justin and Phillip. I'll go to the car and get my checkbook, and we'll get out of here. Is two months' rent enough to close the deal?"

Eight hundred dollars! Camryn could order more chickens, some brown egg layers, maybe even some of those Ameraucanas that Esther had been wanting, the ones that laid the blue and pink eggs. "Yes, that will be fine," she said.

He brought her the check and she slipped it into her pocket.

"Pleasure doing business with you, neighbor," Reed said. "I'm sure I'll see you again real soon."

"Thank you." She watched him walk away,

a sturdy, determined swagger to his step. She didn't for a moment think it was put on. Reed Bolden was a man who knew what he wanted and how to get it. Now if he could just control his boys, the goal he said he was working toward, perhaps Esther would make some lasting friends. Maybe.

She was smiling when she went into the house. She had eight hundred dollars and a renter who only intended to stay until his own barn was built. An ideal situation, right?

AT SUPPER ESTHER picked at her food. Camryn had a good idea what was bothering her. "Is there something you would like to talk about, Essie?" she asked.

Esther put down her fork and stared at Camryn. "Why wouldn't you let me jump from the fence? The boys had been doing it. I wanted to show them I could jump as well as they did."

"I'm aware of that, honey, but if I'd seen them, I would have stopped them. First, and most important, the fence is almost four feet high. Jumping from that height could be dangerous. What if you twisted your ankle…or worse?"

Esther took a long swallow of milk as she thought. Obviously she wasn't buying the danger excuse.

"And second," Camryn said, "the fence was only put in two weeks ago. I don't need rowdy children climbing around on it and putting all their weight on the top rail. What if one of the boards had broken?"

Esther set down her glass and gave her mother an earnest glare. "Then the fence wouldn't be any good, and you would have wasted your money anyway."

Sometimes her daughter's powers of observation astounded Camryn. This was one of those times. "The fence is undoubtedly fine," she said. "But what concerns me the most is that you think you need to prove something to Phillip and Justin. You are an amazing, wonderful girl, and you don't have to prove anything to anyone." She almost added, *especially two chest-thumping, taunting boys*.

Camryn looked away from her daughter for a moment as memories flooded her mind. She wished she had learned that lesson before she'd married Mark and spent a good part of her life trying to live up to his expectations. But Mark had been the golden boy her parents had always wanted for her. Unfortunately the value of gold was not the same to different people.

"The world is changing every day, Essie," she said. "Girls and boys are equal in almost every category." She smiled. "You're a smart girl. Smart enough to know not to jump off a fence."

Esther didn't look convinced. Her bottom lip trembled in a pout. "But they called me an old lady and said I had an old lady's name."

"Those are just words, Es. They don't mean anything. A name is just a name. I've told you before that yours is a very special name. It was my grandmother's, your great-grandmother's. Esther May Bergeron was the kindest, most intelligent, most loving woman I have ever known. When I gave you her name, I believed I was giving you a gift."

Though her grandmother had been gone for more than five years, Camryn still thought about her and missed her every day. It didn't matter that Esther May wasn't a blood relative. Camryn and her twin sister had learned early on that they had been adopted. The Montgomerys were the best parents any two girls could hope for. And the Bergeron side of the family, Camryn's adopted mother's side, had produced the best grandmother.

"I know," Esther drawled. She moved food around on her plate. "I just thought I might be friends with those boys."

"And maybe you will," Camryn said. "You'll no doubt see them at school and here on our farm. But I guarantee you won't be happy with a friendship based on who jumps the highest from our new fence."

Esther took a bite of her macaroni and cheese and mumbled some words Camryn only thought she heard correctly. "What did you say?"

"Nothing."

"Oh, no. You said something. I think it was about Auntie Brooke."

Esther had never been very good at back-pedaling. Honesty was her strong point. She was too much like her auntie Brooke to play coy. So she stared at her mother and said, "I just was thinking that Auntie Brooke would have let me jump off the fence."

No doubt about it. Brooke would have insisted that Esther go over to the fence, shove the boys out of the way and show them how fence jumping was done by a true South Carolina girl. Camryn had always been a bit envious of Brooke's spunk. There was no challenge too great, no goal unattainable, no date with a handsome guy that couldn't be had.

Brooke had always been a doer. Camryn had been a watcher. Still, Camryn wasn't unhappy with the lessons she'd learned by watching and thinking. She often wondered if Brooke wasn't a little jealous of Camryn's ability to nurture all living things. While Brooke made the tastiest salads, Camryn grew the ingredients.

Their parents had stopped calling the girls "two peas in a pod" before their fifth birthday. They'd stopped dressing them alike and allowed them to make their own choices. As the girls matured, their parents had often marveled at how two such different females could have formed such a lasting bond.

But they had. Not a day went by that Camryn didn't talk to her sister in Charleston. Brooke was her best friend, the one person who made Camryn's minor successes seem like world-altering accomplishments, the one person who had Cam's back through the divorce and supported her dream to own an organic farm.

Brooke admitted that she would never feel comfortable on Cottontail Farm, but she'd agreed to try. So far she hadn't been to the farm, but Camryn had sent her lots of pictures. Brooke complimented Camryn on the quantity of eggs her hens produced—as if she knew five a week was a good number—and made Camryn believe she was the strongest, most clever woman around. Cam longed for the day Brooke would show up and she could share the calm and peace of a country life with her best friend.

As she cleared the table, Camryn smiled. If her sister had been faced with renting barn space to a man like Reed Bolden, she wouldn't have blinked an eye. She'd have given him the whole barn and probably thrown in a room in the farmhouse, as well. And Reed's "horrid" little boys would have been schooled in fence jumping.

CHAPTER THREE

THE NEXT MORNING Camryn rose early and discovered a burst of energy she usually didn't feel until she'd had two cups of coffee. She did her chores, woke Esther, prepared her breakfast and lunch, and tamed Esther's hair into two long dark blond braids. Then she walked her daughter to the end of the lane and waited with her for the bus to arrive.

Camryn's phone rang, like it usually did, as she walked back to the farmhouse. Right on schedule. 8:00. Brooke called her about this time every morning when she was driving into work. "What's up, farm girl?" Brooke said.

"Oh, the usual," Cam replied, without mentioning she was expecting two horses and their owner sometime today. "I'll spend a couple of hours on November's *Alphabet Days* magazine and then tend to my garden. Do you have any news?"

"Actually I have an invitation," Brooke said. "Mom just called me and said she wants us both, and Essie of course, to come to dinner on Sunday. She and Dad are taking us to a new restaurant in Ocean Cove. Should be nice. It's on the water."

"That sounds lovely," Camryn agreed. So far she'd managed to stay in touch with her parents at least every other day. "But there's no way I can do it this Sunday."

"Oh, come on, sis. You have to come. I figured we'd have dinner and then maybe do some shopping—you know, girl time. I might even buy you a dress in case you've forgotten what they look like."

"And in case you've forgotten, I used to have a closet full of dresses, fancy ones picked out by my personal stylist, Mark."

"And what did you do with all of them?"

"You know exactly what I did. I kept a couple just in case, and gave the rest to Goodwill. I hope other women are happier with them than I was."

"It wasn't the dresses' fault that you were miserable in your marriage, Cammie. You know that. Being the kind of corporate wife Mark expected just wasn't you."

Old news, Camryn thought. Old and highly accurate. Two miscarriages brought on by stress, three full-blown panic attacks and too many minor anxiety attacks to count were all the details Cam needed to remind her of her old life.

"Tell you what," Brooke said. "If I drop the subject of the dresses, will you come? I haven't seen you since you moved."

"You know where I am, Brooke. I've been so busy setting up my fields I haven't left the farm in two months. And it's only a little over an hour's drive for you."

"Sure, I can come there, I suppose. Can't wait."

Camryn smiled. She figured that when her sister finally visited Cottontail Farm, it would be a spur-of-the-moment decision. One day, Cam would step outside and see her sister's BMW pulling up the drive. With the windows closed, of course, to avoid getting farm dust on the upholstery.

"Look, Brooke, I'd like to come. I really would. But I've got two dozen hens being delivered on Saturday. I want to make sure they adapt to the rest of the flock and get settled in their new home."

"Really? Two dozen new hens! How exciting."

Camryn chuckled at her sister's sarcasm.

"Are you even making money with the egg business yet?" Brooke asked.

"I am. I've got three dozen good layers right now and the new ones coming Saturday. At the farmers market I get four dollars and fifty cents a dozen for my eggs. The ones I don't sell I take to the diner in town. They give me three dollars a dozen for the ones I have left over."

"That's a start, I have to admit," Brooke said. "I've heard that free-range eggs demand a premium. I'm used to paying a dollar eighty-nine at the supermarket."

"And I hope to make between one and two hundred a Saturday with my vegetables. I chose fast growers when I got here and I'm harvesting those plants now. The tomato bushes left by the previous owner just needed some fertilizer, and…"

"Stop, Camryn. Have mercy." Brooke laughed. "I'm about to fall asleep at the wheel."

"Okay. Sorry."

"Is Mark still ponying up with his financial obligations?"

"He's been wonderful, actually. Hasn't missed an alimony or a child support payment. And I got fifteen thousand for that ten-acre parcel I sold."

"Okay, Cam, you're obviously rolling in it—money, I mean. Among other things."

"I've got to go, Brooke. Speaking of rolling in other things, I'm cleaning my chicken coop. And a neighbor is coming up my drive. And you have to be at work in ten minutes, don't you?"

"I do. Talk to you later. Love Essie. Love you."

They always ended their calls the same way. Even if they'd had a disagreement or a full-fledged argument, they didn't disconnect without saying I love you. Camryn was constantly amazed that two little infants could have been so lucky as to have been born together and adopted by the generous and loving Montgomerys.

Sliding her cell phone into her jeans pocket, Camryn went to meet the SUV heading down to her barn. She smiled to think of Brooke's reaction if she were at Cottontail Farm meeting this particular neighbor.

ALL REED WANTED to do was hang up the phone. He had two day laborers in the back of his SUV and a barn to clean before noon. And he wouldn't mind having a conversation with his cute landlady currently walking across her yard toward the barn, that scruffy watchdog following her. But he had to finish with Helen first.

"So you're sure the boys are okay?" she asked for what seemed like the hundredth time. It was all Reed could do not to say, "If you're so concerned for their welfare, why don't you visit them once in a while?" But he held his tongue, knowing he would only instigate another argument.

All Helen ever did was ask the same questions over and over, her attempt to assure herself that her ex-husband was fulfilling his obligation as a parent, the obligation she'd wanted no part of.

"Yes, Helen, they're fine."

"Can I talk to them?"

"What? Helen, I realize Rio seems like a planet far removed from South Carolina, but you are in a time zone only three hours ahead of us. Where do you think the boys are right now?"

She paused. "Oh, right. They're in school."

"Yes, and I've got a lot on my plate today, so…"

"I really wish you hadn't taken them from Bucks County," she said.

Reed sighed. "We've been over all this, Helen. You had left the country, and the judge decided the move would be good for the boys. Case closed."

"Sometimes I wonder if you paid the judge off, Reed. Maybe that sounds cruel, but you got everything you wanted in the divorce, including full custody of the kids."

"Paid the judge off?" Reed almost choked on the words. "This is a new low, Helen. The judge decided on custody based on the qualifications of both parents, and even you have to admit the bar wasn't set very high. I wasn't a perfect parent by a long shot, but I was the one who wasn't leaving the country with a cattle rancher from Brazil."

Helen snorted, a sound Reed found haughty and typical of her. "You never wanted me to be happy, Reed," she said.

"Well, that's all changed, Helen. I hope you're deliriously happy now."

Missing the sarcasm in his tone, she said, "Thank you, Reed. That's very kind. Oh, and by the way, Daddy wants to see the boys. Can you drive them down to Atlanta?"

He shook his head in disbelief. "I'm a little busy here, Helen. You know I'm working to set up a clinic." He parked the SUV in front of the barn and indicated the two workers could get out. When they had stepped away from the car, he said, "Your father knows where I'm living now. And he has a car. Just tell him to call first."

"Do you think that's fair? What has Daddy done to make you so angry?"

Recently, nothing, Reed thought. But he'd spent twenty-two years raising an entitled daughter who thought rules were for everyone else, and the world was her yellow brick road. Unfortunately, Reed hadn't looked deep enough under Helen's shell of charm and spontaneity. He'd fallen for the unpredictable debutante and believed he was the luckiest man alive to be "the chosen one."

"Just tell him to call first," he repeated. "I've got to go." He disconnected, grateful that the workers he'd hired didn't speak English. The last few minutes of conversation hadn't been pleasant.

He crossed his arms over his steering wheel and rested his brow on his forearms. Just a few minutes of calm. That was all he needed. But then he changed his mind when a light tapping on his window made him look up. There was Camryn Montgomery, hair in a messy bun, straw stuck to her clothes and chicken droppings on her boots. She looked adorable.

"Are you all right?" she asked through the window.

And she actually cared about how he was doing.

Wow, Reed looked like he'd just lost his best friend. He stared at her for a moment and then lowered his window. His expression grim, he said, "Hi, Camryn. I was just…"

Whatever he was about to say remained unspoken. "I asked if you are all right?" she said. "I saw you leaning over the steering wheel. Headache?"

"What? No. I'm fine." He gave her a pitiful attempt at a smile. "I was taking a minute before I go inside the barn to tackle what has to be done in there."

That made sense. After seeing the condition of her own barn yesterday, Cam had dreaded the thought of Reed having to remove layers of dust, cobwebs and dirty straw. "I see you brought help," she said.

"I did. And I think we can get the job done by noon. The horses are due shortly thereafter." He opened the car door and stepped out. In jeans, a worn Clemson University T-shirt and a baseball cap, he looked ready to work. His slow gaze traveled the length of her. "I'm guessing you've done a few chores yourself today."

"I'm expecting two dozen more hens on Saturday, so I'm starting a thorough cleaning of the coop. Wouldn't want the new arrivals thinking they were moving into a chicken flophouse."

He laughed. "No. Most of the flophouse details are stuck to your boots anyway."

She scraped her boots on the grass. "Indeed. Hazards of a chicken farm."

He peered toward the barn where the workers stood at the entrance. "Guess I'd better get busy."

Camryn looked across a nearby field. "I don't see my two goats, so I'm guessing they've wandered into the barn. It's fine if you just want to shoo them out. I never really confine them, but I'll try to keep them away from your space."

"No need," Reed said. "Goats are actually considered great companions for horses. You even see a lot of goats at racetracks where the horses are much more temperamental and valuable than the two I've got coming today. The little fellas have a calming influence on horses, believe it or not."

"Okay, then, I'll probably see you later." Calling Rooster to follow her, Camryn went back to working on the coop before she cleaned up to go inside and sit at her computer.

At noon Reed left the farm but was back by 1:30. He led a truck and horse trailer up the drive to the barn. Camryn couldn't hide her curiosity. She went outside to watch the unloading of the new residents of Cottontail Farm.

What an interesting process it was. The horses had been loaded into the trailer head first, so of course they had to be walked out head last. This maneuver required skillful handling. A man in front of the trailer issued encouraging words to the animals while Reed waited on the ground in back. Step by precarious step, each horse made its way into the sunshine.

One horse was huge, or at least Camryn thought so. She'd never been around horses, though her sister had. Camryn had grown up taking care of small creatures, birds and squirrels, even a skunk one time. Her experience with equines was limited to watching them at the arena, where she'd gone to see Brooke ride.

The other horse was much smaller. When both horses were securely tied to a fence post near the barn, Camryn watched Reed take out his wallet and hand over bills to the driver of the trailer. The man backed around in her yard and drove away.

"Hey, Camryn," Reed called. "Come meet my family."

She walked over but stopped several feet from the animals. Both horses seemed agitated. They pawed the ground and made high-pitched nickering sounds. Every so often one or the other would shake its large head.

"I don't think they like it here," Camryn said, realizing that Rooster was dangerously close to those large hooves. She pointed a finger and said, "Go." The dog backed off but still remained vigilant.

"Actually they didn't care much for the ride to get here. They'll like the farm just fine." He smoothed his hand down the white blaze of the large horse. "This is Brute. He's a palomino paint gelding. Came from Texas. Eight years old and fifteen hands tall. A good-size fella, and a surprisingly easy ride." Reed gave Camryn a carrot from his pocket. "Here, get to know him."

Camryn opened her palm and held the carrot under Brute's nose. The horse's lips wiggled around a bit but then he enthusiastically and gently took the treat.

"And this little white jewel is Saucy," Reed said. "She's a three-year-old pony. Only eleven hands high." He stroked the pony's neck. "Justin can handle her already."

"They seem nice," Camryn said, not knowing how a person should compliment a horse. "Like I said at the feedstore, I don't know much about taking care of horses."

"You don't have to," Reed said. "If you think something's not right, just give me a call. I'll be right over. Oh…and I hope you don't mind, but I told my boys to ride the school bus to your place today. They're anxious to see the horses."

"No, I don't mind. That's fine."

Reed looked at his watch. "Speaking of school bus, it's nearly three o'clock already. Should be here soon."

"I'm sure you have things you'd like to do to get your horses settled in." Camryn started to walk away.

"Wait a minute." Reed stopped her by placing his hand on her arm. She waited.

"What do you know about the Bufflehead Fall Festival this weekend? When I was in town I saw posters advertising the big event on every store window."

"Oh, that," she said. "I guess they have the festival every year. I don't know much about it. I'm not even sure what a bufflehead is. A duck, I think."

"Oh, it's a duck," Reed said. "And a very distinctive one. It dives for food and completely disappears in the water. When you think it's lost forever, it pops up again. They are pretty ducks, too. The males have bright white spots on their heads and dark, glistening green and purple feathers."

Camryn smiled. "Thanks, though that might be a bit more than I need to know about a duck."

"Not when it's our community's duck," Reed said. "About this festival. Looks like our new town wants to pay homage to its namesake."

Reed's smile was infectious. "What do you say we take the kids and go on Friday night? We can eat a bunch of junk food, go on some rides and listen to the Dirty Boots Band. I've never heard of them, but they're the headliners on opening night."

"I don't know, Reed," Camryn hedged. "I don't go out much. And I don't date. I…"

His eyes widened. Oh, no. He probably hadn't meant it as a date at all. He probably meant that they'd take two cars and meet there, and she'd assumed… Now she had to figure out a way to get her foot out of her mouth.

"Oh, no, not a date," he said quickly. "It's

just a thing, a way to support our town and our duck. You want to support the duck population, don't you? After all, they'll be flying down to Florida pretty soon, and I have a hunch we'll miss them."

"Sure, that's what I thought you meant," she said, grateful he'd offered a way out of her blunder. "We can meet there if you like."

"Why take two cars?" he said. "Waste of gasoline. Two adults and three kids can go to a 'thing' in one car, can't they?"

Well, yes, they could. But now it sounded like a date. And she was only two months divorced and three months pregnant. She was pretty sure Becky had told Reed about the divorce, but she trusted that Becky hadn't told him about the pregnancy. Besides these two significant facts, dating was nowhere on Camryn's social calendar. Heck, Camryn Montgomery didn't even *have* a social calendar—not since she'd given up being a corporate wife to be a simple farmer.

"What do you say," Reed prompted. "Is it a d…thing?"

"I'll think about it," she said. "The bus is here. I'll go meet it and send your boys over here by the barn." She was relieved to have an excuse to walk away from the invitation, oddly because she was too close to accepting it. But what could it hurt? A simple night out to a country festival with three kids in tow? Esther would probably love the idea. She would do as she promised. She'd think about it. She knew darn well what Brooke would do if she were in this situation, and what Brooke would tell her to do if she asked.

Camryn smiled. She wouldn't tell Brooke. She'd just say yes on her own.

She and Esther went in the house, sat at the kitchen table as they usually did while Cam set out milk and a snack. They'd only gotten through the details of the first couple of hours of Esther's day when the child suddenly looked out the window and bolted from her chair.

"Wow, Mommy, are those Mr. Reed's horses?"

"Yes, they are," Camryn said. "That's Brute and Saucy."

"They're beautiful," Esther said.

"I suppose they are," Cam agreed. "Not that we've seen many horses to compare them with."

"Can I go outside?"

How could Cam say no? Something this exciting didn't happen every day at Cotton-tail Farm. "Sure, go ahead. But don't get in the way. Stay close to the house. And please, don't go near the barn."

"Okay." Esther darted out the back door.

After a few minutes Camryn heard hoots and hollers. She would have figured Reed's boys were welcoming the horses, but one of the voices was distinctly not male. Camryn went out her back door. What she saw took her breath away.

She looked twice. Her anger rose like a thermometer in boiling water. There was Esther, sitting in a saddle behind Justin, her arms around his waist and her heels digging in to the sides of Saucy, the pony.

Esther, who'd never been near a horse, was riding one? And without a helmet, though Reed was holding the horse by a rope. The back door of the farmhouse slammed with a loud bang as Camryn tore across the yard.

CHAPTER FOUR

CAMRYN GULPED BACK an instinctive urge to holler at her daughter. Common sense told her that any loud noise could upset what she determined was a delicate balance between horse and riders. She didn't want to alarm Esther or jolt her with a burst of angry shouting.

Cam reached Reed first and grabbed his arm. He spun around. "What do you think you're doing?" she demanded.

His eyes widened in surprise. "What do you mean?"

"That's my daughter on the horse. My daughter! I don't recall giving permission for her to ride."

He shook his head as if trying to process her distress. "First of all, Camryn, Saucy isn't a horse. She's a pony. Your daughter's feet are all of two feet off the ground."

"A lot can happen in two feet! Besides,

that's a seven-hundred-pound animal, Reed. No match for a tiny nine-year-old girl."

"No match? It isn't a contest, Camryn. No one is trying to win anything, and no one is threatened."

"And how would you know that?" Camryn said. "Yes, you're a vet, but that doesn't mean you know what is going on in an animal's head."

"Well, I'm an especially competent vet, so yeah, it kind of does."

While they'd been talking, Reed had let the rope around Saucy's neck fall to the ground. He picked it up and held tight as the horse circled around him. Camryn felt somewhat relieved that he maintained some control over the situation, but that didn't mean the horse, or pony, or whatever... wouldn't bolt at the first strange noise or unexpected kick. Nearby, Rooster was barking madly, obviously picking up on Camryn's alarm—proof that animals had instincts of their own.

"I want you to get my daughter off that animal immediately," Camryn said. "She's never even been near a horse before."

"That's too bad," Reed responded. "My

two animals are extremely gentle and people friendly. She couldn't be in better hands, or should I say hooves?"

"You shouldn't say anything," Camryn countered. "I'm her mother and you didn't even ask if I wanted her on the horse."

"You're right. I didn't. The truth is, I can't come up with a logical reason why you wouldn't want Esther to experience Saucy for her first ride." He made a clicking noise with his tongue and the pony shook her head and peered over at him. At the same time, Esther saw her mother.

"Look, Mommy, I'm on a pony. Isn't she beautiful?"

Camryn couldn't answer. All at once she felt dizzy and light-headed. In a few moments her breaths would come in short gasps just like it had always happened in the past.

"She loves this," Reed said, unaware of Cam's distress. "Look at her face. Did you ever see such a big smile?"

"Get. Her. Down. Now." Cam clutched her stomach as a shooting pain radiated up to her heart.

Reed stared at her. He grabbed her arm.

"You need to sit down." He started to lead her to a bench outside the barn. "Phillip, come take the rope and stop Saucy from walking. Keep her still."

"Aw, Dad," Justin squawked. "We're still riding."

"Not anymore you're not." Supporting practically all of Camryn's weight with his arm tight around her shoulders, he brought her to the bench and gently pushed her onto the seat. "Put your head between your knees," he instructed. "I'll get your daughter."

Camryn did as he suggested. Suddenly she'd broken into a cold sweat. Her body was trembling. She thought she was having a heart attack. But experience told her that wasn't true. She just needed to concentrate on her breathing. She looked up long enough to see Reed lift Esther from the pony and set her on the ground. And then her first normal breath filled her lungs.

She needed to get complete control. Esther had never seen her have a panic attack and Camryn had always prayed she never would. In the past Cam had always had enough warning to put space between her and her daughter, protecting Esther from witnessing what she would never understand.

"Did you see me, Mommy?" Esther hollered as she ran to the bench. "I was riding a horse."

"I saw you," Camryn managed to say in a normal voice.

"It was so cool, Mommy."

"You should have asked me before you got on the pony, Essie," Cam said.

"Why? Reed was here the whole time."

"Reed…is not your parent."

"But you're here now, and I want to ride again."

Camryn blinked hard to clear her blurry vision. "No, Esther. Go in the house."

"I don't want to." Esther's face was set in a pout of determination.

"Go. Now."

Esther whirled away from her. "Why are you always so mean?"

Camryn didn't answer. She heard Esther's footsteps echo toward the house. And then Cam rested her forehead in her hand and waited for her heart to stop hammering. She knew Esther would ask the question again when they were both in the kitchen.

"Are you okay now?" Reed asked her. "You seemed pretty dizzy for a while there, but you're getting some color back. Is there anyone I should call?"

"No, I'll be all right."

Justin slid off the pony and came over to his father. "Why'd we have to stop riding? I thought you said the right thing was to ask the girl if she wanted to ride behind me, so that's what I did. Now everybody's acting all mad. I would have rather gotten on Saucy by myself."

Camryn stared up into the boy's eyes. "You'll have plenty of opportunity," she said.

"Good. Old lady Esther just kept giggling the whole time like girls do."

Reed turned his son around and administered a little shove toward the barn. "What did I tell you regarding teasing Esther about her name?"

"Heck, Dad, she's not even here now."

"You and Phillip brush Saucy down. The tack box is right inside the barn. You'll find the equipment you need."

Justin turned to give his father one last hard stare of complaint.

"And do a good job!" Reed added.

When the boys had gone into the barn, Reed sat beside Cam on the bench. He took her hand, a gesture she might have found forward from a man she'd only known a couple of days, but instead she let the warmth of his palm tingle along her arm. Now that the attack had subsided, she appreciated having someone near, even if that someone was technically responsible for her discomfort.

"Why do you keep clutching your abdomen, Camryn?" he asked. "Are you experiencing pain?"

She quickly moved her hand. Protecting her babies was what mattered and she often covered her tummy in times of stress. But she could relax now. The baby was fine. Even the slightest of butterfly movements had returned.

"No. Instinct, I guess."

Reed's eyes were kind when he asked, "What's going on? Why the dizzy spell?"

"I told you. I was surprised to see Esther on a horse. And I was upset that no one had talked to me beforehand."

"I was right here," Reed said. "I was watching the children the whole time. I know the pony. Esther was safe, I promise you."

She shot him a glance. "How many times has a parent heard that same statement and lived to see a tragedy occur."

He sighed. "I can't help wondering if something else is going on. I get that you probably don't trust me…" He squeezed her hand. "But you can. I'm not the best disciplinarian in the world, Cam, but I do love my kids. All kids."

"It's not that."

"Then what?"

"It's hard to explain. I feel like I can trust you, but it's fate I can't trust. No one can predict what's going to happen. I feel like I have to protect Esther from anything that can hurt her." Camryn took a deep breath, grateful for the cool rush of autumn air filling her lungs. "Maybe if I had been out here, if I had been warned, if I could have asked questions…"

Reed smiled. "You know what? You're right. No two parents operate the same way. My boys have grown up like wild March hares and look at them. Their mouths don't open that I don't worry about what will come out of them. Your daughter is calm and polite, so well mannered. And I should have asked you before putting Esther on the pony. I get it."

She smiled, too. He'd said just the right thing. "And maybe I can admit to being a bit overprotective. I'm sure Esther would like it if I would lighten up where she's concerned. But it's hard, you know? Esther and I are alone, just the two of us."

"Maybe it doesn't have to be just the two of you," he said. "You have neighbors. I'd like you to depend on me if you need to. I certainly don't want you to distrust me."

"I don't, Reed."

"Good. Are you still thinking about the festival this Friday?"

"Yes, maybe," she said.

He stood. "I'm going in the barn now. You sure you're okay?"

"Yes, I'm fine." *Except for feeling out of control.*

"Oh, Cam, one more thing…"

She waited.

"You might notice some commotion in the next couple of days. I'm having materials delivered for construction of two metal buildings on my property. Plus there will be a backhoe digging a hole, a rather large hole."

She twisted her hands together. "You're digging a hole?" All sorts of strange images came to mind. "What are you doing?"

"I gave up my practice, but I still have to make a living. I'm starting a rehabilitation facility for wounded and endangered low country animals. Got a nice grant from the government. The other building will be a small clinic where I can take a few customers, local people."

His words started to buzz in her head. Rehabilitation facility, wounded animals, low country wildlife. "And why do you need a big hole?"

"Have to provide a habitat for large turtles, maybe a gator or two."

Suddenly she pictured strange, dangerous creatures roaming her land, birds of prey swooping down on her chickens.

He must have read the concern in her face, because he walked back to the bench. "Don't worry. I'm not bringing in more horses. And I'll have proper security all around. That's not to say you won't hear a few squawks now and then."

A few squawks? She could handle that, couldn't she? Heavens, her chickens made noise twenty-four hours a day. She looked up into Reed's eyes. *Please don't make me regret selling your parents that land.*

THE HOUSE WAS QUIET when Camryn went into the kitchen. She took a moment to investigate the refrigerator for dinner possibilities. She put the kettle on for tea. Normal things, much needed for a day that wasn't a bit normal and needed for a person who couldn't seem to find her own normal.

"Esther, would you come out here, please?" she called after a few minutes had passed.

"I don't want to!"

Camryn took a deep breath and prepared her tea. "I'm your mother, Essie, and I want you to. We need to talk."

"I don't want to talk."

Camryn walked to the hallway, stared at her daughter's closed door. "Come to the kitchen now, Esther. I don't want to talk to you through this door. And I don't intend to have an argument about it."

The door opened and Esther stepped into the hall. Turning sideways, she scooted around her mother as if touching her would deliver the always-perilous cooties. Making as much noise as possible with her bare feet, Esther stomped into the kitchen. Camryn followed her. Esther plopped onto a chair.

"Would you like another cookie?" Camryn asked. "And another glass of milk?"

Eyes down. Feet swinging under the table. "No."

Camryn sat across from Esther. "Look, I know you're upset with me. I get that. But there are things you don't understand. It's my job to protect you. And sometimes maybe it seems like I might be taking my job too seriously. But honey…"

Esther lifted her eyes. "I don't need protecting, Mommy. I'm nine years old. I want to do stuff. You don't have to treat me like a baby."

Oh, but I do, Camryn thought. *I lost two babies, but fate gave me you. I will protect you as long as I live.*

"I was having fun outside. The pony was

fun. Justin was being nice to me. And then you came and spoiled it."

"I never mean to spoil your fun, Essie. And I realize you are growing up. But you need to ask me before you do things that might be dangerous."

"Why? So you can say no?"

"Not necessarily. So I can be aware of what you're doing. So I can offer my best advice."

"Riding a pony isn't dangerous, Mommy. It's fun. And Reed was there. He was holding Saucy. We were all laughing and then…"

I know. And then I came outside.

Had she gone too far when she made her daughter get off the pony? Camryn couldn't convince herself that she had. So often her body told her what to do when her mind hadn't processed the situation yet. The panic attack was her body's way of telling her that Essie shouldn't be on the horse, that Essie's health and safety were suddenly in someone else's hands. Camryn simply couldn't put any part of raising her daughter in someone else's hands. Not yet.

She reached across the table and entwined

her fingers with Esther's. "Look, honey, I think we can come to an agreement."

"Yeah, and I know what. I have to do everything you say."

Camryn smiled. "It seems like that, I know. But you're still a child. I know what dangers are lurking around us. I see things that you don't. I don't want anything bad to happen to you, sweetheart."

"But Mom, you don't let anything happen to me at all! Not all things that happen are bad, you know."

"Yes, of course I know that. We live here on this beautiful farm. We have chickens and Rooster and a pair of very fun goats. All of that is good."

The dog, who'd recovered from his need to protect and was sleeping on a mat on the kitchen floor, looked up when he heard his name and emitted a contented whine.

"And I promise I will try to consider your feelings more than I have in the past. I may have overreacted today. But you need to keep me informed of what you are doing. I had just told you not to go near the barn, and the next thing I knew you were sitting on top of a pony."

Esther's eyes narrowed. "So are you ever going to let me ride the pony again?"

"I just might," Camryn said. "If you ask first. But we don't need to decide that today."

Esther thought a moment. "Okay. Can I have that cookie now?"

Camryn realized that all she had really done was buy a little time before the next crisis occurred. Esther was right about one thing. She was growing up, and she would soon reach for greater independence. But for now Esther was satisfied. She ate her cookie and went back to her room to do her homework.

And Camryn did what always felt right to her—she called her sister.

"Hi, Brooke, are you busy?"

"No, you caught me at a good time. Tonight's stories are loaded into the teleprompter."

As a news producer in Charleston, Brooke was always busy, always a perfectionist at her job. She strived to make certain her facts were accurate, her stories for the evening news consequential. She wanted her work to be absolutely right on.

"As long as the creek doesn't rise between

now and five o'clock, I should have a few minutes to breathe," Brooke said. "What's going on?"

"Not much. I just wanted to hear your voice."

Brooke paused. "Okay. And now I've heard yours. What's the matter?"

Brooke had always been tuned in to every inflection, every nuance of Camryn's voice. She wasn't surprised that her sister could tell something was wrong.

"I had a little disagreement with Esther," she said. "I feel terrible about it." She proceeded to fill in the details of the pony incident. "Basically," she concluded, "Essie thinks I'm mean and unreasonable…"

"Of course you are," Brooke said. "You're a mother. It's your job to be unreasonable."

Camryn sighed. "But I think I may have been overprotective."

"Do you trust this man, this Reed fellow, who owns the pony?"

"I do. At least I think I do. I don't know him that well yet. I'm going to have to trust him. I've rented my barn to him for his horses. Plus, he has two boys about Essie's age who will probably be coming over often, and he's living on that property I sold to the Boldens."

"I trust your judgment on things like this, Cam. You must have seen a reason to believe Reed was a good guy. Otherwise you wouldn't have rented him the barn."

"Yes, I suppose."

"But you seem to be losing sight of the most important thing here, Cam. You are a good mother. No, a wonderful mother. Esther is so lucky to have a mom who worries as much as you do. I couldn't care for a cat, and you are involved and nurturing. Don't ever doubt your abilities as a parent."

Cam wiped moisture from her eyes. Brooke always made her feel better. "Thanks. But I'm not sure I believe that cat statement."

"I'm not you, Cam, and vice versa. That's why we work and always have."

"The other thing I didn't tell you was that I had another panic attack while all this was going on."

"A bad one?"

"Bad enough."

Camryn almost broke down and sobbed. "Oh, Brooke, when are things going to change? Months of therapy after each miscarriage, and again when Mark and I decided to split. Now the attacks starting up again."

"What about taking a pill?" Brooke said. "The doctor told you it was okay."

Camryn had a prescription for a calming medication, but she rarely took a capsule. And she hadn't taken one since she'd learned she was pregnant.

"No. I'd rather not."

"You know yourself the best, Cam. Not to mention being the bravest and best grower of anything green."

Cam chuckled.

"I want you to be happy, Cam," Brooke added. "And I think this farm is a real start. You are doing what you love in a place that seems ideal for you and Esther. Don't let a few misgivings about your ability as a parent ruin what you've got there."

"I am happy, Brooke. Truly I am. I'm lucky to have a job with Southern Square Press that allows me to work from home. And I love the farm." Camryn meant the words. She just wished she could live the life.

After a pause, Brooke said, "So, about this guy, Reed. Is he married?"

Camryn smiled. "No, he's divorced."

"Aha…"

"No aha, Brooke. I just told you I barely know him."

"That can change. I've heard stories about what goes on in a barn."

"Brooke…"

"Oops. Gotta go, Cam. Someone is calling me from the production booth. Only thirty minutes to airtime. I love you."

"Love you back."

They disconnected. Camryn took the last sip of tea and thought about her situation. Maybe she could loosen up a bit. Maybe she could stop thinking about the consequences if she let her guard down once in a while.

A good way to begin would be to finally tell Esther about her new brother or sister. As soon as the doctor gave the all clear that the pregnancy was progressing well, Cam would tell her daughter. Again, she'd been protecting Esther from the reality of tragedy if something happened to the baby. It had been hard enough to tell her about the divorce. Explaining about a miscarriage would have been impossible.

Cam took her teacup to the sink and stared

out her kitchen window. As far as she could see, the land was hers. The chickens were rooting around the yard. The crops she had planted close to her house were doing well, and when she could afford to, she would expand her gardens. If she could just stay focused on this place of security and bliss, just her and her children, she could handle anything.

But was that even possible? Not when her thoughts kept returning to Reed Bolden, the way his hand had felt holding hers. He made her think of sacrificing that focus for the possibility of something better.

CHAPTER FIVE

JUST AS REED had predicted, Wednesday was a busy day at the Bolden property. He directed truckloads of building materials to the sites where his clinic and rehab centers would be. He instructed the backhoe operator where to dig the planned water hole. And most important, when he had time to focus on the future, he envisioned the facility that would soon be his—a place where he would earn the trust and respect of the folks in his new community, a place where animals, large and small, would be made whole again, a place where his sons would grow into men.

Midway through the day, his cell phone rang. He checked the number on the screen, frowned and answered. "Hello, Frank. How are you?"

"Hello, Reed," Frank Holbrook said. "I'm quite well, thank you. I'm calling because I want to see my grandsons."

That was his ex-father-in-law. Blunt and to the point. Helen had hinted that her father might be requesting a visitation. Reed had no problem with the man's right to see his grandchildren. He just knew that Frank would expect Reed to drive the children to Atlanta, book a hotel room for a couple of nights for himself and return the boys to Bufflehead Creek. It was too much to hope that Frank, busy attorney that he claimed to be, would assume any of these duties.

"You can see them whenever you want, Frank," Reed said. "Provided they won't miss any school. I have them on a rather strict schedule now, and they are adjusting well to it." Reed hoped his ex-father-in-law would recognize Reed's veiled accusation that Helen almost never kept the boys to a schedule unless it suited her needs.

"When can you bring them to Atlanta?" Frank asked.

"Sorry, Frank, but I won't be able to do that. I gave you my address when I left so you could arrange a time to come to South Carolina. It's only about a four-hour trip. If you want to see the boys, you'll have to come here. Unfortunately I don't have room

to put you up, so if you plan to stay overnight, I can suggest a local motel not far
away." He figured Frank, who was used to
five-star accommodations, was cringing in
his Ferragamo calfskin loafers.

"I see that chip on your shoulder has only
grown larger," Frank said.

"And so has my hope for my new practice."

"Look, Reed, I can understand your re-
sentment of Helen. I'm not happy with her
leaving you and the boys. But I don't think
the kids should suffer because both of their
parents are self-centered enough to only
think of their own futures. Helen is off
somewhere in the wilds of Brazil. And you
are stuck in a town that's barely a dot on the
map. Phillip and Justin aren't used to the environment you've taken them to. They are
accustomed to culture, museums, sporting
venues in grand arenas."

*Yes, and running wild with no apparent
direction in their lives*. The first inkling of
fear worked its way down Reed's spine. "I
don't know what you're getting at, Frank,
but the boys are fine."

"Since you're practically accusing me of

something, I might as well level with you," Frank said.

"That would be nice."

"I'd like to bring the boys back to Atlanta permanently, Reed. Now, before you go off half-cocked…"

Too late. Reed's blood had almost reached the boiling point.

"…just think about it. I have the resources and staff to see to the boys' needs. I have the ability to send them to a private school and the best summer camp programs in the area. You can visit them whenever you want and spend as much time as you desire with dogs and cats and whatever else sort of four-legged creatures you're partial to."

Reed shook his head, resisted the desire to hang up. "You're forgetting, Frank. I'm partial to a couple of two-legged creatures, as well—my sons, and if you believe for one second that I'm going to entrust them to your care…"

"All right, Reed. Calm down. I didn't broach this topic the way I'd planned to. I wanted to first say that Candace and I are both willing and able to take the kids. We both love them. They would have a caring and supportive home with us."

Reed couldn't stop the next words. "Frank, your second wife is two years younger than Helen. I would think you'd have enough of a playmate in her, and you wouldn't need my sons."

After a moment of uncomfortable silence, Frank said, "You're going to regret saying that."

"I already do. I apologize. That remark was uncalled for, especially since I don't spend much time thinking about your personal life at all."

"You remember Judge Olson, don't you, Reed? He was elected to the Georgia circuit court system. He and I play golf at least once a week. I've explained this situation to him, and he has considerable influence…"

"Frank, I'm busy, and this conversation is over. If you'd like to see the boys, plan on no more than an hour or so and call first." Reed disconnected the call. His hand was shaking so badly he thought he might break his cell phone. This wasn't the first time Frank had hinted that he wanted custody of Phillip and Justin, but it was certainly the most blatant.

The threat from Helen's father was one of the reasons Reed had moved from Bucks County. Maybe he hadn't been the greatest dad in the world before now, but he was certainly trying to do the right thing since moving to Bufflehead Creek. No matter what cost or frustration he was experiencing with his sons, no matter the weight of responsibility on his shoulders, there was no way he was going to relinquish his flesh and blood to Frank Holbrook.

It would never happen. Anticipating Frank's power and influence, Reed had consulted his own attorney and was assured that as long as the boys were well cared for, there was no court in the country that would take them from a rightful parent. Still, Frank's call had been upsetting. And Reed didn't need upsetting in his life right now.

He jammed his phone into his pocket and went back to the easy job of merely supervising the construction of a future with his sons.

FROM A DISTANCE Cam watched the activity at the Bolden property. She had planned to pick Esther up at school and run errands afterwards. Her thinking was that if Essie wasn't home, she wouldn't ask about the horse. But she changed her mind and waited for the school bus as usual, her own curiosity having gotten the better of her.

All day the workers put finishing touches on Reed's house. In a little more than a week, the lot had been prepared and the house erected on the flattest part of the property. Reed came to the barn to feed and care for his horses in the morning but didn't stay and didn't come to the house to see Camryn. Just as well, she thought. She'd embarrassed herself enough the day before. She didn't want to discuss the pony incident again.

When Esther got home, she didn't ask to ride the pony again. Even she could tell that other matters were priorities at the Bolden house. Shortly after the bus dropped the kids off, Reed and his boys climbed in the SUV and left for a while. They arrived home in time to see more building materials delivered. Camryn assumed the huge metal panels were for the structures that would make up Reed's clinics.

On Thursday workers arrived to make sense of the piles of construction materials, and a pair of small but sturdy buildings began to take shape. This time when Reed came to see to his horses, he wandered up to the house and knocked on the door.

Camryn couldn't deny that his appearance through her door window made her heart skip a couple of beats. Though the erratic rhythm didn't signal a panic attack. No, this was something much more pleasant. Drying her hands on a dish towel, she opened the door.

Reed grinned at her, said a friendly hello. "How are you feeling?" he asked. "No more incidents like that dizzy spell you had before?"

She didn't correct him. If he thought she suffered from dizzy spells that was better than him knowing she had panic attacks.

"No. I'm fine. I know I overreacted on Tuesday. Sorry if I worried anyone."

"Don't apologize. You were right. I had no business allowing your daughter on that pony without having checked with you first—" the smile stayed in place "—even if she was perfectly safe."

She smiled back. "Okay, you've made your point."

"Anyway, I've left you alone for a couple of days just in case you were still angry."

"I'm not angry. I'm over it. Still I wonder when our children are ever 'perfectly safe'?"

He leaned against her doorframe. Cam wondered if should she invite him in? Should she step outside? He settled the issue by peeking around her and staring into her kitchen. "What's that smell?" he asked. "Delicious."

"Nothing fancy. Just beef stew." She opened the door wider. "Would you like a lemonade?" She laid her palm over her still flat tummy. "I don't have anything stronger in the house."

"That would be great." He stepped inside. "I like this kitchen. It looks like many great meals have come from this room."

"Unfortunately from people other than me," she said. She looked around the space, trying to see her kitchen from his point of view. Yes, it was cozy with its old wooden cabinets, tiled countertops, practically ancient appliances and ruffled curtains at the windows. The kitchen had been Cam's favorite room when the Realtor had shown her the house. She felt strangely gratified that Reed appreciated it as well.

She gave him a drink, and he pulled out a chair and sat. "I can only stay a minute. Got a whole lot going on over at my place, including delivery of furniture in about an hour. Took my boys out yesterday to a store in Bluffton and we picked out a houseful."

She sat across from him. "You certainly work fast," she said. "A house, buildings and now furniture."

"Too fast according to my mother, who didn't have a say in picking the furnishings. I don't know if she'll ever forgive me. I'm thinking I may never invite her over. She's probably going to find fault with everything we men picked out." He chuckled. "Although probably not, because furniture of any kind means we're getting out of her motor home."

"I'm sure you're anxious to get settled, too," Cam said.

"I am. I made sure I got each of the boys a desk to do his homework. Hope the power of suggestion works." He leaned back in his chair. "But anyway, here's why I stopped at your house. Tomorrow is Friday night, the opening of the Bufflehead Fall Festival. I'm hoping you've decided to say yes to my invitation. Since we're both relative newcomers to the area, we should be there and show our support for the town's namesake."

"Nothing like supporting the local ducks," Camryn said. "Until you gave me a lesson on buffleheads, I wasn't even sure what they were."

"But now that you know…"

She paused. Why not? She wanted to say yes. She wanted to prove to her daughter that she could be fun. So she smiled and said, "Now that I know, how can I say no?"

He slapped the top of her table. "Great. The Bolden men will pick up the Montgomery ladies at six tomorrow night. Don't eat supper first. Dinner of corn dogs and funnel cakes is on me."

She walked him to the door. "See you tomorrow."

He gave her a crooked grin. "Right. This is a dream come true. I've always wanted to go to a bufflehead festival."

She watched him through the screen door. Camryn had formed casual relationships with a few people in town—store clerks, Esther's teacher, the local doctor, the nice waitress at the diner—but she'd never before felt excited about going to a festival. Maybe Reed Bolden was the reason.

CAMRYN AND ESTHER climbed into Reed's SUV when he arrived a bit before six in the evening on Friday. The kids sat in back and Camryn settled in next to the driver. She was instantly aware of her close proximity to Reed.

"We can't stay out too late," she said. "My hens are arriving around ten in the morning, and I have to make a run to the feedstore before they get here. A dozen of my new chickens are brown egg layers and two are Ameraucanas. All my new residents need special nutrients added to their diet to produce the best eggs."

Phillip leaned forward from the back seat. "What are American chickens?"

"It's Ameraucanas," Cam said. "They lay pastel eggs the color of Easter eggs. Blue, pink, green."

"Can you eat them?"

"You bet. Because the hens cost more to raise, some people consider their eggs a delicacy. I'm hoping to get five dollars a dozen for them."

Phillip snickered. "I wouldn't give you five dollars for eggs."

"That's probably because you don't have to pay for eggs at all," Reed said.

Cam looked over her shoulder into the back seat. She was pleased to see that both boys had taken some care with their appearance tonight. Their dark hair was neatly combed, though Justin's curls had begun to spring into a halo around his head. They had on clean jeans and brightly colored T-shirts. Each boy had a jacket bunched on his lap.

Esther had insisted on wearing her best jeans and a ruffled blouse. She twisted her single braid, which ended in a pink ribbon in an almost flirtatious flip. Another way Es was more like her auntie Brooke.

Camryn had chosen slimming jeans knowing she might as well wear them when she had a chance. In a few weeks she wouldn't be able to close the button. She completed her outfit with a formfitting white T and a denim jacket.

"So who's hungry for corn dogs?" Reed asked.

"And French fries," Justin chimed in.

"And Cokes, extra large," Phillip said.

"I've never had a corn dog," Esther said.

Camryn cleared her throat. "Surely you have, Essie." She paused. "You must have had a corn dog. Maybe when you were with your dad."

"Nope. He always said you wouldn't want me to eat one of those. He said they were unhealthy."

Camryn looked out her window to avoid looking at Reed's smile. Another embarrassing moment she had to live through.

They arrived at the Bufflehead Creek athletic field, which had been transformed into a magical land of neon and noise. Reed parked and they all piled out of the car. At the entrance gate a man in a bufflehead hat sold them tickets.

"So that's what a bufflehead looks like," Camryn said, staring at the volunteer's headgear.

"Well, yeah," Reed said. "If the bottom half of the duck were human. They all have black feathers with a distinctive white spot. Although the ducks wear the colors better than a man whose head is too big for his hat."

They passed a stage where a band was playing country music. Older folks sat around in lawn chairs. Teens danced on the makeshift wooden platform. The littlest kids rolled around in the grass. They were surrounded by bufflehead mementoes, even T-shirts that said, "I'm a Bufflehead, are you?" and "Buffleheads know how to duck."

Every volunteer had on the traditional bufflehead hat.

"Anybody want to hear the music?" Reed asked.

"Heck, no." Phillip pointed up the midway, past a few white canvas tents that protected the crafts fair. "There's the food trucks. Let's go there."

"Maybe we should do the rides first," Camryn said. "I don't know if it's such a good idea to eat and then go on rides."

Both Bolden boys stared at her as if she'd spoken a foreign language. "Why?" Phillip asked. "In case we puke or something?"

"Well, yes, exactly," she said.

"No one's gonna puke," he said. "Unless it's old lady…"

"Phillip…"

His father's controlled voice cut him off.

"What would you like to do, Essie?" Camryn asked her daughter. "Would you like to eat or maybe ride the carousel first?"

Justin hooted. "The carousel? That's for babies. We want the real rides."

"Yeah, Mom," Esther said. "Let's eat first and then find the real rides." She gave Justin a look that was a combination of accord and admiration. "Carousels are for babies."

"Okay, then." Camryn consented because eating would buy her some time before having to argue with Esther about the rides that might be too thrilling for her nine-year-old. She hoped that the height limits would prohibit Esther from going aboard. Essie had never been on a thrill ride before.

Reed deposited everyone at a picnic table with strict orders not to move. Then he went in search of corn dogs and fries. When he returned, he not only had the desired food, but he'd bought three kid-size bufflehead hats. Esther and Justin put theirs on right away. Phillip insisted that the hats were lame, but he finally slapped his on top of his head.

Esther cautiously picked up the stick of

her corn dog. Camryn wondered why she didn't dig into the strange treat, but then she figured out why. Her gaze on Justin, Esther waited until he'd decided whether to dunk his dog into ketchup or mustard. Ketchup won out. After Justin had covered the tip of his corn dog with ketchup, Esther did the same. Between corn dogs and French fries, ketchup was the popular condiment of the evening.

When they'd all finished their dinner, the boys squirmed in their seats, anxious to get to the adult ride area on the midway.

Camryn took a pamphlet from her purse. "I picked this up when we came into the festival," she said. "There are rides you've always liked, Essie. They have the pirate ship, the teacups, a new Star Wars plane ride..."

"Those aren't rides," Phillip said. "Every one is like a baby's tricycle. They don't go fast and they barely leave the ground."

"Yeah, we don't like those," Justin added.

"Well, maybe Esther does," Reed said. "Can't you go on a couple of the tamer rides first? Then you can use tickets for the faster ones."

"Do we have to?" Phillip groaned.

Esther looked up at her mother. "I want to go on the fast rides, too, Mom. Can I?"

Camryn glanced at Reed. He shrugged his shoulder, leaving the decision up to her.

"I suppose we could check them out," she said. "I'm not promising anything. I doubt you'll meet the height requirements, Es."

I hope you don't anyway, Camryn thought.

They stopped at a ticket booth where Reed purchased twenty dollars' worth of ride tickets. Then they headed to the most colorful and exciting part of the midway, the area where music was loud and screams were prevalent. These rides should have been classified as fast and furious.

"I want to go on the Flying Chair," Phillip said.

Camryn studied that ride a moment. Each chair held only one occupant. A giant wheel lifted the riders higher and higher and spun them out and away from the center. "Let's not start with that one," she said.

"How about the Octopus?" Justin suggested.

Each car zoomed in a circle at the end of a long octopus arm while spinning on its axle at the same time. "No," Camryn said. "Pick another."

"Mom, those are both neat rides," Esther said.

Reed pointed toward a pendulum ride called the Hummer. "That one doesn't look too bad," he said. "It just goes back and forth, and Esther can be between the boys. What do you think?"

"Yeah, Mom, the Hummer! I want to go."

The pendulum was swinging at a relatively slow pace. Of all the choices, Camryn decided this seemed the tamest. "Okay," she said, reading a sign about the ride. "If you meet the height requirement of forty-eight inches, you can try that one."

"Oh, she will," Justin said, standing in front of a growth chart. He was at least fifty-two inches, and Esther was nearly as tall. "See?"

Camryn sighed.

"Are you going on, Mom?" Esther asked her.

"No, I think not. But you go. And have fun."

Reed gave each child ride tickets and they ran to get in line. "We'll be right here on this bench," he hollered at them. "Come over here when you get off."

Reed took Camryn's elbow and they walked to the bench. After sitting down, Cam had a good long look at the Hummer. Its pendulum motion had increased to daredevil heights.

"I don't know about this," she said to Reed.

"Your decision, Cam. If you want me to, I'll go get her out of the line." He started to rise.

"No, don't do that. She'd never forgive me."

Reed took her hand. "She'll be fine, I promise." He smiled. "Besides, this gives me the chance to be alone with her mother. As alone as any two people can be in the middle of a crowd of five hundred buffle-head enthusiasts."

She looked down at their joined hands. Once again, the warmth of Reed's palm was soothing. "I can't watch, so if anything happens you're in charge."

"Nothing's going to happen. By the way, they're getting on now."

He let a moment pass before turning the

conversation in a different direction. "Oh, did you see the work done on my property today? One metal building, the one I'll use for my clinic, is up. Just need to install air and heat and good electric lighting. Of course, before I can open, I'll need an operating room, exam tables, cabinets for storage and about a ton of medical supplies. But the shell is there, and the rest will come."

The calm tenor of his voice comforted her. She only glanced once at the Hummer, and concluded no one had fallen out. "When do you think you'll be operational?"

"Maybe a couple of weeks. The other metal building, the one I'll use for rehab, should be done the first of the week. Then I just need some rehabilitative outdoor areas—fences, a pond, some cages, that sort of thing."

"You sound excited to get started."

"I am. I think this will be good for my boys, too. It's no secret that they need some sense of routine and responsibility in their lives. I hope that helping me care for the animals will do that."

Camryn wanted to ask Reed about the boys' mother. Not wanting to invade his privacy, she said, "Have the boys always lived with you?"

"In one form or another," he said. "Before my wife and I divorced, I was at my clinic in Georgia for long hours at a time. Can't say I was the best father in those days. But since I've had the kids full-time for more than a year, I've made some changes that I hope work for all of us." He squeezed her hand. "One of those changes is relocating to Bufflehead Creek, where the nicest neighbor rented me barn space. I'm thinking I'd like to get to know her better."

He'd been divorced for a while; Camryn, only two months. Of course Reed wouldn't know this. "There isn't much to know," she said.

"I doubt that." He smiled. "I'm a good listener if you'd like to tell me your story, Cam."

Oh, sure. Tell him that she and her husband had lived in separate bedrooms for three years before getting divorced? Admit that she'd slept with him one unscripted night and now she was pregnant with his child? Confess to having panic attacks brought on by two miscarriages and an inability to cope with the pressures of her husband's job?

What man starting his life over wouldn't love to know the intimate details of a life as screwed up as hers was?

She took a deep breath. "Um…let's talk about this another time, okay?"

"Sure. Here come the kids anyway."

The conversation had accomplished one thing. Camryn hadn't focused on the perilous danger her daughter was in during the four-minute ride on the Hummer. All three kids ran to the bench.

"That was so cool!" Justin said.

"Yeah, cool," Esther echoed.

Phillip, unfazed by anything as mundane as an amusement ride, didn't comment.

"Did you like it, Phillip?" Reed asked him.

"It was okay."

Esther quietly took Camryn's hand. "Can you come with me a minute, Mommy?"

"Of course." Camryn got up and followed her daughter a few feet from the boys. "What's up?"

"I hated it, Mommy," Esther said. "It went

fast and high and I was scared. I don't ever want to do that again."

Camryn gently tugged her daughter's head to her chest. "You don't ever have to, Essie. You never should do anything because someone pressures you to do it. You know that, don't you?"

Esther looked up. Her bottom lip was trembling. "Mommy, I think I'm going to throw up."

Cam quickly ushered Esther to a bank of bushes nearby. They just made it in time. She held her daughter's head as Essie spewed up bits of corn dog and lots of fruit punch and ketchup, colorful proof of her tummy's revolt.

"Oh, look!" Phillip hollered. "Gross. She's puking."

Justin pointed at the bushes. "Gross!"

Reed grabbed both boys by their T-shirts and turned them away. "Stop that right now," he said. "As I recall, both of you have lost your cookies several times. It's no fun. Sit down on the bench until I see if I can help."

"We're not going home, are we?" Phillip moaned. "Not just 'cause of her?"

"If we go home, it'll be because of you two!" Reed said.

A minute later he appeared next to Camryn with a glass of water and a bunch of napkins. "Come here, sweetie," he said to Esther. He swept her bangs from her face, wiped her forehead and mouth, gave her a few sips of water. "Feel better now?"

She nodded. "Yeah. I just had to do that."

He chuckled. "Happens to the best of us," he said.

Camryn had a brief flashback to another time when Esther had vomited. She had brought the eight-month-old baby to Mark's office on a day she had planned a lunch date with Brooke. The office drop-in was meant as a surprise. Mark was consulting with an important client. The older man was immediately taken with Esther.

"What a beautiful baby," he'd said. "Can I hold her?"

He took the baby, held her away from his obviously expensive suit and jiggled her in the air. Esther had burped loudly and promptly thrown up mashed peas and carrots all over the man's lapels.

"Good God, Cam!" Mark had hollered.

"Look what you've done." He handed his daughter back to her mother and called for his secretary to bring towels and cleaning solution, all the while promising to replace the suit.

"It's all right," the client said. "I should have known better. Had four kids of my own."

Cam had bundled Esther into her stroller and quickly wheeled her out of the office. That wasn't the end of the episode. That night Camryn had to hear Mark's lecture about an office not being an appropriate place for a baby.

Now, as Camryn watched Reed smooth his hand down Essie's hair and encourage her to drink sips of water, she was amazed at the difference between the two men. Esther was actually laughing at the explosive timing of her stomach incident, and Reed was telling her about a similar experience from his past. She knew he was exaggerating. She didn't believe for an instant that Reed had thrown up during an audience with the Queen of England.

"Why don't we try some skill games

down the midway," Reed suggested. "I'll bet Esther will win a giant stuffed bear."

"We want to ride," Phillip said. "You can't make us do girl stuff."

"I can make you do anything I want," Reed said. "But I won't." He gave them the rest of the ride tickets. "Watch your brother every minute," he warned. "And, Phillip, what time does your watch say?"

"Seven fifteen."

"Right. At fifteen minutes until eight I will be back here to meet you. That's thirty minutes. And you'd both better be here. Let's go, ladies."

Esther walked between Reed and Camryn, her hands in each of theirs. "I want to pop some balloons with darts," she said.

"Excellent idea. And I plan to threaten some milk bottles with a baseball." Reed glanced over Esther's head at Camryn and winked. "Having fun yet, Mom?"

She smiled because, quite unexpectedly, she was.

CHAPTER SIX

AN HOUR LATER and sticky from dripping soft ice cream, Reed's boys and Esther climbed into his back seat. Despite the drama of the evening, Reed thought the trip to the festival had gone well. He'd spent fifteen dollars to win what was no doubt a three-dollar teddy bear for Esther, and she had cuddled the fuzzy black-and-tan animal the rest of their stay at the fair.

"I'm naming him Saucy," she'd announced. Justin had argued that she couldn't borrow a name. She had to think of a new one. However, *Saucy* stuck.

Reed enjoyed his fleeting moments with Camryn. When she relaxed and wasn't worried about Esther's well-being, she'd become chatty and enthusiastic about the fair. She'd stopped to talk to several people, including neighbors she claimed to have run into for the first time outside of the grocery or feedstore. One lady she introduced as the housewares manager at Value Center, Cam's favorite place to shop. She talked about the folks in their bufflehead hats and T-shirts. Reed liked this Camryn, the easygoing, smiling woman who was as determined to make a success of her new life as she was to be a good mother. And as he was to establish a successful clinic.

Reed couldn't help wondering what she would be like if suddenly they were alone and all her attention was on him. And all of his on her. Too bad that wouldn't happen tonight. The stars were brilliant, the country music coming from his radio soft and mellow, the moon full... And three kids in the back seat.

"Hey, are we here already?" Phillip asked.

"Yes, this is Camryn's house," Reed said.

"You're not going to make us go to bed, are you? It's only nine o'clock."

"That depends."

"On what?"

"On the kind of behavior you guys show when we get to our house."

From the corner of his eye, Reed caught Camryn's smile in the dashboard light.

"What do you think my chances are?" he asked.

"All three of them should be tired," she said.

Reed parked his vehicle, opened the door for Esther to get out and waited for Camryn to come around to join them. When they got to Camryn's door, Esther hurried inside. Good kid, Reed thought. *That's exactly what I was hoping she'd do.* Not that it mattered. His own kids were staring out the window of the SUV watching every move he made. They had rarely seen their father with a woman other than their mother, and those encounters had been fraught with tension for many years.

"Thanks so much," Camryn said. "Esther and I had a really nice time. I definitely owe you and the boys a home-cooked meal after this."

"You don't owe me anything," Reed said. "But if you're offering, I'm accepting." He smiled at her, resisting the urge to take her hand as he'd done several times already. "It was a fun evening."

"I'm glad you talked me into this. There are some nice people in this town, and I'm pleased I got to see so many of them. And so many duck enthusiasts."

"Buffleheads all," he said. After a short pause, he added, "You know, I really have the strongest urge to kiss you good-night."

Her gaze darted from his car to his face. "Oh, no, that can't happen."

"I know that." He reached up and twisted a strand of her blond hair between his fingers. "I promise I will tamp down my reaction to the overwhelmingly tempting observation that you look about as cute as a bufflehead duck floating on a quiet pond."

She chuckled. "Such flattery."

"Besides," he said. "This isn't a date. We made that clear when I asked you to come with me. I especially know that because if this were a date, we wouldn't have brought any kids along, we wouldn't be ending it at nine o'clock and we would have already kissed once or twice."

He was glad she'd left her porch light on—he could see the color rise in her cheeks.

"Good night, Camryn."

"Good night."

"If you need any help with your chickens tomorrow, let me know."

"I'll be fine." She turned and started to go into the house. As he stepped away, he heard her say, "If you need any help with your horses, don't ask me."

He was laughing as he walked to the car.

"I NEED CHICKEN FEED, corn and sugar-free grains," Camryn told Becky.

"Coming right up. Heard you are getting new chicks today."

"Who told you that?"

"That handsome Reed Bolden, the one whose gorgeous smile has no doubt brightened up Cottontail Farm in the last week. He just left here a few minutes ago. Said you were coming in."

Just the image of Reed's face popping into Camryn's mind made her smile. She hadn't stopped thinking about him since he'd dropped her off after the festival. "Can't anybody have some private business around here?" she said, feigning impatience.

"Sure." Becky winked. "Lots of stuff is private and should be, but probably not hen orders."

Esther tugged on Camryn's shirttail.

"Mommy, can we stop and buy apples and carrots for the horses?"

As much as Cam didn't want her daughter wandering into the barn, she couldn't say no. Besides, she had to stop at the farmers market herself for lettuce and blueberries. Her new chicks were going to appreciate their fancy buffet when they arrived. "Yes, you can get treats for the horses, but you can only go in the barn with an adult."

Esther gave her a bit of a pout.

"This is the way it's going to be, Es. Promise me."

"Okay."

Camryn paid her bill and hurried Esther to the truck. "No dawdling at the market, Esther. Apples and carrots, and that's it. We have to be home before ten when the chickens are supposed to be delivered."

They arrived at Cottontail Farm with fifteen minutes to spare. An open-air truck pulled in right on time. The driver unloaded three crates of Production Reds, beautiful birds with red feathers and earlobes. Happy to be released into the yard, the new arrivals wandered around, flapping their wings in what appeared to be an appreciation of their freedom. Next they progressed to pecking at grubs and insects on the ground.

"Ew, Mommy, give them some blueberries," Esther said. "Look at the gross stuff they're eating."

"It's not gross to them, Esther."

The final crate was unloaded from the truck, and the driver released two fluffy, young Ameraucana Blues and a pudgy, clucking Easter Egger. All three hens immediately waddled over to Esther, who promptly sat on the ground and took one in her lap. Known for their friendly demeanors, the hens didn't disappoint. Esther and the chickens were soon fast friends.

"I'm glad you're getting to know these birds, Esther," Camryn said. "Because you are going to be responsible for gathering their eggs every morning…even on school days."

"And they'll be blue and green, right?"

"Yes, they will. And maybe some pink."

"Then that will be fun."

Camryn paid the driver for the delivery and twelve dollars each for the twenty-seven birds. Besides missing the chance to sell produce at the market this morning, she was burning through Reed's advance rent money pretty quickly. But all the new hens were good layers, and she'd make the money back soon enough. She hoped each new hen would give her four to five eggs a week.

Plus she'd finished her cover for the next edition of *Alphabet Days*. Quirky the Thanksgiving Turkey would be ready for delivery a week before the holiday, and Cam would get a nice check and one hundred copies to donate to Esther's school.

Camryn and Esther spent the next hour acclimating the chickens to their new environment and feeding them the goodies from the feedstore. Camryn noticed that there was no aggressive behavior between the new hens and her original ones, and was thankful for that.

Reed and his boys came over at noon to care for their horses. The boys went into the barn, but Reed walked over to the chicken yard and complimented Esther on her new feathered friends. After paying attention to the birds, Reed headed to the barn, but not without placing his hand on the small of Camryn's back and wishing her a good day. A simple gesture, but one that temporarily made Camryn forget which nesting boxes she'd neglected to put food pellets in.

Get a grip, Camryn, she told herself. *Just because a man is nice to you, just because your daughter seems to bloom when he gives her his attention, it does not mean you should jump to any conclusions. Don't forget that any relationship with Reed would come encumbered with all your baggage, especially the one in your tummy he doesn't know about. And that doesn't take into account the two rambunctious bits of baggage of Reed's own...the ones currently in your barn.*

Satisfied that she'd put her mind back on track, Camryn began changing the straw in some of the nesting boxes. She barely heard Esther call, "Mom, somebody's coming up the drive!"

Camryn came out to the yard. Oh, boy, not just "somebody," she thought…a very special somebody driving a pearl gray BMW. Despite all her protestations, Brooke Montgomery had finally graced Cottontail Farm with a visit.

"Brooke!" Camryn had opened her sister's car door before Brooke had even turned off the engine.

"Auntie Brooke!" Esther bounced on her toes, waiting for Brooke to exit the car.

Brooke managed to hug both ladies in one giant embrace. "If I had known I'd get this kind of reception, I'd have come to this farm before today."

"I'm just glad you're here now," Camryn said. "In fact I can't believe it. Why are you here? What made you decide to make the drive?"

Brooke smiled. "Had to see those new chickens for myself. When you're this excited about something, Cammie, I have to participate."

"I thought you were going to dinner with Mom and Dad."

"Yep. Still am. But that's not until tomorrow. You and I are going to have that girl time I promised you today." She looked at the farmhouse. "So this is the place. Looks just like the pictures—all cute and charming. Can a girl get an iced tea before she dies of thirst?"

"Of course. Let's go in the house." Camryn stared down at her dirty blouse and pants. "I'll just brush off my clothes and

I'll be right in. Essie, take Auntie Brooke inside."

Esther sidled up close to her aunt. Brooke put her arm around Esther's shoulders and they headed toward the front porch. As she swatted chicken feathers and feed from her pants, Camryn watched the two go inside.

As usual Brooke looked fantastic, her makeup artfully applied and her gorgeous blond hair, kissed by the skilled hands of Charleston's finest hairdresser, hanging down her back in lush, loose curls. One side of her hair had been pulled up and was held by a chic tortoiseshell clip. Brooke wore a pair of tight-fitting, stylishly ragged jeans that probably cost more than three pairs of the sturdy brand Camryn owned. A white blouse and dark blue jacket completed her outfit.

Camryn smiled as she followed the girls to the house. She'd managed to get most of the chicken remnants off her clothes. Even if she'd stopped to change clothes completely, she knew she'd never match Brooke's high fashion taste. Brooke had always been the stylish one. Cam had never minded playing the girl next door to Brooke's cover model.

Esther and Brooke were chatting easily when Camryn came into the kitchen. She got the iced tea pitcher from the refrigerator and poured them each a glass.

"This kitchen is really adorable," Brooke said. "I love the vintage look."

"Thanks," Cam said. "But sometimes the vintage look means I need to have a repairman come out. Someday I will replace the appliances."

They caught up on family news, and Esther got to tell of all her adventures, especially her ride on the pony with a "cute boy" named Justin.

"Oh, my, this sounds serious," Brooke teased.

After a few minutes, Brooke gave her sister a serious glance.

"What?" Camryn asked. "Is something wrong?"

"No, nothing. But remember when I mentioned girl time? I was just going to suggest that maybe you and I could have a few minutes alone. Would that be okay with you, Essie?"

"Okay." She looked at her mother. "Can I go outside?"

"You can, but no pony rides when I'm not around. You understand, right?"

"But can I give Saucy one of the apples we bought this morning?"

"I suppose. But only if Reed is there to show you how to feed the pony. You can't approach the horses by yourself."

Esther grabbed an apple from a basket on the table. Cam sliced it for her, and Esther ran outside, excited to be anywhere near the pony.

"All right, sis. Girl time," Camryn said. "What do you want to talk to me about? It must be good to have brought you all the way from Charleston."

Brooke methodically twirled her glass of tea. "I think you'll agree that what I'm about to tell you was worth the trip."

"I must admit," Camryn said, "my curiosity is definitely piqued."

"So hear me out. Don't go ballistic on me before I can state my case."

Camryn pretended to be insulted. "When have I ever gone ballistic…? Oh, wait, there was that one time."

"Yeah, one time," Brooke repeated. "Promise?"

"Yes, I promise. Now, tell me, for heaven's sake."

Brooke took a deep breath and settled more comfortably on the old wooden chair. "Sometimes it pays to be a news producer," she said.

"I'm sure it does, but why are you telling me this now?"

"We had a guest in the studio a couple of weeks ago. He was interviewed during the six o'clock news about an ongoing lawsuit involving a homeowners association at a local condo complex. The HOA is suing the condo owners for not living up to their contracts."

"This is all very interesting," Cam said, "but what does it have to do with your visit today?"

"Well, the condo thing has basically nothing to do with my visit. I'm not here to talk about the lawsuit. But this lawyer—the guy who was interviewed, Bill Rappaport is his name—is kind of a big deal in Charleston. He can open doors and get answers if you know what I mean."

"I do. And I'm assuming you had a question for him."

"Right." Brooke took a couple of deep

breaths. "You know that for years I've wanted to find out anything I could about our biological parents..."

Realizing where the conversation was headed, Camryn sat stiffly in her chair. "I've known, yes, but I never understood why. Have you forgotten that I told you countless times to let it go? Those adoption papers were sealed. That's the way Mom and Dad wanted it, and all parties agreed to the terms."

Brooke held up her hand in a placating gesture. "Of course I haven't forgotten, Cammie, but this has always been an issue between us. You don't want to know about our parents..."

"I know everything I need to know. Linda and Craig Montgomery are our parents, and we should both count ourselves lucky that they took us when our mother obviously didn't want the responsibility of a pair of twins."

"I agree with that one hundred percent, Cam. I love Mom and Dad every bit as much as you do. But aren't you curious? Just a little?"

"No, I'm not. And I don't get why you are."

Brooke exhaled, taking a deep breath.

"You never have. Okay, let me try to explain it to you. There is something missing from our lives. We don't have the pieces that can make us whole." As if she sensed that Camryn wasn't buying her explanation, she took another deep breath. "Remember when we were in middle school and had to make a genealogy chart of our ancestors?"

"Yes, I remember. I used Mom and Dad's family as ours because that's exactly how I think of them. I loved Gran with all my heart."

"I know, but I felt like the project was a lie. Every name I added to that chart was a fabrication. None of those names had anything to do with me. The entire chart was filled with substitutes for all the missing pieces, the pieces that make up you and me. The other kids in our class had real families and real ancestors. Maybe it's my reporter's instincts kicking in, but I want…no, I *need* to know what my missing pieces are."

"But I don't, Brooke. I wouldn't do anything to hurt Mom and Dad, and I think prying into this piece of history would hurt them badly. Also, I feel pretty certain that what I would discover about our birth parents would only result in pain for everyone involved, but especially for you and me."

Camryn paused a moment. "I hate to be so blunt, Brooke, but I believe that uncovering this particular molehill would only reveal a mountain of regret. My instincts tell me that the people we have become, thanks to Mom and Dad, are probably the exact opposites of our biological parents and the values they would have instilled in us."

Brooke frowned. "It's not like you to be such an elitist, Camryn."

"Elitist! That's ridiculous." She spread her hands to encompass her kitchen. "Would you look where I live?" She plucked a few feathers from her blouse. "How about this shirt I bought at the Value Center in Bufflehead Creek? If I were any kind of an elitist, I would still be living with Mark and entertaining the upper echelon of the corporate world."

"Whoa, whoa," Brooke said. "I picked a poor choice of word. It just sounded like you are afraid our parents would turn out to be poor or uneducated."

"That's not what I meant. People's values aren't tied to their income or how long they've spent in school." Camryn stood, pacing around her small kitchen. "No, Brooke, I don't want to know anything about them."

Brooke lowered her head and spoke so softly Camryn couldn't hear her. "What did you say?"

Brooke leaned in. "I said, it's too late. Bill Rappaport was able to track down the records and have them unsealed. I asked him how he'd managed that and he simply said, 'Don't ask.' But if you or your sister is ever in front of a Charleston judge, and asked how either of us is feeling after discovering our link to a genetic childhood disease, we should say we're doing much better."

"So he lied to get the records opened," Camryn said.

"I prefer to call it creative persuasion."

Camryn sat heavily on the chair again. "I can't believe you did this, Brooke. Against my wishes."

"What about my wishes? Don't they count as much as yours?"

Camryn didn't have an answer, so she kept silent.

"It was just too great an opportunity for me to have a past, a real past, with names that mean something," Brooke said. "A genealogy that actually exists! When I met Bill, and he said if I ever needed anything… well, I started telling him."

Camryn drummed her fingers on the tabletop. "I don't want to know my past, Brooke. If you do, that's your business. But I believe it will only bring me heartache. And I suggest you forget you ever opened this Pandora's box. Throw the information away and try to forget it."

"I'm not going to do that, Cammie. You know me better than that, just like I know you better than you give me credit for."

"What's that supposed to mean?"

Brooke took some papers from her shoulder bag. "It's all here in black-and-white, at least the details about our mother. And now that you're aware that all you have to do is look at the name and the address, I know your natural curiosity will get the better of you. It always has. You've always dug another few inches into the dirt to find buried treasure. And that's what this could be, Cam—buried treasure about our lives."

Camryn gave her a hard stare. "Don't play

me, Brooke. Don't try to anticipate what I will or won't do."

Brooke paused and ruffled the papers, an annoying act that seemed designed to hold Camryn's attention. After a few moments, she said, "She lives in Myrtle Beach, Cam. Less than an hour's drive from here."

Cam wanted to stay angry. She'd always vehemently objected to searching out their parents. And now Brooke had betrayed her by pursuing the search on her own. But the sight of those papers, the knowledge that her history was hidden inside them… Could she do this? Maybe she could just see the woman from a distance. Maybe that would be enough. Bottom line, though, she should ignore the proposition Brooke was presenting. That's what she should do. But those papers, so tempting…

Camryn sighed. "Give me your word, Brooke, that you will never tell Mom and Dad we did this. You have to promise. Otherwise…"

"Of course, Cam. I don't want them to know any more than you do. I don't believe that finding our mother is a betrayal of what Mom and Dad mean to us, but they could read something into our quest that simply isn't so." She reached across the table and took Camryn's hand. "I will never tell them, Cammie. Never."

In the end, this was Brooke, the sister she'd loved forever. "One trip to Myrtle Beach, Brooke. One time. If we don't find her, that's it. I won't go back."

"Understood." Brooke put the papers away. "Pick a day this week. Essie will be in school. You'll be home before she is."

Camryn's mind was spinning. Pick a day. Choose a time to do something that had the potential to hurt people she loved. She shook her head. "Wednesday, I guess."

"Great. I'll arrange to get the day off work. I'll meet you at the highway rest area at the Myrtle Beach exit at nine o'clock, and we'll drive one car from there. Can you be on time?"

Camryn simply nodded. Her throat felt too dry to utter any words.

Brooke stood and came around the table. She folded Camryn in a fierce hug. "Oh, thanks, Cammie. I need this. I really do. And I need you beside me, presenting a unified front. I love you," she whispered in Camryn's ear.

"I love you, too," Camryn said.

And then the quiet of the kitchen was broken by an ear-splitting cry for help.

"Mommy, come get me! Help me, Mommy!"

Camryn shot to her feet and sprinted for the door. With Brooke following her, she ran to the barn.

CHAPTER SEVEN

"I'M COMING, ESSIE!" Camryn screamed as she tore across the yard. Her heart was racing so fast she hardly heard her own words and just barely noticed the chickens squawking and fluttering in confusion.

The barn doors were wide open. Camryn's first thought was that one of the horses had gotten out of its stall and had injured Esther. She flew into the open doors and stopped dead. There, above her head, were Esther's two legs, hanging down from an opening in the hayloft at least twenty feet above the barn floor.

"Esther, I'm here, baby," she called out. "What happened?"

"I fell through, Mommy," Esther said, her words muffled by tears. "I stepped on a board, and it went crack and I went through the hole."

"Try not to move, Esther. You have to stay real still until I can get to you."

"But my arm hurts, Mommy."

Camryn searched frantically for a ladder. There must be a ladder. She finally saw it leaning against the loft. A pair of large feet at the end of two long legs balanced on one of the top rungs. She could just see Reed's head above the hayloft. Hay rained down onto the barn floor as he scooted across the boards, scattering everything that blocked his path to Esther.

"I'll get her," Reed called out. "Stay calm, Esther."

Camryn clenched her hand over her mouth. "Don't wiggle, baby. Reed's coming to get you. Can you hold on?"

"I think so. My arms didn't go through."

"If you feel like you're going to fall, I'm right here underneath you. Auntie Brooke is here, too. We'll catch you."

"What hurts, Essie?" Brooke called out.

"Just my arm. It's not so bad right now."

Reed's legs disappeared from view. Camryn had to imagine the rescue taking place by just watching a path of dust motes as he made his way to her daughter.

"I'm here behind you, Esther," he said. "I

can almost reach your arm. Be still, sweet-heart. I'll pull you up."

"Please hurry, Reed," Camryn yelled. "She's going to lose her grip and fall."

A few seconds later, Camryn heard the words that allowed her to finally take a nearly normal breath.

"I've got her, Cam," Reed said calmly. "I'm pulling her up right now."

Slowly, a few inches at a time, Esther's legs ascended through the hole, and she was soon back on the unstable flooring of the hayloft.

"Be careful, Reed," Camryn said. "Those old boards are obviously not safe. I don't need both of you falling through."

"I'm sending Esther down first," he said. "I'll hold her while you climb partway up the ladder. Just position yourself a rung or two underneath her in case she slips. But her legs seem fine."

Esther's thin frame appeared at the top of the ladder. Reed held tightly to her upper arms as Esther found her footing on the top rung. Camryn climbed as fast as she could to meet her daughter. "You can start down now, sweetie," Camryn said. "I'm right here."

She kept her hands on Esther's hips, guiding her down the ladder. Seconds seemed to drag until Camryn reached the bottom. Brooke was waiting to grab Esther. When her boots touched the floor, Camryn hugged Esther and they both collapsed on the straw-covered planks. Camryn's hands wandered quickly over Esther, checking her arms and legs. "Are you okay? I don't think anything's broken."

"I'm okay, Mommy. I just scratched my arm."

Brooke stood with her cell phone in her hand. "Should I call 911?"

"Hang on a minute, everybody," Reed said, reminding Camryn that he was still on the precarious landing above them.

"Oh, Reed, be careful," Camryn said. "Don't injure yourself."

"I don't intend to." He began a slow descent down the ladder. Dust and straw billowed around him in the breeze coming through the barn. He was filthy, and so was Esther. Camryn figured no one had been in that loft for decades.

He hopped the distance of the last few

rungs and came over to the women. "Let me look at you, Esther."

"Is he qualified to determine her injuries?" Brooke asked. "I mean that was a daring rescue and all, but Esther might need a doctor."

"I'm the closest thing here," Reed said. "I'm a vet."

"Okay, that's better than nothing, but since my niece is not a horse I still say we should call the paramedics."

"Stop it, Brooke," Camryn said. She gently urged Esther into Reed's waiting arms. "We're lucky that Reed was here today. He got to Esther before we did, and I'm thankful for that." She turned to Reed. "How did you know Esther was in trouble?" she asked.

"I heard her calling for you, and I came running from the paddock. Believe me, Cam, after she fed Saucy the apples, I made her go away from the horses."

"Esther, you came back to the barn?" Camryn asked. "I told you to stay away."

"But I wanted to," Esther said.

The eventual punishment for disobeying was the farthest thing from Camryn's mind.

Reed asked Esther a few questions and

soon had her laughing. "She's fine, Cam," he said. "She was mostly scared."

"I wasn't scared," Esther insisted.

Camryn ran her hand down Esther's hair. "Of course you weren't, honey."

"Yeah," Brooke said. "That's why we all heard you from a few hundred yards away."

Esther giggled. Camryn thanked Reed for rescuing Esther, and then she finally relaxed. She'd never been so happy to see someone's boot heels as she'd been to see Reed's from the loft.

Reed seemed focused entirely on Brooke. "You two look alike," he said after a moment.

"Oh, sorry," Camryn said. "Reed, this is my twin sister, Brooke. Brooke, this is Reed Bolden. He rents my barn."

"So this is the guy you…"

Camryn immediately interrupted her. "This is the guy who rents my barn. I just told you that."

"Right. The barn renter," Brooke said.

"Twins," Reed said. "I should have guessed."

Camryn frowned. Sure. *Because my hands are all callused. I have muscles where girls should have soft curves. And my hair hasn't been styled in months and is covered in barn dust. Brooke, on the other hand, never did manual labor, has gorgeous curves where they ought to be, and has nothing in her hair but a pricey tortoiseshell clip.*

"You here for a long visit?" Reed asked Brooke.

"Nope. In and out in one day. But at least I didn't miss all the excitement."

"Speaking of excitement," Camryn said, "Esther, we need to talk about why you came to the barn by yourself. I told you…"

"I wasn't by myself," Esther said. "Phillip and Justin were here with me."

Camryn immediately sensed this story would end badly. "Why did you climb up to the hayloft in the first place? And how did you even get the ladder over there where it needed to be?"

"Phillip and Justin brought it over."

Reed's face changed in an instant. A small vein throbbed in his temple. "They did what?"

"They brought me the ladder so I could climb up. They said they had already been in the loft, and if I wasn't a scaredy-cat I would go up, too. They said they would come up right behind me."

Camryn's head buzzed with the first spark of anger. "And did they...come up after you?"

Esther shook her head.

"Oh, Esther, you believed them? What have I told you about taking dares from Phillip and Justin? Don't you realize how foolish it was for you to..."

Reed's boot steps made her pause. She spun around to see the back of him as he exited the barn.

"Where is he going in such a hurry?" Brooke asked. "And who are Phillip and Justin?"

"Reed's sons," Cam explained. "He's a single father, and if he's got any sense at all, he's on his way to find his sons and punish them. This isn't the first time they've goaded Esther into doing something she shouldn't."

"Obviously they like you, Es," Brooke said.

Esther grinned. "Do you think so?"

"Absolutely. Your mother knows all about chickens. But I know a thing or two about men. And my instinct says..."

"I hope it's telling you to be quiet," Camryn said. "I don't need to hear such nonsense right now."

Brooke smiled. "As a matter of fact, that's exactly what it's telling me."

A HALF HOUR later Camryn left Esther soaking in the tub and returned to the kitchen, where Brooke was waiting.

"How is she?" Brooke asked, nursing another glass of iced tea.

"She's fine. A few bruises. One minor abrasion. But she was lucky. I know that. She could have fallen all the way through and hit the barn floor."

"I suppose," Brooke said. "But she didn't."

Camryn brought some lunch meat and bread to the table. She couldn't eat a thing but figured Brooke must be hungry after driving from Charleston. Sitting down, Camryn took a couple of deep breaths. "I don't know where she gets this bold streak all of a sudden. Esther has always been such a quiet child. She has never been a discipline problem, and now she has defied me more than once in just a few days."

Brooke reached in her bag and took out

a compact mirror. She fluffed her hair with exaggerated movements. "Can't imagine where she gets it, Cammie, but I'm starting to think she looks a bit like me, too."

Camryn laughed. "She looks like both of us, and I never broke any rules."

Brooke dropped the mirror back in her purse. "Karma will get you for that lie, sister."

Camryn sighed. "I'm going to have to make some adjustments around here. Esther hasn't learned to stand up to those boys of Reed's, so I don't have a choice. I have to monitor the times she sees them. They can't come over here whenever they want to."

Brooke slathered mustard on a slice of bread. "You don't want to inflict the same rules on their father, do you?"

Cam didn't know what she was getting at.

"Speaking of Reed," Brooke said. "Let's talk about him for a minute…or an hour or two. He's absolutely scrumptious, Cam, a fact which you neglected to tell me when you explained this barn rental agreement."

"His looks had nothing to do with my decision to rent him the barn," Cam said but couldn't hide a smile. "Though I have to agree with you. I simply needed the eight hundred dollars he offered me. How do you think I paid for those new chickens in the yard?"

"So, in essence, Reed paid for your chickens. Besides being gorgeous, he's a true romantic. No man has ever given me a chicken, not a live one anyway." She took a bite of sandwich and spoke around the food in her mouth, something Brooke rarely did. "Tell me you're appreciating this guy on every level, Cam. I mean it's great that he rescued Es, but surely you've discovered his other attributes."

"I'm not about to admit to that, and don't read anything into him being my new neighbor. We are friends I suppose, but that's it."

"Friends who are both single. I'm assuming he still has red blood pumping through his veins, though at times I wonder about you."

Camryn rubbed her tummy. "It's that dang red blood that got me in this situation."

"How is that going anyway?"

"Okay, I guess, and thank goodness. I only have a short time until the critical period is over. Then I hope I can relax." Unable to discuss the tragic details of her other pregnancies, Camryn stared down at the tabletop and shook her head. "I know I've been a bit uptight about this baby, Brooke. But delivering a strong, healthy child is all I think about these days."

"Understandable. But when you finally can relax, I hope you'll allow your thoughts to wander to that handsome neighbor. He seems like a great guy, Cam. And he's obviously interested in you as more than a landlady."

"I don't know how you could tell that in just the few seconds you spoke with him." But Camryn didn't bother to deny Brooke's observation. Reed had definitely shown an interest in her last night at her front door. She'd thought about his words over and over again before falling asleep, and she'd wondered about what would have happened if their children hadn't been present.

"Okay, I'm guessing, but it's an educated guess."

"Even if he is interested, I can't encourage any relationship with Reed now, Brooke. You know that. I'm barely two months divorced. I'm three months pregnant. I have no business thinking about starting something with Reed. Besides, he's raising those two roughneck boys…" She patted her stomach again. "I have this bundle of joy to consider. And I can't imagine that Reed would welcome a fourth child between us."

Brooke frowned. "Now who's reading minds?"

"It's not just my pregnancy." Camryn paused and took a deep breath. "I had one of my spells in front of him the other day. I covered it well. He assumed I'd gotten dizzy and I let him believe that. Bottom line, if he knew about even half the baggage I'm carrying around with me, he would run for the hills."

"He doesn't seem like the running kind to me," Brooke said.

"You're drawing conclusions, Brooke. I barely know the man and you just met him."

"True, but maybe you should give him a chance before assuming that it could never work between you. In fact…" Brooke stopped, took a sip of tea. "You should level with him. Tell him everything. I know I'd feel better if you did, and Mom and Dad, too."

"Why would my telling Reed about my pregnancy make you feel better?"

"We all worry about you out on this farm with no one but Esther. We'd all like to think someone close by is watching over you."

Camryn shook her head. "Honestly, Brooke, do you think I would tell Reed what's going on in my life so I could guilt him into being my babysitter? Or to satisfy you and Mom and Dad?"

"I didn't mean that the way it came out," Brooke said. "I sense that you like this guy. It's quite possible he likes you, too. You might as well start the friendship off with the truth. He's going to know you're pregnant in a couple of months anyway. You can't hide it forever."

"I don't intend to hide it. I just don't want to involve anyone in my problems. Things are going well for me. I'm getting a grip on my panic attacks…or I was."

Brooke finished her sandwich. "Okay, it's your life. But please, if you see more of Reed…and I can't even begin to imagine why you wouldn't…he's handsome, he's educated…"

Camryn grew impatient. "What's your point?"

"My point is that you should confide in him. If you don't, and he's interested in you, he's going to wonder why you kept so much of your situation a secret. And even if he's not interested in starting something with you, a nine-year-old girl is not qualified to help you if you suddenly need assistance. You need a vet nearby." She gave Camryn a coy smile. "What are neighbors for anyway?"

"I have friends. And neighbors don't exist so we can take advantage of them. But I'll think about your advice," Camryn said.

"Good, and I'm leaving now. I came. I saw. I conquered—which reminds me... I'll see you on Wednesday at the highway exit to Myrtle Beach. You're not going to back out on me?"

"No, I'll be there. Reluctantly."

Brooke stood, came around the table. She leaned down and gave Camryn a hug. "This really is a charming little house, Cam. And your farm looks like it's thriving to me, though I haven't seen many farms to compare it to."

Cam walked into the living room with Brooke. When they passed the dining room table, Brooke suddenly stopped and stared at boxes filled with glass jars. "What is all this?" she asked. "I didn't notice it when I came in."

"It's blackberry jam, four dozen jars of it."

Brooke pulled a jar out of a box. "Don't tell me…you made these yourself?"

"I absolutely did. And I plan to sell them at the farmers market. Go ahead, take one. Blackberries grow wild around here, and if I do say so myself, the jam I make with them is delicious."

Brooke tucked the jar into her bag. "Oh, my gosh, Cam, it's like you're in a play or something." In her most dramatic voice she added, "Come back to us, dear sister, before we lose you forever."

"Don't be silly. Now pop into the bathroom and say goodbye to Esther."

Camryn was still smiling as Brooke drove down the lane to the road. Brooke wasn't all wrong. Cam had changed, made decisions that had surprised her entire family. She had given up a big house and a life in Charleston for the sweet smell of grass in the country. There indeed was a big difference between the refurbished condo in a nineteenth-century house in Charleston, where Brooke lived, and a small farm in Bufflehead Creek.

AFTER SUPPER, CAMRYN and Esther played a game and watched a bit of television until Esther's eyes would no longer stay open. Cam tucked her daughter in bed, turned on the night light and left the bedroom door open a crack.

Now was Cam's time. She showered, washed and dried her hair and slipped into her comfy chenille robe. After the day she'd had, she really wanted a glass of wine, but with a baby on the way, that wasn't possible. So she poured a glass of white grape juice, added ice and went onto the front porch to enjoy the sounds of night time settling around the farm.

She didn't turn on the porch light because she didn't want to attract bugs. But she lit a couple of citronella candles and sat in her favorite rocking chair. A fresh, cool breeze swept over the porch but the robe kept her warm and cozy. She rested her head on the back of the rocker, listened to a nearby owl in a tree and the melodious rhythm of crickets, and thought, *I really do love it here.* An idea for her Christmas magazine cover occurred to her. "Carl the Christmas Cricket," she said aloud.

After a few minutes, the peace of the evening was interrupted by a vehicle coming up her drive. Camryn had no idea what time it was, but certainly it was too late for visitors. She sat upright in the rocker and peered into the darkness. The vehicle was a large SUV, black in color. Camryn's heartbeat escalated as the SUV came closer. Reed's car.

He parked in front of her porch and got out of his car.

"Evening," he said. "Mind a little company on a pretty night?"

She waited before answering to see if his sons got out of the back. They didn't. "Sure. Pull up a chair."

"I noticed you hesitated before issuing the invitation, and I can't blame you. The boys are home with my mother. She's probably using a cattle prod to get them to bed right now."

He chose a comfortable wicker chair and scooted it close to Camryn. "How's Esther?"

"She's fine. A couple of bruises, which to my dismay she is proud of, but she's no doubt sleeping peacefully by now."

"That's good." He sat, crossed his legs so his ankle rested on the other leg. "Speaking of my boys, they didn't have a good evening."

"Oh? Why is that?"

"Because they learned they were denied video games for a month and have to do their homework immediately upon getting home from school for a week." Reed smiled. "That last one probably hurts me more than it hurts them. I had planned to take full advantage of the lax child labor laws in this area and work their butts off in the barn."

Camryn nodded. "I guess it's not unusual for our punishments to backfire on us once in a while."

Reed pushed the sleeves of his denim jacket past his elbows, revealing strong forearms with a light covering of dark hair. He shifted as if trying to get comfortable on the plush cushions and released a long breath. "I came to apologize," he said. "Again."

Cam smiled. "Why? What did you do?"

"What I did was contribute fifty per cent of my DNA to those two hooligans and then basically ignore their upbringing for eleven years. But what I'm apologizing for is their behavior. Their actions were dangerous and mean. All I can say to you now is that I think they understand that what they did was wrong for so many reasons."

He leaned toward Camryn, resting his forearm on the arm of her rocker. "But at the most basic level I think this was an example of boys and girls testing each other, trying to prove themselves and strutting around until they establish dominance. In other words, I think my boys actually like your daughter." He smiled. "Justin said, 'But she did it, Dad. She's not a baby after all.'"

Justin's comment was little comfort to Camryn. She shook her head while her gaze remained on the tendons of that arm so close. "Funny, that's what my sister said, but I'm not sure I buy it."

"That's okay. Finding a reason for bad behavior does not excuse it. And in my capacity as a single father, I've learned a thing or two about bad behavior."

Camryn looked up, focused on the deep brown of his eyes. The entirely female part of her wished she had eyelashes even half as thick as Reed's. His hair, still damp at the ends from a recent shower, glowed golden in the candle light. She couldn't let such sensory pleasures influence her. While she'd been sitting on the porch, she'd reinforced the conclusion she'd reached earlier.

"Reed," she began. "You understand that I must think of my daughter before anything else."

"Of course."

"I've made a decision. It would be best if your boys didn't come around my farm unless they are supervised. One of the two of us should be present whenever the kids are together. If that is a hardship on you... If you want to cancel the rental agreement..."

"I don't. I'm happy with our situation. And my horses tell me they love it here."

She smiled. "You're not angry? This hopefully isn't forever, but for the near future..." She took a deep breath. "I understand that your sons are children, and all children test authority, but what happened in the barn today…"

"I get it, Cam. Believe me, I know how bad it could have been. Phillip and Justin will be occupied with homework after school for the next week anyway, so they will not be near Esther. Maybe they'll surprise us both and come to regret their actions. That's my hope anyway. I have no problem with keeping them from coming over here. But I don't want to punish myself, as well. I want to see you, Cam. I tried to tell you that last night. Maybe we can go out to dinner next week, with or without the kids, whatever makes you comfortable."

She considered the open-ended invitation. A dinner out might be nice, and with both parents there, all the children could be trusted to behave in a restaurant, couldn't they? "I actually owe you a dinner," she said. "But if you let me pay the bill for myself and Esther, I think we could do that."

"We can talk about the details later. And don't worry about owing me a home-cooked meal. I intend to make you live up to that promise. But I'm just now thinking that you agreed too quickly to that part about taking the kids along." He grinned at her. "I was kind of hoping you'd argue that point."

"You don't want to take the children?" she asked.

He placed his hand on her arm over the sleeve of her robe. "What do you think?"

"Well…"

"Has Esther planned any sleepovers in the next little while?"

Camryn smiled. "Are you seriously suggesting ways of getting rid of our children, Reed?"

"Life isn't all about the kids, Camryn. We adults need to find time for ourselves. Let's make this dinner about just you and me. Good food. A good bottle of wine."

Camryn's hand went instinctively to her tummy. "I don't drink, but you can certainly have a glass." If Reed was serious about wanting to take her out, the perfect solution for Esther had been presented this afternoon. Mark had called to say he wanted to drive down and pick up Esther on Friday for the weekend. Camryn certainly couldn't deny Esther and her father time together, so she'd told Mark that he could come.

Camryn bit her bottom lip. She suddenly

wanted to go out to dinner with Reed, and the details were falling into place. Still she questioned whether she should do anything to further this relationship. Reed had responsibilities on his shoulders right now. There was so much about her life that Reed didn't know. Maybe Brooke was right and Cam could tell him about her past, and present, when they went out.

"The bottom line is this, Camryn," Reed said. "My horses aren't the only living, breathing creatures who like it here. I consider the day I met you at the feedstore to be a stroke of pure luck." He took her hand and held it in both of his. "I like you, Camryn, more than I expected to that day and perhaps more than I should considering those two boys over there are doing everything they can to make the Bolden men look bad. But it is what it is, and I do like you."

Continuing to hold her hand in one of his and gently massaging her knuckles with his thumb, he shifted his free hand to her nape. His fingers threaded through her loose hair, tickling her neck in the most delightful way. His palm was warm, sending waves of pleasure through her shoulders. When he pulled her close, she knew he was going to kiss her. And she knew she wouldn't resist.

He pressed his mouth to hers, gently but persuasively. She sighed, releasing the tension of the last moments to the feel of his lips on hers. Once she had decided to accept his kiss, the urge to feel him so close was overwhelming. Even when she'd been with Mark that one last time, he hadn't kissed her. And right now she wondered if anyone, anytime, had ever kissed her like this. Reed's kiss was potent, manly and yet somehow pure, as if he valued what she was giving him.

When he drew back, she ran the tip of her index finger over the moisture on her bottom lip. She could still feel his mouth, the sweet press of his tongue. She sat back into her chair, released a deep sigh and clutched the lapels of her robe more tightly at her throat. She could lose control with a man who kissed like Reed Bolden.

He lightly stroked her bangs with his fingertips. His thumb repeatedly brushed her forehead. "That was nice, Cam. If I didn't know my mother was dealing with issues at my house, I'd be trying to think of ways to beg you to let me stay a bit longer."

And she might be thinking of ways to beg him to stay. The practical side of her, the part that protected herself and all she held dear, spoke. "It's probably for the best if you go," she said.

"Probably. Dinner on Wednesday? Just the two of us?"

Wednesday... Wednesday...something was happening on Wednesday. She suddenly remembered the trip to Myrtle Beach. "That's not a good day for me this week. I've made an appointment I can't get out of."

"No problem." He stood, bent over her and kissed the top of her head. "I'll be in touch."

He got in his SUV, drove down her lane until his taillights disappeared into the dark. And Cam, who felt deliciously warm under her robe, did not realize for several minutes that the temperature around her had dropped.

CHAPTER EIGHT

CAMRYN DIDN'T SEE Reed at all on Sunday, but she knew he'd been over to care for his horses. The outside water troughs had been filled and fresh hoofprints remained in the dirt at the rear of the barn.

Monday, as she gathered eggs from her coop, Reed waved at her from Brute's saddle, heading into the pasture for a ride. She'd never have believed she was a "cowboy sort of girl," but seeing him with his hat pulled low and his back straight, his hands loose on the reins, she wondered why she'd overlooked the obvious appeal of a man who loved horses. Or maybe she was appreciating this particular cowboy.

Reed had told her on Saturday night that he would be in touch, and she was ready with her answer. She would go out to dinner with him, allow herself to have a good time and maybe even wear one of the two dresses she'd brought from Charleston. Brooke would be so proud.

On Monday afternoon, when the school bus pulled up to the lane leading to Cottontail Farm, Camryn and Rooster went to meet Esther. Esther got off the bus, barely spoke a word and stomped past her mother. Rooster whined at being ignored by his favorite playmate, and Camryn stared after her.

"Hold on there, kiddo," Cam said. "What's going on? Did something happen at school today?"

Esther stopped, spun around. "At school? No. On the bus coming home, yes!"

Camryn caught up to her daughter and slipped her arm around Esther's shoulder. "Want to tell me about it?"

Esther looked down at the ground. "I hate them!"

"Who? Who do you hate?"

"Justin and Phillip. They're awful."

Oh, dear. Images of a romantic dinner seemed to vaporize in Camryn's head. "What did they do?"

"They told everyone on the bus that I ratted them out." She paused, sniffed loudly.

"I guess that means tattling. They said I fell through the wood in the hayloft and blamed it on them. Phillip said I was such a big baby that I couldn't even climb up to a hayloft without getting hurt."

Esther stopped, glared up at Camryn. "It's not true. I did climb up to the hayloft, all by myself. And I didn't get hurt." She glanced at a bruise on her lower arm. "Not hardly anyway."

Remembering the incident from two days ago made Camryn cringe all over again. "Yes, I know you did. Even though you had disobeyed me, you were very brave."

Esther whirled out of Camryn's hold on her shoulder. "Why did you let me tell Reed that his sons made me do it? Now everyone thinks I'm a baby *and* a tattletale. I'm never getting on the bus again!"

Camryn took a deep breath. "You told Reed because that is exactly what happened, and you are not a girl who lies. I had warned you about letting the boys goad you into doing things that weren't safe, and taunting you into climbing the ladder to the hayloft is just another example. You could have been seriously hurt, Essie, and it's my job to see that you are safe, that you don't take unnecessary chances."

Esther remained silent a moment before her bottom lip quivered. "Well, now you've made it so I can't ride the bus again!"

"What about Justin? What did he say on the bus?"

Esther grudgingly shrugged. "He wasn't as bad as Phillip. At least he didn't say I was scared."

"We'll talk about this later, Esther. But you know you have to ride the bus again."

"I knew you'd say that!" Esther headed up to the porch, went inside and slammed the front door.

And once again Camryn decided that she would have to make this all right for Esther.

Esther did board the bus again on Tuesday with strict instructions to sit as far away from the boys as possible, and if they teased her again, she would ignore them and pretend she didn't hear. "Nothing shuts down mean teasing better than acting like their words don't bother you at all," Camryn had told her.

Midmorning, Camryn got in her truck with Rooster riding shotgun and drove over to Reed's property. Since all the children would be in school, this was a good time to tell him what happened yesterday and get his solemn word that he would speak to his sons—again.

She didn't like making such demands, especially when children were involved, and especially when this might mean that the date she'd decided to accept would probably never happen now. Camryn knew how difficult it was to be a single parent, and she could sympathize with the struggles Reed was having, but what happened on the bus was a clear case of two against one, and she had to do something.

When no one answered her knock on Reed's front door, Cam went around to the back of the house, where she spotted him a few hundred yards away. He was tending the cages that had recently been constructed on his land. As she approached, she heard strange squawks and cries from assorted birds who apparently didn't like her intrusion.

Reed turned to see what caused the commotion. When he saw Camryn, his mouth split into a grin. The cowboy was gone this morning, replaced by a casual man in shorts, a long-sleeved shirt, a ball cap low on his brow and a sturdy leather glove on his right hand.

"Hey, Camryn, welcome. You're just in time to see our newest residents." He removed the glove, stuffed it in his pocket and explained that he'd been filling feed bowls for the birds. When he walked over to her, he took her elbow and led her to the cages. "I got three birds from the Low Country Rehabilitation Center. Each of these guys needs prolonged recovery before they can be released. I'm hoping I can get them well in time to fly to Florida before the cold weather sets in for good."

The loud squawking continued as she got closer. Thinking Rooster was the problem, she ordered him back from the cages.

"It's okay," Reed said. "These birds have to get used to all kinds of wildlife, not that Rooster is so wild."

Reed seemed to stand taller and straighter as he paused in front of the first cage. The large, screened area was meticulously clean with new shavings on the floor, and various branches and stuffed toys to occupy the bird's time. As Camryn stared into the cage, a sleek, reddish bird perched on a tree limb opened his beak and screeched at her. She jumped back.

Reed chuckled. "First time you've seen a Cooper's hawk?" he asked.

She nodded.

"This guy has a broken wing, but I'm pretty sure I can get him to fly again."

"So he can circle over the heads of humans and scare them half to death?" she said.

"He doesn't care about humans," Reed said. "But I guarantee you he can scare a field mouse."

She moved on to the second cage, where a small-headed foul with a kingly bearing peered at her from hooded eyes. She could have been convinced that this bird made all the management decisions for the entire farm.

"This is a falcon," Reed said. "They have quite a history dating back to medieval times. They are revered."

"What's wrong with him?" Camryn asked.

"An alligator took a bite out of his neck, but the clever bird managed to get away. He didn't fly far before a camper found him lying in an estuary and brought him to the center. He needs a good month of rehab here with me."

She moved on. "And this last cage?" The bird inside stared at her with quiet intensity. She recognized that it was an owl. In fact it looked very much like Ollie the October Owl.

"Your average barn owl," Reed said. "Just wants to be left alone to ponder the universe. For some reason he stopped eating, but I plan to give him some true delicacies, crickets and grasshoppers, and bring his appetite back." Reed smiled. "He needs to get in touch with his hunter side again before he can be released."

Camryn was impressed, both with the facility and with the man who dedicated his time to birds that needed help. She forced herself to remember her reason for coming over here this morning.

"I hope they aren't too loud," Reed said. "Nighttime seems to be when birds of prey like to make the most racket. I tried to establish them far enough from our boundary to keep you from being pestered at night."

"I'm sure it will be fine." Did she just say that? Squawking and screeching would be fine?

Reed pointed to a metal building not far

away, which had been built in just a day or two. "That will be my clinic," he said. "Hope to be open in a week or so when all my equipment is delivered." He leaned down and rubbed Rooster's ears. "There's a new doc in town, boy," he said. "And he treats neighbors for free."

Taking her arm again, Reed led Camryn to the back door of his modular home. "I'm actually glad you showed up this morning," he said.

"Oh? Why is that?"

"I wanted to show you our place. It's not much, but for three guys it should do for a while." He opened the door and held it while she stepped into the kitchen.

The room was smaller than her kitchen, but everything a cook needed seemed to be there, including a microwave and a dishwasher. If Camryn missed anything from her old life, it was the dishwasher. She envied Reed the beautiful stainless steel appliance. "Looks good in here," she said.

"Truthfully it looks rather spartan," he said. "We need some things—curtains on the windows, some place mats, real plates instead of paper. I thought I might persuade you to make a trip into town with me to pick up some essentials."

"You could probably do that," she said, running her hand over the new Formica counter top. "You should have a cutting board, too, so you don't damage the surface."

"Sure. Make a list. Whatever you suggest. I mostly mentioned the shopping trip as a way to rope you into seeing me."

Her mission in coming here suddenly came back to her mind. She turned, finding herself backed into a corner where the counters met. Reed was very close. She could see places on his face where his skin had bronzed under the Carolina sun. His time in Bufflehead Creek had made him appear strong and vital. The fact that he hadn't taken time for a haircut was just one more interesting aspect of the man in front of her. Her fingers itched to glide through that dark hair which seemed almost coppery thanks to the sunlight coming in the window.

She swallowed. "Reed, there is something I need to talk to you about…"

He smiled. "I hope it's an answer to my asking you for a date."

"Well…"

"Because in case you haven't noticed, I kinda sorta like you, Camryn. I'm finding myself thinking about you an awful lot." He wrapped his hands around her upper arms and stepped closer. "I've especially been thinking about that kiss, and when I saw you just now I had a strong urge to see if it was as great as I remember."

She held her breath. "Are you asking for permission?"

"No, ma'am." He moved his hands to cup her face and threaded his fingers into her hair. "I'm just giving you fair warning that I'm determined to find out."

His head tilted. She blinked an instant before his lips settled on hers. And then she let her eyelids flutter closed and her mouth melt into his. He moved his lips slowly, temptingly, teasing her with his tongue until she opened to let him in. The kiss was absolutely perfect, full of promise. She sighed happily as the kiss continued.

He pulled back but kept his hands on her cheeks. He grinned, a long, lazy, satisfied expression of his appreciation. "Yep. Every bit as good as I remember." He pulled her face close and kissed her forehead. "Now, what did you want to talk to me about?"

"I… I wanted to tell you…" She struggled to draw in a deep enough breath to get the words out. "I want to say…well, never mind. We'll talk about that later. For now, I'll just say that I'd love to go out with you." Those were not the words she'd planned to say when she came into his drive minutes ago. But they certainly expressed her desire now. And really, why make a big deal out of something that may not even be a problem today? Kids teased. Kids forgot. She would see how Esther felt today.

"Great. Let's plan on Friday night if you can find someone to watch Esther."

"I've got it covered," she said. "My ex-husband is picking Essie up Friday afternoon and taking her for a weekend in Charleston. How about you and the boys?"

"I think I can bribe my mother with some of those fancy cupcakes from the bakery in town."

"Well, then, it seems we can actually go on that date."

Reed grinned. "Super. A real date this time. We can even stay out after dark."

With a gentle caress down her cheek he stepped away. "I know you said you had something going on Wednesday. Is it anything I can help you with?"

Wednesday...tomorrow. The trip to Myrtle Beach. Suddenly the decision to accompany Brooke didn't seem so distasteful. In fact, at this moment she didn't feel there was anything she couldn't accomplish. "No, I can handle it." And she left Reed's property without "ratting out" his sons.

THE REST OF the afternoon Camryn worried about how she would help Esther cope with the teasing on the bus. She hadn't complained to Reed, so now Esther would just have to do the best she could with only her mother's advice to guide her. Camryn did not regret her decision not to tell Reed. Maybe it was time that she and Esther both grew up a little.

As the time for the school bus drew near, Camryn and Rooster walked to the end of the lane as usual. Rooster sat back on his haunches, panting excitedly. Camryn hoped Esther didn't disappoint him again.

When the bus arrived, Esther did not get

off immediately. Camryn had thought she would be sitting by the driver for extra protection. Eventually Essie climbed out, gave Camryn a quick hug and threw a stick for Rooster. The child and the dog raced up the lane. When they landed on the front porch, Esther was laughing.

Camryn had to catch up with them. She sat on the porch step next to her daughter. "How did things go today?" she asked.

Esther gave her a confused stare. "Fine. I got a B on my spelling test."

Camryn didn't know whether to laugh or gasp. "That's good, but I was talking about the bus ride. Yesterday you told me you were never going on the bus again."

"Oh, that. Everything was great today. Justin was transferred to my class. He got an A on his spelling test. Our teacher said there were too many kids in his class."

Camryn wondered if that were true. Maybe Justin was transferred because Esther's teacher was a more accomplished disciplinarian. "How do you feel about that?" she asked her daughter.

"Okay. And you know what?"

"What?"

"The teacher was picking out a desk for Justin and he asked if he could sit next to me."

Sure. So he could pull your pigtails or call you names. Camryn couldn't help her skepticism. "Did Mrs. Glover let him sit next to you?"

"No, she didn't. But I thought it was nice that he asked." Esther jumped up from the step. "I'm hungry. Can I get cookies?"

"Yes. And then what would you like to do?"

"I wanted to go over to Reed's and play with Justin and Phillip, but Justin said he has to do his homework before he plays. Reed must be a really mean dad."

"Oh, no, I don't think that's true."

"Anyway, I guess I'll play with my Easter Egg chickens."

Esther bounded inside. Camryn sat a moment longer trying to analyze what had just happened. She decided that apparently Esther had grown up a bit today. Or maybe this was the perfect example of the way kids acted. Forgive-and-forget blending into a delightful coping mechanism of "Oh, that was so yesterday." And kids didn't know the meaning of the word "grudge." Now it was Camryn's turn to take a lesson from her daughter. She would work on that once she got through the ordeal at Myrtle Beach.

CHAPTER NINE

THE NEXT MORNING Camryn hurried Esther through her school-day routine. By the time 7:45 arrived, both Esther and Camryn were dressed for their day. Esther didn't ask why her mother was wearing black dress slacks and a tailored white blouse. Maybe she just figured Cam was dressing up for the chickens. At any rate, Camryn didn't tell her the plan for the day and quickly ushered her onto the bus. If she drove the speed limit, Cam could make the nine o'clock meeting time Brooke had set.

Camryn pulled into the rest area by the Myrtle Beach exit at five minutes past nine. Brooke's BMW was already parked. Brooke, holding a coffee cup in both hands, waited outside the car. She looked nice in a mid-calf printed skirt and turquoise blouse. But then Brooke always looked nice. The sisters hugged.

"I still can't believe I agreed to this," Camryn said.

"Of course you can believe it, Cammie. You agreed because I asked you to do it."

Camryn couldn't argue. All their lives the sisters had faced victories, problems and challenges together. Camryn's acceptance of Brooke's plan wasn't a sign of weakness. She would do anything for Brooke and vice versa. Just the way it was.

Camryn locked her old truck and got in the passenger seat of Brooke's car. "Have to say I always like riding in this beauty," she said, smiling across at her sister. "I've never heard you say the same about my vehicle."

Brooke smirked. "That's just because I haven't ever ridden in it."

They were silent as Brooke navigated onto the highway that would take them into Myrtle Beach. Camryn's anxiety level spiked, but not to a dangerous level. She'd never had a panic attack with Brooke. Cam actually thought, and hoped, that this trip might be for nothing. Marlene Hudson might not be home. Heck, she might not even live in Myrtle Beach any longer. Anything could have happened. If they didn't meet their biological mother, Camryn would be fine with that outcome. She would feel badly for

Brooke because her sister had pinned such high hopes on this meeting and would be devastated for a while.

Brooke set her cruise control to sixty-five and relaxed for the twenty-minute drive. "So what's going on with you and the amazing Mr. Bolden?"

"Oh, noth—" Camryn cut off her words. She was simply too excited about Reed to hide the truth. "He kissed me…twice!" she blurted out.

Brooke squealed. "Why didn't you tell me?"

"I was afraid you would squeal," Cam said. "Obviously you're surprised."

"That he kissed you? No. That you let him? Definitely."

"You make me sound like an old prude," Camryn said.

"Hardly, Cammie-girl. Though you are older than I am."

"By five minutes."

"Yes, and now you're starting to act like the red-blooded young thing you are. I'm assuming you kissed him back."

Camryn released a contented sigh. "Guilty as charged. We're going out Friday night. To dinner, without kids."

"That's a positive step." After asking about plans for Esther, Brooke doubled back to the topic of Reed. "So—" she arced the flat of her hand over her stomach "—did you tell him?"

"No, not yet. I'd like to see how the date goes first."

"Okay, I get that, but not too much stalling, sis. The man obviously likes you, wants to spend time with you. Putting off telling him the truth will only make it harder to admit when you think the time is right."

"That's not necessarily true," Camryn said. "If I wait I'll know Reed better. It will be easier to talk to him."

"Or your feelings will be so wrapped up with him by then that you won't be able to find the words." Brooke's eyes left the road long enough for her to give her sister an earnest stare. "The whole thing about the divorce isn't so important," Brooke said. "Who cares if your divorce was final two months ago or twelve months ago? You haven't been happy for years."

"So true," Cam said.

"But the issue of the baby could be a

roadblock in your relationship, you've got to admit."

Camryn stared down at her tummy. "Yes, I suppose it could be."

Brooke looked into Camryn's face again. "And…?"

"Oh, all right!" Camryn said. "Sometimes you get lucky and make sense. I'll tell him Friday night. If he's not accepting of my child, then at least I'll know. I'll be able to walk away without getting terribly hurt. It is still early in our so-called relationship."

"Good for you, Cammie. It's the right thing to do." Brooke focused intently on the road. "Now get out your phone and log on to the GPS. Marlene's address is sitting on the dashboard. You've got to guide us in."

Camryn did as Brooke suggested. "Says we only have two miles to go to reach Garfield Street. Only a couple of turns."

They followed directions through a neighborhood of dry cleaners, pawnshops and convenience stores until they came upon a large apartment complex of gray buildings, each more tired-looking than the one before. Ironically, the name of the complex was Sunshine Meadow. A few worn-out signs with letters that were barely readable identified streets in the maze of buildings.

"Garfield is just ahead," Camryn said. "We need 1501."

Brooke selected a parking space with faded yellow letters spelling "Guest." The rest of the lot was mostly empty. This was obviously a working-class project, and the residents were at their jobs. The few remaining cars were older-model compacts. She and Camryn got out of the car and faced a double row of solid white doors.

"Marlene is in unit G," Cam said. "Looks like that's upstairs."

Brooke nodded. "You ready?"

"I guess so."

They climbed the concrete steps to the second floor. As they proceeded along the catwalk, they passed tricycles and other assorted toys as well as lawn chairs flanking the doors. "I hope the children who live here have a green area where they can play," Camryn said.

Brooke didn't comment. She stood in front of unit G and wiped her hands on her skirt. Camryn had rarely seen her sister nervous. This was almost a first for her. A Magic

Marker placard on the door read Hudson. So much for discovering their mother had moved.

Brooke inhaled deeply. "Here goes," she said and knocked lightly on the door.

After a minute an elderly woman opened the door. She wore a cotton dress that reached below her knees. The cornflower blue flowers might have been bright and cheerful at one time. A white scarf covered her head but didn't prevent coarse strands of gray hair from peeking out everywhere.

Camryn looked at Brooke, who was staring at her. Brooke straightened her back.

"Are you Mrs. Hudson?" Brooke asked.

"Land sakes, no," the woman said. "Marlene had to go into the coffee shop this morning. She called me to watch Harold while she was gone. I just live downstairs, and I do that for her sometimes if he's had a bad night."

"Harold is her husband?" Brooke asked.

"Who's at the door?" a man called out from another room. "Is it Meals on Wheels?"

"It's too early for Meals on Wheels," the older woman said. "That's not till dinnertime."

"Is it someone selling something?"

"I don't know, Harold. Be patient." Turning her attention to the visitors, the woman said, "Yep, that's Marlene's husband. Got dementia. No sense of time any longer." Grasping the knob in obvious preparation for slamming the door shut, the woman said, "If you are selling something, you're wasting your time…"

"No, nothing like that," Brooke said. "We were just hoping to speak with Marlene. We have a connection with her from years ago. When will she be home?"

The woman peered over Brooke's shoulder. "In about five minutes, I'd say." She pointed down the block to the street below. "That's her coming now. Must have worked the five-to-nine shift this morning."

Both girls looked down. A middle-aged woman wearing a ruffled band on her head and a pink-and-white restaurant uniform was headed to the building. Her hair, bound in a barrette at her nape, was dark, so black it was almost blue, a sure sign that she covered the gray with powerful dye.

"That's Marlene?" Brooke asked.

"That's her," the woman confirmed. "Thought you said you knew her."

"Not well," Camryn said.

Brooke backed up a step. "We'll just go down and meet her."

As the girls made their way along the catwalk again, the woman called over the railing. "These ladies want to talk to you, Marlene!"

Marlene shaded her eyes. "Who are they?"

"I don't know. Said they know you from way back."

Marlene's shoulders slumped, and she suddenly appeared tired. "Tell them to hurry. I've got to soak my feet."

They met in a small courtyard with a tile-top table and benches for seating. The few scrawny trees provided little protection from the sun. Camryn wondered if the complex had a pool for the kids to play in.

Marlene sank onto one of the benches and stared at Brooke and Cam. "Make it quick. Gilda charges me by the hour."

Brooke and Camryn sat across from her. Brooke cleared her throat. "Mrs. Hudson… Marlene," she began. "My name is Brooke Montgomery, and this is my sister, Camryn."

Marlene squinted her eyes nearly closed and pressed her lipstick-free lips together tightly. For a moment she didn't seem to be breathing. Camryn resisted the urge to squirm. She couldn't remember when she'd ever felt so uncomfortable, so unprepared to meet the demands of a difficult situation. Once again she questioned the merit of this whole trip. For sure, she wished she hadn't agreed to come.

"I'm happy to pay you for any extra amount that Gilda might charge," Brooke said. She took a ten-dollar bill from her purse and slid it across the table. "We won't be long. Will this cover it?"

"Should." Marlene took the bill and stuffed it down the front of her dress. "Now, what do you want?"

"My sister and I were born thirty-two years ago," Brooke said. "We were given up for adoption."

"Why should that interest me...?" Marlene's eyes widened in undeniable recognition. Her attempt at a bluff wasn't working. "Thirty-two years ago, you say?"

"We don't want anything from you," Camryn said quickly. "Our lives have been good. The Montgomerys were wonderful parents."

"Well that's just ducky," Marlene said.

"But I learned long ago that nobody just suddenly steps out of the shadows of your past without wanting something."

"All we want is to know you," Brooke said. "You're our mother. We have questions, that's all. We thought you would answer them."

Marlene clutched her handbag in both hands. "How did you get my name? Those records were supposed to be sealed."

"Does that really matter?" Brooke said. "The point is we just want to get to know you."

"And what makes you think I want to get to know you?"

Brooke's face dropped as if she'd been slapped. "Haven't you ever wondered about what happened to us, how our lives turned out?"

"No. I heard you stayed together and went to a good family. I did what I did because it was the right decision. I never looked back. And if you think there is anything to be gained from making a relationship with me now, you're about as wrong as you can be."

She glanced up at her apartment. "This is where I live. I've got a sick man I care for on what I make in a coffee shop. But I make do.

I don't need anyone else hanging on or asking me for anything, even my time. I don't have it to give."

"That's not our purpose in coming here," Camryn said.

"You don't have a purpose that interests me," Marlene said. "You're obviously well-off girls who think you're entitled to whatever you want in life, especially to know where you came from. I know it's the popular thing these days for adopted kids to seek out their real parents. Too bad they don't think about why they were given up for adoption in the first place."

"We're curious, that's all," Cam said. "It's not fair to call us entitled. We are both working women."

"Tell you what," Marlene continued. "If you're so curious about your past, swab your cheek and send it off to one of those hereditary places. That will tell you more than I ever would. My past is my past. It's over. I couldn't tell you one thing about the people that came before me. I've got all I can handle to make it through each day of my life right now."

Camryn noticed a spark in Brooke's eyes,

and she sensed trouble ahead. She reached for Brooke's hand.

"But aren't you even the least bit sorry?" Brooke said. "Aren't you the least bit happy to see us now? Doesn't it matter to you that we've grown up, and we're okay?"

Marlene stood, slipped her handbag under her arm. "If you want me to say something that will make you feel all warm and cozy, then yeah, I'm glad you're okay, glad you didn't end up in a situation that would have been worse than being raised by me. I would have only brought you up in misery." She started to walk away. "Now I've got things to do."

"We're sorry we bothered you," Camryn said. She didn't trust Brooke to speak.

"Yeah, me, too. Don't do it again. There's no point." She walked several steps away and then turned back. "I don't know how you found me, but let me give you one warning. Don't go looking for Edward, or whatever his name is now. Not everyone wants to be found."

Brooke scurried to catch up to Marlene. She grabbed her arm. Her voice was low and threatening when she said, "Who's Edward?"

Camryn caught up, spoke softly in Brooke's ear. "Let's go. We found out what we came for."

Brooke didn't seem to hear her. "I asked you a question, Marlene. Who's Edward?"

Marlene's face flushed crimson. "You didn't find that out, too?"

"Find what out?"

"Forget I said anything. I just figured the records would have revealed…"

Brooke's eyes narrowed. "I'm asking you one last time. Who is Edward?"

Marlene released a long, trembling breath. "I already had a kid when you two came along. He was three. I didn't even have a steady paycheck then, so I gave him up, too."

"Where is he now?" Brooke's voice had taken on a breathless quality, as if she were having a hard time getting the words out.

"How should I know? Last I heard he went into the foster care system. He wasn't so adoptable. He was older and wild."

"We have a brother?" Brooke said, the sudden realization giving her voice almost a reverent quality.

"Half brother. You had different fathers, both of them losers."

"Don't you care about anything, Marlene?" Brooke's voice now shook with anger and hurt. "We are your children!"

"I care about my next meal, and I care about that man upstairs. I loved him once. Would have done anything for him. Still would, I guess." She jerked her arm away from Brooke. "Don't judge me, not unless you've been in my shoes. Now go on back to your nice lives. You've got nothing to stay here for."

Marlene headed for the stairs. Camryn took Brooke's hand and led her to the car.

"Don't you dare say it," Brooke warned. "Don't you dare say you told me so."

"I wasn't going to," Camryn said. "I know you had expectations. I know this hurts."

"Do you, Cam? Do you really?" She got in the car, started the engine. The air conditioning whirled around them. And then Brooke fell into Camryn's arms. Cam could count on one hand the number of times she'd seen her sister cry.

CHAPTER TEN

"WILL YOU BE okay driving home?" Camryn asked Brooke after they'd arrived at the rest area again.

"I'll be fine. Don't worry about me."

"I'm sorry this didn't work out the way you wanted it to, Brooke. Marlene is just a bitter woman who probably has never made peace with her past."

Brooke turned in her seat and gave Cam an intense stare. "She gave away three children, Cammie. Can you, in your wildest dreams, ever think of doing that and then ignoring it as if it never happened?"

Camryn shook her head. "Of course not, but my life has obviously been very different from Marlene's. I've always had support and family to love me. And you know my history with miscarriages. Nothing is more precious to me than a child. That's why I'm so overly protective of Essie, and why I'm panicked half the time about losing this next baby."

Brooke put her hand on Camryn's shoulder. "You're not going to lose this baby, Cam. In a few months I'm going to be a proud auntie for the second time. And Esther is going to make a wonderful big sister."

They hugged. "Thanks for going with me, Cam," Brooke said.

For the first time Camryn was glad she had. "Sure. Just tell me again that you are okay."

"I am." Brooke smiled. "I look at it this way. One mother down, but one brother to go."

Camryn couldn't stop her jaw from dropping. "You don't mean it? You're not going to try and find this Edward? He's a stranger to all of us. Who knows what his life story has been. For all we know he could be in jail, or living in another country, or…even be dead. His name may have been changed. He may have lived in too many foster homes to count. I beg you, Brooke…"

"You're right, Cam. I don't know what got into me. This journey into the past this morning should be enough to convince me to leave well enough alone."

Brooke said the words, but she was looking out her car window and not at Camryn, so Cam knew she was merely saying what

Cam wanted to hear. "I don't want you hurt again," Cam said.

"I know, and I love you, sweetie. Now go on and drive back to your chickens and jam and whatnot. And for heaven's sake, Cammie, dress up on Friday night. Do you need me to overnight you a dress?"

"I have dresses, so no." Camryn lifted the door handle. "Call me later," she said. "And drive carefully."

"Oh, I'll call you, probably a dozen times between now and Friday when you go out with the gorgeous Mr. Bolden." She gave Cam a wicked little grin. "You do want all my dating advice, don't you?"

"Only the advice I specifically solicit."

Brooke laughed. "But Cam, seriously, tell the guy you're pregnant. He has a right to know that this adorable, glowing creature you've become in the last three months isn't the real you."

"Okay, I'll warn him not to expect much glowing after the baby is born." She glanced down at her blouse. "Even this impressive chest will go back to normal." Cam got out of the car. Before shutting the door, she leaned back in. "I guess you can call me with a little advice," she said.

Getting a thumbs-up from Brooke, Camryn got in her truck and headed back to Cottontail Farm, glad that this journey was over but still worried about Brooke.

CAMRYN RAN INTO Reed a couple of times on Thursday and Friday morning. Each time she saw him, he mentioned the date, adding details as they became necessary. By Friday afternoon she knew that Reed was picking her up at seven, and they were going to the best restaurant in Harborside, South Carolina.

Mark was due to pick up Esther at four o'clock, which gave Camryn plenty of time to shower, shave her legs, do her hair and dress. However, in typical, super-busy Mark fashion, he was a half hour late. Esther had grown tired of waiting for him and was playing in her room when he got to Cottontail Farm.

"So this is the country estate you've been bragging about?" he said when he came into the house he'd never seen before.

"This is it," Camryn said. "What do you think?"

"It's cute. Are you sure Essie is happy here?"

Oddly, that was the first time Mark had asked that question. "Find out for yourself," Cam said. "I haven't coached her on her answers."

Mark clapped his hands loudly. "Where's my beautiful daughter?" he called out.

Esther raced from her bedroom. "Daddy!" She threw herself in his arms. "I thought you were never going to get here."

"Sorry I was a little late, pumpkin." He twirled Esther around. "Good grief, Es, you're twice as big as the last time I saw you, and that was only a month ago when Mom brought you to Charleston."

"Kids grow fast, Daddy," Esther said in a surprisingly grown-up voice.

He smiled. "So I've heard. Are you ready to go?"

"Just have to get my suitcase," Esther said. "I'm all packed."

"Why don't you go to your room and make sure you didn't forget anything," Mark said. "I need a minute to talk to Mommy."

Esther went back to her room. Camryn offered Mark a chair and hoped he didn't want to chat long. "What do you want to talk to me about, Mark?"

He sat, crossing his very tanned legs that stuck out from his perfectly pressed shorts. Mark had always prided himself on his golf course tan and naturally sun-lightened blond hair. "First I want to know how the latest bun in the oven is going, Cam."

"Everything is fine," she said. "Nothing to worry about." Nothing for Mark to worry about, but she worried constantly.

"That's good. I know a healthy baby is the most important thing to you now, Cam."

"Isn't it important to you, too, Mark?"

He had the decency to look a bit sheepish. "Of course."

"Well, you're right. I want a healthy baby, and the safety and security of our firstborn."

"Nothing more than I want," Mark said. "That's partly what I want to talk to you about." He cleared his throat. "I got a promotion, and it's a pretty darn good one."

"Congratulations."

"I'm telling you because I don't want you to worry about money. I got a sizable raise."

"That's nice, Mark, but I'm not worried about money. I still have my job with Southern Square as well as other sources of income. You've been prompt with your support payments."

"Well, Esther's my kid. I want the best for her. And for you, Cam, even if you don't believe it."

Camryn remained silent.

"When the second baby comes, I'll increase my payments by seventy-five dollars a week. I figure you're going to need that at least."

"Thank you. I appreciate it."

"It's nice that we can talk about these things without having to go to court, don't you agree?"

She nodded. "Of course. Is that all you wanted to tell me?"

"No. There's one other thing." He glanced into the hallway, presumably to make sure Esther wasn't coming out of her room yet. "The thing is, Cam… I've met someone. This woman is new to our office, a recent hire recommended by one of the headhunter corporations. She's working in our financial department."

Keeping her voice level, Cam said, "I'm happy for you, Mark."

"Esther will meet her this weekend. I'm sure they'll get along great. The best part is,

Paula has a daughter, Zoey, just a couple of years younger than Es. A built-in playmate."

Camryn tried to see the advantages of this situation, but instead all she envisioned were more problems. "Mark, you have to promise me that Esther will be your main priority this weekend. You won't force her into relationships she's not ready for."

His brow furrowed. "I'm her father, Cam. Do you think I want her to be unhappy?"

"No, but…" Camryn got up from her chair and paced in her small living room. "This divorce is still new to Esther. She may not be ready to accept you with another woman yet. And what if Esther and this other child have completely different interests? What if they don't get along?"

Mark drummed his fingers on his knee. "Still the same old mother hen, I see," he said. "When are you ever going to trust anyone but yourself with our child, Camryn?"

"I do trust you, Mark, but by adding Paula and Zoey to your life, you've added a whole new dynamic to your relationship with Esther. I just need to know you will be aware that this situation might be difficult for her.

You may have to be patient and more understanding…"

Mark stood, glowering down at Camryn. "I get it, Cam. You're the only perfect parent in the entire world." He called down the hallway. "Come on, pumpkin. Let's get going."

"Coming, Daddy." Esther came into the living room carrying her suitcase and a couple of stuffed animals. "I'll see you on Sunday, Mommy. Don't forget to feed my Ameraucanas."

Camryn bent down and kissed the top of Esther's head. "I won't forget, sweetie. You have a great time with Daddy."

They left the house, chatting all the way to the car. Camryn didn't realize until they were halfway down the drive that she'd been clasping her hands so tightly the knuckles hurt. She suddenly felt so alone, as if the best part of her, the part that made her stable, had just been ripped away.

She took several deep breaths. "You don't have time for a panic attack, Camryn. You only have two hours, and who knows how many times Brooke will call before Reed gets here."

WHEN REED ARRIVED at seven, Cam stood at her bedroom mirror one more time. "Not bad," she said aloud. She smoothed the scoop neckline of her basic black dress, checked her hair one more time, deciding she had done wonders with the flat iron she'd almost forgotten she owned, and adjusted the strap on one of her high-heeled sandals. A minute had passed, just long enough for Reed to have waited at the door, and for Camryn not to appear overly anxious.

She was anxious of course, about two important issues. Mark may never have tried to understand her. He may have coaxed her into being someone she wasn't, and let her know whenever he was disappointed in her performance. But he did love his daughter. *Don't let your worry for Esther ruin this evening*, she said to herself. *Your apron strings don't reach all the way to Charleston.*

The second consideration on her mind was whether or not to tell Reed about her pregnancy. Part of her knew that Brooke was right. How could she expect this friendship…or whatever it was…to continue if she wasn't honest with Reed beginning right now, tonight? But another part of her was so excited about this date, and the prospect of more, that she didn't want to risk her momentary happiness with news that might change everything. She'd just have to wait and see how the date progressed and what her instincts told her.

"You look beautiful," Reed said when she opened the door.

The perfect compliment, simple and elegant. She wanted to return the praise, for he did look handsome in black dress jeans, a light blue shirt and a tan sports coat. "You look nice, too," she said. "I hope I don't fall off these shoes. It has been a while."

"Don't worry," he said. "Those heels just give me a good excuse to hold on to you all night."

She went to the sofa to pick up her bag. "I just need to put on some lipstick…"

"I wish you wouldn't," he said.

"What? Why not?"

"I haven't kissed you yet, and if only one of us is going to wear lipstick, I'd rather it's not me."

She waited for him to cross the living room and take her in his arms. His kiss was sweet and warm and made her think of what might come later, what she'd allowed herself to actually wish would come later.

"Our reservation is for eight," he said when he stepped back. "We should make it in plenty of time. It's cool outside. Do you want to bring a coat?"

"I should, yes." She took her coat from the closet and he helped her into it.

She turned on the porch light and locked her front door. Reed came around the SUV to open the door for her. Somehow she just knew he would follow the rules of polite courtship. Courtship…was that what this was? An old-fashioned word for emotions that had become entirely new.

Reed turned his vehicle around and drove to the end of the lane. "Nice night," he said.

"Yes, very nice."

Before entering the road, he looked at her. She was staring out the front window but felt his gaze on her, warm and caring. "Is everything okay, Cam?" he asked. "Esther went with her father without complaint?"

"Yes. She was happy to see him."

"And my boys are with Grandma eating cupcakes." He pulled out of her lane. "I relented and gave them a video game reprieve tonight. I figured why make my mother suffer with two bored boys?"

She smiled. "That was probably a good idea."

"So, our kids are fine. You look like a goddess, and I couldn't be happier to be with you. I'm thinking this night will end up every bit as great as it has started out. Here's the plan…no talk of kids or chickens or birds of any kind. I want to get to know all about you, and you can get to know as much about me as you want. It's 'open book' night, okay?"

Oh, goodness. He didn't know what he was suggesting. She'd already come close to promising Brooke that Reed Bolden would hear all the important details about her life, for good or ill. And once he did, would this evening end up as great as it had started? Or would Reed decide that she simply had too much baggage for him to consider seriously? She wished she would receive a sign from above about what to do.

"Okay," she said, forcing her mind to respond to his suggestion. "Open book it is."

He took her hand, settled it on his knee while he drove. Camryn felt young and desirable and on the verge of something truly wonderful. And yet scared. The whole truth and nothing but the truth did that to some people.

CHAPTER ELEVEN

THE DINNER AT Wayfair's Dockside Restaurant was elegant, even more, it was perfect. The restaurant staff had set up standing heaters that sent waves of comforting warmth over all the tables. Like the other customers, Camryn removed her coat. Reed took off his sports coat. Beyond the heaters the temperature might have registered in the fifties. But here, on a deck at the shore of the Atlantic Ocean, the comfort was ideal.

Reed ordered a glass of red wine. Camryn ordered sparkling water. "Is there a reason you don't drink?" he asked her.

"Actually I do drink," she said. "Sometimes, though, I lay off for a while." She looked longingly at his crystal wineglass. "Have to say, that wine looks awfully good." Later, if she followed through with her current decision to tell him everything, he would know exactly why she wasn't having a drink herself.

"So tell me about yourself," he said. "How does it feel to be a twin?"

A safe topic, and one that opened the door to talk about growing up with a look-alike sister. She admitted that she and Brooke were very different, but that hadn't stopped them from being close their whole lives. She ended by disclosing that they had been adopted as infants.

"In fact," Camryn said, "our adoption was the reason for that little errand I told you I had to run on Wednesday." Reed was so easy to talk to. He was attentive and considerate, commenting when it was appropriate and letting her get her story out without interruption. She ended up telling him all about meeting Marlene and the disappointing ending for Brooke.

"Sounds to me like your biological mother has a guilt complex," Reed said. "One that has turned her into a bitter, unfulfilled woman. I hope Brooke is able to realize this and put the past behind her."

"I'm hoping she'll try," Camryn said.

When the main course was served, Reed began talking about his relationship with his sister, Penelope. "She's so smart she's almost scary," he said with unmasked pride. "She's a professor at Rutgers, specializing in family counseling and marital problems." He smiled. "Unfortunately she wasn't able to save my marriage, but I doubt the most brilliant psychologist in the world could have."

That remark led naturally into a discussion of both Reed and Camryn's failed marriages. Camryn understood Reed's guilt at not being the most responsible father and his disappointment with his wife's failures and infidelity. She summed up her divorce by explaining that she was never happy being a corporate wife always striving to live up to Mark's high expectations. "Honestly," she said, "it was never a good match from the beginning."

She took a breath, stared at the candle in the center of the table for a moment. "And then there were the miscarriages," she said.

"Plural?" Reed said. "You lost more than one baby?"

"Yes, two. Each time was horrible. I felt like such a failure. After the first one, I thought I would never conceive again, but I did, and Esther was born healthy, thankfully." She smiled. "I couldn't wait to try again, but the next pregnancy, two years later, failed also. I'm afraid I didn't recover well from that one."

While she talked, he finished his meal. She'd practically forgotten her own meticulously prepared salmon. Reed took her hand. "I'm sorry you had to go through that," he said. "How did Mark react?"

"As well as he could, I suppose," she said. "Mark was seriously working his way up the corporate ladder by that time. He was busy, distracted much of the time. But my sister and parents were there for me. Even so, I don't think I could go through that loss again."

Reed's eyes were kind as he said, "You know, Cam, your history explains a lot about the woman, the mother, you are now."

She chuckled. "Yeah, like why I'm such an over-the-top fanatic about protecting Esther?"

"Yes. I've never lost a person who was close to me. But you lost two babies, and I get it. But Cam, Esther's a bright girl. So when you can finally accept that she's growing up and can make decisions on her own, and those decisions will be the right ones for her, or she'll learn from them, you'll loosen up on the reins a bit. Maybe there just hasn't been enough time."

He squeezed her hand. The feeling was so comforting and reassuring that Camryn almost believed that anything was possible. How different her life might have been if she'd been married to someone like Reed instead of… She closed her eyes, drew a deep breath. No use speculating about what couldn't be changed.

He took the last sip of wine from his glass and tipped it toward her plate. "Listen, lady, you haven't finished your meal. Don't you like the salmon?"

"It's delicious," she said. "I guess I've been talking too much." She took a bite of fish and relished the lemony, mild flavor. "I think I might finish it now, though."

"No hurry," he said. "We have the whole evening."

The mischievous glint in his eyes told her he was happy to be thinking about the hours ahead.

After dinner they bundled up again and went for a walk along the city's seascape. The moon was full and bright and lending what warmth it could to the crisp evening. Camryn didn't notice the cold. Her jacket was enough protection and her hand was comfortably secure in Reed's. They stopped in the shadows of one of the historic streetlamps, and

Reed kissed her, a long, lingering embrace that she wished could go on forever. When he ended the kiss, Camryn tucked her head under his chin and breathed in the woodsy scent of his aftershave.

She felt his breath in her hair as he spoke. "You know, Camryn, I didn't expect to feel this way about anyone when I moved here. I came because my parents were here, and I thought it would be good for my sons. I never had expectations of meeting someone as wonderful as you, or of feeling as strongly about you as I already do."

She smiled, though he couldn't see it. "My sister always says that the best options are the ones that sneak up on you."

He chuckled. "I wouldn't call the effect you've had on me a sneak attack," he teased. "When I saw you in the feedstore that first day, I was drawn to you, and wanted to get to know you better. And now that I do know you better, I realize that the first reaction I had was real and honest. I don't want to push you into anything you're not ready for, but Camryn, I'm falling for you." His breath ruffled her hair. "Unless you tell me to back off, I intend to keep getting to know you, the little things, the big things, everything you want to tell me."

He'd given her the perfect opening, and his honesty made her realize that he deserved the same from her. She stepped back, looked up into his eyes. "There is one thing you should know," she said.

"I'm listening."

"Okay." She let a couple of moments pass while she gathered the thoughts she had rehearsed for this moment. "My divorce is fairly recent. In fact, Mark and I only split up a bit over two months ago." She studied Reed's face for any sign of shock or disappointment. Finding none, she continued. "That explains why I've only been in Bufflehead Creek such a short time. When the divorce was final, I took the money I settled upon and immediately bought Cottontail Farm."

He nodded his head in quiet contemplation. "I see."

"Are you disappointed to hear that?" she asked.

"No. I am a bit surprised that this move was such a sudden one. You made a few major decisions at a stressful time in your life."

"I know it seems that way, but the decision to leave Mark was not sudden. We hadn't had a real marriage in years. Without a firm purpose in mind, I stalked Realtor.com on the internet, looking for properties in the southern part of the state. For a long time it had been my dream to get away from Charleston and settle quietly with Esther on my own piece of tranquility."

He smiled, a slight upturn of his lips. "And no regrets?"

"None. I didn't question my decision, and I've never been sorry. The four walls I inhabited with Mark, as lavish as they were, never felt like home. With one step into that little clapboard farmhouse where I live now, I knew I'd arrived where I'd always wanted to be."

She took hold of the lapels of his jacket and ran her hands down the fine material. "I hope I haven't shocked you. It must be difficult to accept that my marriage ended so recently. But I felt you should know how and why I ended up at Cottontail Farm, the place where I plan to be for many years."

"I've never been fixated on dates, Cam. Two months…two years. Doesn't really matter. What does matter is that we've found each other now and what we've found is worth exploring. I hope you agree."

She wondered if he could read the sincerity, the promise in her eyes. "Reed, haven't I shown you that I agree one hundred percent?" Rising up on her toes, she kissed him lightly. "If I haven't, then I'm doing this all wrong, and I promise to do better."

His arms came around her, enveloping her in warmth. The kiss he returned was exactly what she needed. "Let's go home," he said, his voice husky. "Because you are doing everything right."

Oh, my. In the car heading back to Bufflehead Creek, Camryn's anticipation grew. What was Reed expecting would happen when they got back to her place? She would ask him in. She wanted to and it was the polite thing to do, and besides, she didn't want the evening to end so soon. But if he thought… No, she wasn't ready for anything more than a few of those spectacular kisses.

She could offer him a cup of coffee or a lemonade. Those were the only choices she had in her house besides one lone bottle of whiskey in the cabinet above the fridge.

Camryn had brought it all the way from Charleston thinking that if she became too anxious some night, she could take a few sips. She never had.

She would offer him the whiskey. She would turn on some music softly in the background while they talked. Maybe they would snuggle a bit under the afghan her Grandma Esther had given her on her fifteenth birthday. And they would kiss. My, yes, they would kiss. He would stay a while. They would get closer. Perhaps because she'd told him how recent her divorce was, Reed would understand her reluctance for anything more than kisses right now. He had taken the news quite well.

Reed turned on the car radio to an easy listening station. Once she had planned the rest of the evening out, Camryn relaxed into her seat. She felt cozy and safe. Totally stress free. And then she thought of Brooke.

"You have to tell him, Cammie," Brooke had said. "He's got to know that you're pregnant."

Well, yes, she did. After they'd both opened up to each other tonight, it was the right thing to do. And as Brooke so truthfully pointed out, Reed would know soon enough about her condition anyway. He had taken the news of her divorce practically in stride. Would he react the same way to this news? At least a girl could hope.

Reed turned off a four-lane highway onto the country road that led to Bufflehead Creek. Camryn sat up straight in her seat. "How much farther?"

"About five miles," he said. He smiled over at her. "I thought for a minute you were going to fall asleep."

"I think I could have," she said. "But I'm having such a nice time I don't want to miss any of it."

He reached over, patted her hand.

"Reed?"

"Hmm?"

"There is one thing I haven't told you. And before we go any farther with this relationship, I think I should."

"Okay. Sounds serious, so don't keep me guessing."

"You remember I told you about the two miscarriages I had?"

"Of course."

"Because of that, Esther is so special to

me. For a long time the only situation I could imagine where Esther wouldn't be my sole and top priority was if I were to have another child."

The car swerved slightly. Reed righted it immediately. "Whoa, Camryn. The conversation we've been having tonight has suddenly taken a sharp turn. I'm not ready to talk about children. I've only just confessed my feelings…"

She felt like a fool. Her face flushed hot and tingly. She'd said that all wrong. Of course he thought she was pressuring him about future children.

"No, no. I didn't mean… I'm not talking about you and I having children. Oh, Reed, you must think I'm being ridiculous… I didn't mean that at all." She was babbling and needed to speak in complete, logical sentences soon.

He glanced over at her. She noticed his hands were wrapped tightly around the steering wheel.

"I'm glad to hear that, Cam, because I'm just embarking on a long and difficult path with the two I've got. So, what exactly did you mean?" he asked.

"I intended only to tell you that…" Suddenly the words that meant so much to her seemed stuck in her throat. This baby, this second child was all she thought about. But how could she explain the situation so he would understand?

She thought about changing direction, making up a topic completely unrelated to the one she'd started. But she'd already said too much, forgotten everything she'd rehearsed, and her brain just wasn't working properly. So she took a deep breath, looked at his rigid profile in the low light from the dashboard and said, "I'm pregnant, Reed."

"What?" His voice had risen an octave.

She knew he'd heard her. Still she said, "Pregnant. Three months. I'm going to have a baby."

"But…but you're divorced." After a pause, he said, "You are divorced, aren't you?"

"Yes."

"Then do you know who the father is?"

His question cut like a knife into her heart. "Of course I do! How can you even ask me that?"

"How can you not have told me?" he snapped back.

"Frankly it didn't seem like it was your business to know," she said. "But then, tonight—the restaurant, the moonlight, your words to me—I realized you should know."

"Well, fine. So who is the father? And more importantly, *where* is the father?"

"The father is my ex-husband," she said.

"But you told me the marriage hasn't been good for years."

"Yes, I did, but there was one time…"

A vein thrummed in Reed's temple. "Does he know?"

"Yes, he knows. You don't think I would keep this information from the baby's father, from the man I was married to?"

"I don't know, Cam. I don't know anything right now. I don't know why you waited to tell me."

"I was obligated to tell my ex-husband," she said. "I was never obligated to tell the man who is renting my barn!" She didn't want to become angry, but a slow burn had begun in her stomach and seemed to be traveling through her bloodstream.

"Wait a minute…" They'd reached Cottontail Farm. Reed pulled into the lane and stopped the car. He swiveled in his seat and gave her a hard stare. "So how do you explain that you hadn't had a real marriage with Mark for something like three years? Isn't the act of producing a baby part of a real marriage?"

"Yes, of course. But what I told you is true."

"Then how did you ever end up…?"

She gathered her thoughts as best she could. Unfortunately her tumbling emotions didn't allow for logical expression right now. "We went to a marriage counselor, Mark and I. We thought that because of Esther we should try to save our relationship. But there was nothing to save."

He looked down at her stomach as if some alien monster was about to burst forth and make a mockery of everything she said. "Apparently there was enough to save if you managed to sleep together. And apparently without any thought to pregnancy prevention."

"The counselor advised us to try and recapture some of the intimacy from our earliest years together," she explained. "We did try, that one time. We both got carried away…"

"Carried away? You aren't teenagers, Cam."

"We didn't even kiss! But we did, well, make a baby. The night we spent together didn't mean anything to either of us. We still went ahead with the divorce. I didn't even know I was pregnant when I signed the papers."

Several moments passed when Camryn didn't know whether to run from the car or burst into tears. "Will you please say something?" she finally asked.

"I don't know what to say," Reed answered. "I suppose I'm still processing this news. Did you and Mark discuss your options? Did you even think about staying together?"

"In truth, no. I had already accepted the divorce as the logical road to take with our marriage. When I found out I was pregnant, I was happy. I turned my focus into preparing for this baby, into assuring that I would have a successful pregnancy."

She stared at his profile, wishing he would turn toward her, that she would see that warmth in his eyes she had seen just an hour ago. But he didn't move. "There is still an element of risk," she said. "But with each passing day, that risk diminishes. I'm now hopeful that I will carry this baby to term."

He nodded, a slight, barely discernible movement of his head. "That's good. I wish you the best."

He wished her the best? That sounded so final, as if he were saying goodbye and good luck. As if he were telling her that he wouldn't be a part of this new miracle coming into her life. She reached for the door handle. Fine. It was better that she understood now. She'd known this baby for three wonderful months. She'd only known Reed for a few weeks.

"Wait. I'm coming." He got out of the car and came around to open the door for her. He offered his hand and she took it. And then they walked, without touching, to her front door.

All her plans for inviting him in suddenly vanished in the smoky haze of her disappointment. "Thank you for dinner," she said, putting her key in the door lock.

"Do you want me to come in with you… to make sure everything's okay?"

She stared at him a moment. What did that even mean? Everything was miles away from being okay. Besides, why wouldn't everything in her cozy home be okay? Because he wasn't part of it? She shook her head. "Rooster's inside. Don't you hear him whining?"

"Yeah, I do."

"He would be barking if anything was wrong."

"Okay." He paused a moment. "I'll be in touch in the next couple of days." He turned, started to walk away, but stopped and looked back at her once more. "Oh, and Cam, take care of yourself."

The first tear gathered in her eye. "I'm sorry you're disappointed, Reed."

He shook his head. "I don't know what I am. I just know that this was a shock, one I can't deal with right now."

Not trusting herself to speak, she simply nodded her understanding.

"If you need anything…" He never finished the sentence.

"I won't." She stepped inside. "Good night Reed."

She went into her house, crouched down on the floor to ruffle the fur behind Rooster's ears. The night hadn't turned out as she had planned, and she would have two more days to think about what this all meant before Esther came home. She didn't want to cry, but her eyes welled with tears.

After all, what had she expected? That a man she'd so recently met, a man who was trying to start his life over, a man who had problems of his own, would suddenly rise up at her announcement and declare, "Wow, that's great!" Even if her relationship with Reed wasn't so new, those expectations would have been unrealistic.

"Don't let foolish dreams cloud the reality of your life, Camryn," she said out loud. "You did not leave Charleston and move to this farm to find a man. No, you left to discover an absence of stress and a healthy environment for your two children." And she had. Because of Esther and this baby, she had so much to be thankful for.

So she rubbed her eyes dry and patted her tummy. "It will all be okay, little one. Just keep getting ready to come into the world. I can't wait for you to get here."

CHAPTER TWELVE

REED'S PARENTS DIDN'T expect him home until quite late. He hadn't expected to be home until late, as well. The clock in his SUV read 10:30. The boys would have turned in, and perhaps his folks would already be asleep in his bed. Reed didn't feel like hurrying home to stretch out on the couch. So he drove past his house and kept going.

For an hour he twisted around country roads, stopping occasionally to view some sample of South Carolina wildlife, a bird, or small creature darting across the road to forage in the bushes on this dark night. He'd gone over his conversation with Camryn several times. He couldn't bring himself to regret the words he'd spoken, though he knew he had upset her. She had shocked the heck out of him. How did she think he would react?

But he did regret the way the evening had ended. He'd so hoped… He'd been thinking about this night for so long, imagining what it would be like to sit next to Camryn on her sofa and talk about the near future, a future that he'd begun to think of sharing with her as more than friends. He'd allowed himself to think that Camryn Montgomery could be the one to make him forget the bruises of his last marriage, the one to make him believe in a life of calm contentment, the one who would warm his bed each night.

He supposed he'd blown that image all to heck now. But how was a guy who didn't have too many skills at fathering supposed to react to hearing another baby was on the way? If his relationship with Camryn was to lead to a trip down the aisle, how was that guy supposed to share in the responsibilities of another person's child, especially when that person was Camryn, the most uptight mom he'd ever met?

No, he'd said what his instincts urged him to say, what his sense of self-preservation dictated, and he'd protected the life he'd established for him and his sons. He pulled into his drive and drove to the darkened house.

He walked slowly up his porch steps and

went into the living room. His mom had left a light on by the couch where she'd arranged a blanket and pillow. Nice, but he probably wouldn't sleep much. Tonight with Camryn, he'd been hoping for so much more and now, as he looked back, he wasn't at all certain he wasn't the one who blew it. He had spoken harshly, perhaps, but he'd spoken the truth.

Early the next morning, after his parents opted for the peace and quiet of their motor home, Reed put his sons in his car and drove to the barn. Before letting the boys out of the back seat, he turned around and issued a strong warning. "You guys stay in the barn, got it? Don't come out unless the building is on fire."

"What are we supposed to do in there?" Phillip asked.

"I've got that all figured out." Reed smiled. "Each of you take a Curry Brush from the trunk and give Saucy a really good cleaning."

Phillip, with the disdain of an eleven-year-old, scowled. Justin popped up and down in his seat. "I like doing that! And Saucy likes me best."

"Whatever, just do it." Reed brought

Brute from his stall and threw a saddle on his back. He needed a short gallop to clear his head. He'd just fastened the cinch when he saw Camryn out of the corner of his eye. She came out of the small gardening shed behind her house with a bucket in each hand. Reed looped Brute's reins over a fence post and marched toward her. Might as well break the ice with a good deed.

He stopped a few feet from her. "What are you doing with those?"

"Good morning to you, too," she said, her facial features registering only a bland indifference.

He took both buckets. "Give me those. You shouldn't be carrying heavy loads."

She let him carry the chicken feed to the grazing lot. "Where were you yesterday? I've been carrying these buckets for weeks."

"Yesterday I didn't know you were..." He stopped, frowned.

"Pregnant?" she said.

He kept quiet, not wanting to bring up the subject again.

Once they reached the grassy area where several dozen chickens waited impatiently, she began throwing handfuls of the grain onto the ground.

After a moment of uncomfortable silence he scattered a handful of feed, as well. "Do you remember that day we discussed my renting the barn?"

"Of course."

"Well, when I was trying to get in your good graces, I said one of the advantages to having me rent was that I would be around your place often and I would help you when you needed it."

"I believe you did say that." She threw another handful of feed.

"It wasn't just idle talk," he said. "I meant it. So don't hesitate to ask me to do things for you."

Without looking at him she said, "Sure." She glanced at the second bucket, which was still full of pellets. "We can feed the goats now."

He followed her and participated.

"Where are your sons?" she asked after they were finished.

He didn't mind telling her he'd brought the boys. He was here to watch them, and besides, Esther wasn't even home.

"They're in the barn. I made them promise not to come out."

She frowned at him. "That's not necessary."

"I know. But you don't want them anywhere near Esther without supervision, and…"

"As you know, Esther's not here. Would you ask the boys to come out, please? I'd like to talk to them if that's okay with you."

"Sure. I'll get them." He walked with a fast stride to the barn. This was the last thing he'd expected. Was she going to yell at his boys or offer them milk and cookies? When he looked back at her, she was carrying the empty buckets to the shed, giving no indication of what she had in mind.

Reed stood with a son on either side, his hands on each one's shoulder. If they tried to run, at least he could collar them. Camryn came from the shed. She wiped her hands on her jeans and stopped in front of the trio.

"Hey, boys, how are you?"

"Fine," Phillip said.

"Okay," Justin said.

"I like those cowboy hats."

Reed had just bought the hats yesterday at

the Route 90 Western store outside of Bufflehead Creek. The boys had been ecstatic
to get them and had tried them on all sorts
of ways in front of their mirror. This morning they'd added jeans and authentic leather
boots to their look, along with a light jacket.
They looked ready to ride the range.

Camryn smiled at them. "I asked your
dad if I could talk to you a minute. Hope
that's okay."

Phillip shrugged. Justin nodded his head.
"Where's Esther?" he asked.

"She's with her father in Charleston."

"Oh, cool," Justin said. "We never get to
be with our mother."

"Who cares?" Phillip said. "If she were
here we wouldn't be able to wear these
clothes and get dirty like we can with Dad."

Reed knew he was right.

"Can we sit down?" Camryn asked. She
led the boys to the same bench where she'd
suffered that dizzy spell. She sat in the middle with a boy on each side. "I wanted to talk
about Esther, and now, with her in Charleston, seems like a good time."

"What do you want to say?" Phillip asked.

"I don't know if you can tell or not, but Esther is very impressed with you two guys."

Phillip looked up at his father as if to say, "See, I told you she didn't mind the teasing."

But neither boy spoke, so Camryn continued. "Unfortunately, with her being a girl, and a small girl at that, and living most of her life in a house in the city, she isn't quite as adventurous as the two of you."

"Yes, she is," Justin said. "She's done everything we told her to, or at least she wanted to if you didn't stop her."

"Well, yes, I know," Camryn said. "But she really shouldn't have. She's not as strong as you guys. She hasn't tried as many things as you have." Camryn looked from one to the other. "I don't doubt for a minute that she'll catch up to you soon enough, but for now, this country life, being around horses, going on the big-people rides…it's all new to her."

"We just wanted to in—" Justin looked up at his dad "—what's that word you told me the other day?"

"Include?"

"Yeah, that's it. We just wanted to include Esther so she wouldn't feel bad."

"I'm sure that's partly true, Justin, and I thank you for thinking of Esther's feelings. But while you tried to include her, you also issued a number of dares that she shouldn't have done."

Justin nodded. Phillip was obviously holding his opinion for later.

"But I think we need to give Esther some time to get used to the way boys do things. Because she looks up to you both, she's not likely to say no to anything you ask her to do. But you both know that's not the safest way for Esther to behave, right? I mean she doesn't have your skills and experience at this point in her life."

"She's a girl," Phillip said. "She'll never be able to do what we do."

"I wouldn't be so sure," Reed said. "One day you'll turn around and Esther will be wearing a cowboy hat and scoot-bootin' all over this farm. She might even grow taller than both of you."

"Like that's ever going to happen," Phillip said.

"She could," Justin said. "Dad knows this stuff."

Camryn gave Reed a look of sincere appreciation. "Who knows?" she said. "But for now, here's what I would suggest. I know Esther and I both want you guys to come to our place whenever you want. She missed seeing you this week. But to be really fair…" She paused, looked at Reed again. He gave her a nod of encouragement.

"Maybe you could ask Esther what she likes to do once in a while."

"Like play with dolls?" Phillip groaned.

"Not necessarily. Esther is raising her very own chickens. And she feeds the goats and runs around the pasture with them so they get exercise. Goats are very fun animals. They can be silly at times. Esther loves that."

Both boys were listening.

"And she can make chocolate chip cookies and her very own jam to use with PB and J sandwiches. And most of all, she likes to share. With you being the only kids around, well, who else will she share with but you?"

"I like chocolate chip cookies," Justin said.

"I hope you understand what I'm saying," Camryn said. "I want you kids to play together, but to do that you have to do things Esther likes once in a while. And you can't expect her to keep up with you guys all the time. What do you say? We'd really like to have you back at Cottontail Farm whenever you want to come."

Justin looked up at his dad. "What do you think, Dad? Can I come back sometimes even if you're not with me?"

"If you agree with the rules, sure." He stared down at Phillip. "How about you?"

"If Justin comes, then I guess I will, too. But I'm never playing dress-up or anything like that."

"I doubt that's part of the deal," Reed said.

"Great." Camryn put a hand on each boy's knee and pushed up from the bench. "Esther gets home tomorrow, probably too late to play, but maybe after school on Monday…" She waited for Reed to say something.

"I suppose we can put off the homework until after dinner. Now go finish brushing Saucy."

The boys ran off. Reed went to Camryn, lightly brushed her hand with his index finger. "Thanks for that, Cam. It was a great start in helping our kids to get along. You've already won over Justin. And Phillip will follow soon."

"We'll see. I don't want to keep Esther from the boys."

"You've got some admirable skills at this parenting business."

"I don't know about that. But maybe it's a way to mend some fences." She started to walk back to the house.

"Wait a minute."

She turned back. "Yes?"

"One other thing before you go in…"

She stared up at him with bright, luminous eyes.

"I'm sorry things got so awkward last night."

"In a way I don't know how we could have expected any other outcome," she said, sticking out her hand. "Friends?"

He grasped it in both of his. "The best. And I meant what I said. You need anything, I'm here. Just ask, Cam. In spite of the words between us, I want you to have a healthy, beautiful baby. I'll help in any way I can."

"Thanks. I'll see you around, then."

"You bet. Looks like you're going to see all three Bolden men."

She turned and walked back to the house. He stared after her, hoping she would turn around and give him one last, meaningful smile. But she didn't. Obviously the words they'd spoken last night were still between them.

AROUND NOON, CAMRYN sat down to eat a sandwich. Her cell phone rang and she took it from her pocket. Brooke. Finally. Cam had wondered why her sister hadn't called at the crack of dawn. "Hey, Brooke," she said.

"How are you? Did you and Mr. Dreamy have breakfast together?"

"Of course not. We went to dinner. He liked my dress. I confessed everything. And now it's all history."

"I hope that doesn't mean what it sounds like."

So did Camryn, but she answered honestly. "Pretty much. We'll talk later, okay? Right now I'm still sort of processing."

"Sure, fine. There's someone here who wants to talk to you."

A few seconds later, a cheerful voice said, "Hi, Mommy, it's me, Esther."

"Esther? Where are you? Where is Daddy?"

"Daddy is at his house I think. I'm at Auntie Brooke's apartment."

You think? Camryn swallowed the first hint of panic. Everything was fine. Esther was with Brooke. But something had definitely not gone according to plan. "Sweetie, why are you at Auntie Brooke's?"

"Because she came and got me."

"Why did she do that?"

"Because I called her."

"Are you okay? You're not sick?"

"Yes, and I'm not sick."

Getting very little information, Camryn said, "Do you think I can talk to your aunt a moment? And then I'd like to talk to you again."

"Sure. I've got to change clothes anyway. Auntie Brooke and I are going to a fancy place for lunch."

The next voice was Brooke's. "Everything's fine, Cammie. Don't worry."

"Tell me what happened, Brooke."

"I will. But first Mark wants you to promise not to say 'I told you so'."

Camryn was just beginning to understand. "You can tell him that 'I told you so' is the least of what I think I'm going to say to him."

"Yeah, I understand, but it has all worked out. Essie just wasn't having such a good time at Mark's. He's kind of hooked up with a woman who has a kid. Apparently Es and this girl have very different outlooks on life."

"What are you talking about, Brooke? They are children. They don't even have outlooks yet."

"True, but Essie believes in the philosophy of sharing. This other kid believes in 'Give it to me, it's mine.' Basically it just wasn't working out. Es called me this morning and asked if I could come get her."

"Did she ask Mark first?"

"She did. He approved the phone call."

"Did she even tell Mark why she wanted to leave?"

"Look, I don't know. The thought of Esther being unhappy was enough for me. I got confirmation from Mark and left right away to go get her. You can ask her all these questions later."

Yes, she could. It was enough for now to know that Esther was with Brooke. Her voice sounded bright and cheerful. She was going to a fancy place for lunch. Whatever disappointments had existed this morning had obviously been replaced with girl-time joy. But Camryn couldn't forget the warning she'd given Mark. She'd told him to go slow with this new relationship, that Esther was still vulnerable to changes in her life. Seemed like Mark was a bit like his girlfriend's daughter. Everything was about him.

"So you think Essie is okay?" Camryn asked.

"Yep. All good here. You can talk to her again. But Es is staying with me tonight, and I'll return her to Mark in time for him to bring her home."

"What fancy place are you going for lunch?"

"Charles Burgers and Gourmet Shakes at the Palladium Hotel. They have twenty-one combinations of milkshakes."

Camryn laughed. "I owe you, Brooke."

"All you owe me is another beautiful niece or nephew. I love being with Es."

"I know, but this is Saturday. You must

have plans for tonight that include someone gorgeous."

"Actually, no," Brooke said. "It has been a few weeks since my Saturday night has included a date of any kind. Guess you can say I'm in a slump. Popcorn and a movie with my favorite niece will be more fun than I've had in a while, though Mom and Dad will holler when they find out Es was here and I didn't bring her over."

Brooke in a slump? Why hadn't she mentioned this to her twin? That was a conversation the sisters would have to have soon.

"Anyway, Brooke, thank you so much. You don't know what it means for me to know that my daughter's backup plan includes the second most wonderful twin in the world."

"Ha! Very funny. I'll call you when I drop Es off with Mark. Then you can explain about last night's date."

And you can explain about the slump, Camryn thought. "Tell Esther to call later this afternoon, okay?"

"You got it."

They disconnected. Camryn wished she were with her sister and her daughter. They could all enjoy popcorn and a movie together. Remembering a quote she'd heard once, Camryn said aloud, "Being lonely isn't so bad unless you have no one to share it with."

Then remembering a couple of goats and several chickens that would be happy to share her company, not to mention four lush acres of radishes, carrots and baby gold potatoes, she hurried through her sandwich. Grabbing the keys to her gardening shed, she went outside just in time to see Reed coming across her property.

CHAPTER THIRTEEN

As Reed got closer, Camryn noticed the double-handled cotton bag he was carrying. She wondered what was inside, since the flowery print seemed out of place in the hands of a sensible, structured veterinarian.

"Back so soon?" she called to him as she walked toward her plants.

"I've got something for you," he said. "From my mother."

She stared at the bag, breathed deeply and nearly fainted with delight. Whatever was in that bag smelled heavenly.

"It's Brunswick stew," Reed said. "My mother is Irish, and when she makes it, she makes enough for every Irishman in County Cork."

"And it's for me?"

"Yep."

Camryn put down her gardening tools and took the bag. "I knew I liked your mother."

"And she likes you. When she asked about

our date last night, as I knew she would, I said it was great. So naturally she asked when we were going out again. I said you weren't feeling too well."

"But that's a lie," Camryn said. "I'm feeling fine."

"I know but did you want me to tell her the truth…that you are pregnant? That's definitely your news to tell, Cam."

Camryn was impressed that Reed was guarding her privacy but thought he might have come up with a more plausible explanation. Who goes out on a date when she's not feeling well? "Actually I am keeping it a secret for now," she said. "There is one person in Bufflehead Creek who knows. Becky at the feedstore. And it's enough to have one mother hen watching out for me."

"Two mother hens," Reed said. "Although I don't want to be gender-specific since I'm the second one."

"You don't have to watch out for me, Reed. I told you last night that I face less risk with every day that goes by. Soon I'm going to tell Esther she's having a baby brother or sister."

He took his cowboy hat off and brushed

his hair off his forehead. "You know something has been bothering me."

She gave him a small smile. "I sort of figured that out last night."

"No. It's not that you're pregnant. It's that fainting spell you had when Esther was up on Saucy."

He remembered that? Well, why not? It was not every day that a seemingly healthy woman practically swoons at the sight of her daughter on a pony. She shrugged. "I was just upset, unreasonably so, I guess."

"I don't think so. It was something else." He grinned. "I am a doctor, you know."

She chuckled. "How many fainting animals have you treated, Reed?"

"I can't tell you for fear of violating doctor-patient confidentiality," he teased. "But I can guarantee you that I'll keep anything you tell me confidential, too." He offered to take the bag from her. "Can we walk up to the house and deliver the stew to your refrigerator?"

"Sure, I guess." She fell into step next to him. When they reached the house, he followed her inside and waited while she put the stew away. When Cam noticed he was seated at the table, she sat across from him. "Are you still wondering if I'm in good health?"

"Yep. And I have a couple of questions."

"Okay."

"Are you really feeling well, Camryn? Did your miscarriages have anything to do with a medical problem you're experiencing?"

Truly, the miscarriages did not stem from a medical problem. Her gynecologist explained each loss in scientific terms that could have applied to any woman. The problem Camryn suffered from had to do with her reaction to the losses, and her inability to adjust to Mark's social-climbing goals. She debated about telling Reed the truth. Let him believe she had a serious condition or admit that her problems were due to something else?

She opted for honesty. "I am in excellent health," she said. "In fact, since moving here, I've never felt better in my life. Getting out of the city has done wonders for both myself and Esther."

"Okay. That's good to hear." He sat quietly, drumming his fingers on the tabletop.

"So why the fainting spell?" she said. "That's what you want to know?"

"Yes." His eyes, as brown as the rich earth in her garden, focused on her with caring intensity.

Her admission would not be easy, but she and Reed had agreed earlier that they would be the best of friends. She took a deep breath. "I suffer from panic attacks," she said. "Not often, but when they happen they can be anywhere from slight to severe. The day you're talking about, the stress factor was serious. I didn't handle it well. Usually I can tell when an attack is coming and I have learned coping skills to deal with it." She looked straight into his kind eyes. "Esther doesn't know. Somehow I've avoided having a full-blown attack in front of her."

He reached across the table and took her hand, reminding her of the walk they'd taken by the waterside last night. "Who have you seen about these attacks?" he asked.

"Medical doctors. Therapists. Even a hypnotist once. Each has helped me in one way or another." She needed him to believe that the attacks did not affect her abilities as a mother or a landowner. "I'm a fully functioning adult, Reed," she said. "Panic attacks are simply a small part of my life, a part

I've learned to deal with. They don't last long, and I believe the frequency is diminishing. Since I left Mark I'm much better than I was."

He nodded, squeezed her hand. "Okay. I'm glad you told me."

She wasn't ready to admit the same thing to him. What would he do with this very private information she'd just given him? Thank his lucky stars that he'd broken off with her? Or watch her as if she were about to self-destruct?

"Again, Camryn, I'm sorry about last night. You caught me by surprise. It's no secret that you and I feel quite differently about bringing another life into the world. My success with the two kids I've got is questionable, to say the least. But I'll tell you this much…" He paused again.

She waited breathlessly.

"I really do want you to have a healthy, happy, beautiful baby. So you'd better get used to having me around."

She felt tears forming in her eyes. He didn't want her. He didn't want to be any kind of father to her child. But he was a good man. He cared about her, and if she couldn't let her mind wander to more, maybe in time, that would be enough.

"You don't have to…"

"I'm here most days anyway. When I'm not, I'm right across the field, Cam. I can be here in five minutes." He smiled. "Keep calm and focused on what's important, and in a few months, you'll have one perfect, full-term baby."

"I'm sorry about last night, too," she said, her voice wavering. "And thank you for what you've just said today."

He stood, placed his cowboy hat back on his head. "Hope you like the stew. Now I'd better go check on those boys." Smiling one more time, he said, "See you later."

MARK BROUGHT ESTHER home around dinnertime the next day. Carrying her overnight bag, Esther burst through the front door. "Mom, where are you?"

Camryn came from the kitchen, held her arms open to hug her daughter. "Welcome home, peanut."

"This was the best weekend ever!" Esther blurted out. "We went to Charles Burgers in a huge hotel. And we watched movies and this morning we went to a petting zoo. So much fun!"

No mention of having fun with her father.

"I'm glad you had a good time," Camryn said. "Why don't you go to your room and unpack? Supper will be ready in a few minutes, and I want to talk to Daddy."

"Okay." Esther gave her father a hug. "Thanks for bringing me home, Daddy."

"Sure thing," he said, and watched her go into the hall. Then he turned back to Camryn. "All those adventures you just heard about… I guess you know she didn't go to any of those places with me."

"Yeah. Brooke called and told me what happened. I was afraid something like this might…"

"Don't go there, Cam. I've had a tough enough couple of days without you piling on more guilt. You have to know I feel terrible about all this."

She exhaled, cutting off the rest of her sentence. She no longer felt angry with Mark. In fact she felt sorry for him. Esther had had a wonderful weekend, and he'd been no part of it.

"I thought Esther and Paula's daughter,

Zoey, would get along great. But I was wrong. They are very different kids. Raised differently, you know. I guess Zoey doesn't adapt well to the word *no*."

"Maybe when they're older, Mark," Camryn said. "In the meantime it might be best if you take Esther only when the time with Zoey will be limited. You need to make Essie feel like she's the center of your universe when you're with her."

"I get it," he said. "I blew it this weekend." His face grew stern. "But just so you know, I'm not letting Paula go. She's been very good for me. We think the same, want the same things."

The words he didn't say hung in the air between them. *She's what I need when you never could be.* "You don't need to justify your life decisions to me, Mark. You found someone who complements you and I'm happy for you."

He rubbed the back of his neck. "I wish it had been you, Cammie."

She shrugged. "It was good for a while, Mark. Let's remember the happy times. Do you want to stay for dinner?"

"No. I've got plans for later in Charleston. Got to get back. But before I go…"

"Yes?"

"Who's Reed? And what's the story with those two kids of his, Phillip and Justin?"

Camryn smiled. "I see you were with Esther long enough to learn that we have new neighbors."

"Is that all they are? Esther said this Reed guy will have all sorts of animals roaming around his place."

"He's a veterinarian, Mark. And this is the country. Animals are everywhere."

"You like him? You like the kids?"

"I do. I'm adjusting to the boys."

"No, I mean… Esther said you talk to this Reed a lot and you've all been out together."

"We're neighbors, Mark. Bufflehead Creek is a friendly community."

"Nothing else you should tell me about?"

She glanced toward the kitchen. "Nope. Nothing else. I've got to check on dinner."

"And I've got to get going," he said.

"Call Esther once in a while, Mark. Or send her an email. She loves getting email."

"I will." He took a step toward Camryn, then stopped. "Well, bye, Cammie, till next time. Keep me posted on what's happening with the baby. If you need anything…"

"I'm fine," she said. "I have good neighbors watching out for me." Okay, that last line was a bit snarky, but she wasn't sorry she'd said it.

THE NEXT COUPLE of weeks were like a contest between the seasons. Autumn seemed determined to turn the trees into works of art before winter ushered in its first snowflakes. The ground became covered in drifting leaves that stuck to the grass and the lane and required raking. Each time Camryn tried to get ahead of the chore, one of the Bolden boys was there to remove the rake from her hand. Once even the elder Mr. Bolden assumed leaf-raking duties.

In the mornings Camryn turned on the modern electric furnace to heat the house. Now that winter was approaching, she'd been thankful that the previous owners of her farmhouse had realized the sense in updating their oil-burning heater.

She'd installed a safe, coil-type heater in her chicken coop and so far her hens had not stopped laying eggs. The diner in town still looked forward to her arrival with dozens of free-range eggs. And Camryn enjoyed her time with the waitress she'd met when she first came to town. Plus, her produce at the weekend market was drawing praise. But there would be no more harvests now until spring, so Cam spent her gardening time turning the soil and adding nutrients for the next growing season. She'd completed two more issues of *Alphabet Days* and was planning the next one. She was busy, and for the most part, content.

Esther had introduced Phillip and Justin to her adored Ameraucanas, and the boys had been suitably impressed. The three kids had even devised a few chicken-and-children games that gave both groups exercise and made Esther squeal in delight. While the children followed the rules of the games, the chickens didn't know they were playing one.

And at least once a day the Cottontail Farm goats received more attention than they ever had before. The kids fed them leftovers and watched the goats climb on bales of hay and ramble about the farmyard bleating gleefully.

A glorious fall was almost over. The holidays were drawing near. Thanksgiving had passed with the Boldens and the Montgomerys sharing cooking duties. Camryn's November magazine cover had been a hit. And her tummy was expanding as it should, making it necessary for Cam to wear larger, bulkier clothes. This could have been the most wonderful, fulfilling time of Camryn's life except for one thing.

She missed Reed desperately.

Oh, he came around a lot, nearly every day. She talked to him about what was going on in town and how his animal farm was growing. He asked her if the noise from his patients kept her up at night. She lied and told him no. That was what friends did—helped to make life easier for those who mattered to them.

And she was running out of answers to his continuous questions… "How are you feeling? Can I do anything for you? Do you need a ride to the doctor?"

It wasn't that Camryn didn't appreciate Reed's interest. Of course she did. But her apparent, and mistaken, helplessness, and his concern wasn't at all how she'd pictured their relationship, especially that night in Harborside when he'd held her hand and smiled across the candlelit table at her.

She found herself dreaming much too often about coming up with the perfect solution to spark his interest again. If only she knew the feminine wile, the flirtatious gesture that might make him take her hand for a reason other than helping her down some stairs. But as the weeks ticked by, Reed remained the exemplary friend. And Camryn became more obviously pregnant.

Camryn sat Esther down one night and told her about the baby. Esther reacted as Cam knew she would, with excitement and joy, and a few significant questions. "Can you have a baby with someone when you're not married anymore?"

To that Camryn had said, "Daddy and I were still married when we decided we wanted this new baby. And we both still do, very much. We may not be a family like others you know, but we will all love this baby and you will be a wonderful big sister."

Thank goodness Esther had taken the news without worrying about her mother's health or the potential problems with the pregnancy. Esther didn't ask how her mother was feeling, or if she needed help in the field. She simply talked about how different and terrific life would be in a few months when the baby came.

Sometimes Camryn wished for a break in her routine. She wanted, perhaps even needed, something to happen to change the flow of her days. Since she accepted that Reed was in her life as a protector and guardian and would never be anything more, she longed for something to occupy her mind.

Something came along on a cold afternoon in early December. Esther was in school when Camryn saw the large and impressive automobile come up her drive. Two men, whose corporate appearance reminded her of Mark, got out of the car. Both wore dark suits and overcoats, fine-looking leather gloves and polished shoes. One was slightly taller and burlier than the other, and he seemed to be in charge as he led the way to Camryn's front door.

She might have been frightened except for the fact that Becky was with them and she didn't seem worried.

CHAPTER FOURTEEN

"Miss Montgomery?" the taller man said when she opened the door.

"Yes, that's right." Camryn quickly greeted Becky before turning her attention back to the man who had removed his gloves and held his hand out to her.

"My name is Vincent Palermo," he said. "I represent a company called Agri-Crops out of Atlanta." Motioning to his partner, he added, "This is Tom Speer, my associate."

"What can I do for you?" Camryn asked.

"May we come in? We brought along a friend of yours to make you feel comfortable. I hope that was all right."

"It's okay," Becky said. "I know this seems strange, but these men explained why they are here. I wouldn't have led them out here if I'd suspected anything was wrong."

"Well, at least three of us know what this visit is about," Camryn said, uncomfortable that she was the only one in the dark about this unannounced arrival. "But yes, you may come in." She stood back and let the men and Becky inside. She wondered what they thought of her warm living room with the Christmas tree lights adding a soft glow to the fire in the fireplace. She and Esther had just decorated the tree, a beautiful Fraser fir, last night.

Vincent Palermo, with graying hair stylishly cut, and a body that looked sculpted from an expensive gym membership, took a seat when Camryn offered it to him. His associate, Tom, younger, blond, with alert green eyes, seemed eager to please.

"What's this about?" Camryn asked. "What is Agri-Crops?"

"We're a conglomerate of food growers," Vincent said. "Our corporate office is in Atlanta, but we have subsidiaries across the southeastern US. Our goal is to produce the best quality food through technology and smarter labor practices. We want to grow larger food staples and rarer vegetables."

He smiled, presumably at the confused look on Cam's face. She was suddenly suspicious of the man and his slick way of talking.

"Let me explain," he went on. "There is a saying in modern farming these days. If you're not moving forward, then you might as well be going nowhere. Our goal is to move farming into the twenty-first century with state-of-the-art equipment and data gathering.

"In short, Mrs. Montgomery, we want to cut labor costs in half by developing newer and smarter farming procedures." He paused as if waiting for her to catch up. "Have you seen a modern combine, Camryn?" He smiled again. "May I call you Camryn?"

"That's fine. No, I haven't. I don't have the need for a combine. I harvest my crops with hand tools. If I eventually need big machines, I can always hire someone to come out and help."

"Yes, you probably could," Vincent said. "But the combines I'm talking about have computer screens on board. They continuously collect data, map the layout of the farm and measure productivity of crops. It's quite amazing, really."

She couldn't argue. Farming machines with onboard computers probably were a sign of the future. But how in the world did that affect Camryn's small acreage? "I'm sure you have a point," she said. "I suggest we get to it."

"We are developing three hundred acres adjacent to your hundred acres," Vincent said. "As you probably know no one lives on those three hundred acres. We were able to purchase the land without displacing anyone. And we were also able to get a soil sample from just across the property line. The sample is from your soil, Camryn."

"If you are going to tell me my soil is rich, I already know that," she said. "I have 'sampled' it myself by actually growing crops and selling my produce at the local farmers market."

Vincent gave her an indulgent smile, almost as if he were finding her folksy ways charming but not effective. She glanced at Becky, whose face revealed nothing.

"I'm here to offer you a deal," Vincent said. "Your soil, being so close to the estuary nutrients of the low country, is more than rich, Camryn. It's what we like to call agricultural gold." He shifted on the chair, crossing his legs. "I want to buy your acreage, Camryn. It's perfect for introducing crops that have previously been rare in this country. We can produce vegetables that would be considered delicacies." He turned to his partner. "Tell her, Tom."

"That's right, Miss Montgomery. In your soil we can grow pomelos, cherimoya, Chinese cabbage, vegetables that have always been considered too expensive to import for the average market."

She sat straighter. "Interesting, but my property is not for sale, Mr. Palermo."

This time when she looked at Becky, her friend nodded. "I told him that, Cam."

"Real estate deals are public record, Camryn," Vincent said. "I know what you paid for this parcel, and I'm willing to offer you twice that amount."

Twice! Camryn shuddered as she took a deep breath. What she could do with three-hundred thousand dollars! And then her senses returned and she answered her own question. Nothing. She would no longer have her farm, the way of life she'd established here. "I'm sorry, Mr. Palermo," she said. "But my family lives here, on this property, in this house."

"We're not interested in displacing you, Camryn. You may keep the farmhouse, your chicken coops, the barn. All we want is the land. But we want all of it. We won't negotiate for parcels smaller than what remains of the entire one hundred acres."

Camryn had been sitting on a straight-backed chair, but she stood now and faced Mr. Palermo squarely. "I appreciate your interest," she said. "But my land is not for sale. I know my gardens seem small to someone like you, but I have plans to expand." She smiled. "Besides, I love it here, even without the technical know-how of growing exotic vegetables."

Mr. Palermo took her hint and stood, as well. He reached into his pocket and withdrew a card. "Keep this anyway, Camryn. If you change your mind, the offer will still be good."

Without having any interest in contacting the man again, Camryn did accept his card. She set it on an end table and opened her front door. "If you gentlemen will leave us alone, I'd like to talk to Becky a moment."

The men headed outside. Becky grabbed Camryn's arm. "Don't be mad at me, sweet pea. I told those hucksters you wouldn't sell one square foot of your property."

Camryn glanced at the card she'd set

nearby. "Is that what you think, Becky, that they are hucksters?"

Camryn's friend tucked a loose strand of graying hair behind her ear. "Mercy, I don't know, Cam. All that talk of computers and soil data. I never heard anything like it. We don't farm that way around here. I just came with them because they stopped in the feedstore to ask the directions to Cottontail Farm. I didn't want those city fellas to waltz right up to your door. Figured they might scare you half to death."

"It's okay, Becky," Camryn said. "I appreciate your loyalty. If I hadn't seen you I probably wouldn't have let them in. Do you know if any of our other neighbors have heard of them or received similar offers?"

"I haven't heard of anybody. I knew you wouldn't let them in, and I think they knew that, too," Becky said. "Probably thought that if you saw me, you'd think I was in favor of this nonsense. Well, I'm not. I just figured you ought to be aware of the offer."

"At least this made my afternoon more interesting than it would have been," Camryn said. "It's not every day a girl is offered three hundred thousand dollars. But

I searched long and hard for this land, and I'm not leaving, not yet anyway."

The business card seemed to wink at her from the end table. She shook her head to dispel the weird sensation in the pit of her stomach and gave Becky a hug. "I know you have to get back to the store," she said.

"I do, and this is your decision to make, but I sure wouldn't like to see you leave us. Other folks feel the same. Debbie at the diner says you brighten her day every time you come in. And the kids at the elementary school like getting those magazines. You're part of this community, Cam."

"And I don't want to go," Camryn said.

The visitors left but Camryn barely had time to contemplate the amazing offer before Reed came in her back door. "Camryn, are you here?"

"Yes, Reed. I'm in the living room."

His footsteps sounded on her wood plank floor seconds before he appeared in the doorway. "Are you okay? I saw a strange car in the drive. I was at the birdcages so I ran over just to make sure everything was all right."

Wearing gloves, a baseball hat and an old

barn jacket that he'd probably picked up in a secondhand shop somewhere, he looked like he'd been cleaning cages again. She couldn't help smiling. Dressed up like he'd been that night at dinner, or dressed down, like he was now, he was a pleasure to her eyes. And an ache to her heart.

"Everything is fine," she said. "Can I offer you some hot chocolate? Two men came to see me, but they've left now. I'll tell you all about it if you're interested."

"Absolutely, I'm interested." He grinned at her. "And not just because I can practically taste that hot chocolate."

They went to the kitchen. Camryn made the drinks and they sat across from each other at the old table as they'd done many times in the past couple of months. To Camryn, staring across at Reed seemed as natural as the first sip of hot chocolate. She'd often, though not lately, thought about sitting just like this every morning, Reed on one side of the table and her on the other, for a long time to come. Now she simply accepted that the chair he now occupied would remain empty unless he came to visit.

Cradling the steaming mug between his

hands, Reed got the obligatory questions out of the way. "How are you feeling? Did that baby grow another pound overnight? You aren't working too hard, are you?"

Healthwise she'd never felt better. Yes, in the small of her back, she was beginning to feel the extra weight she was carrying around, and her stomach made some chores cumbersome. But now that she was looking toward the end of the second trimester, her energy was boundless, her appetite voracious and her hopes for this baby blossoming each day.

"The two men who came to see me today were from a corporation called Agri-Crops," she began.

"Never heard of it."

"Neither had I, but apparently they are horticultural scientists who apply their knowledge to growing food. They study soil conditions, monitor growing times. In short they farm with a computer and fancy combines." She sighed. "And make a great deal of money or so they want me to believe."

"What did they want with you?"

Camryn didn't mind telling him all the details. Reed no longer had a personal interest in her, but he was, and might always be, a good friend. She trusted him and his judgment. And like her, he was a newcomer to Bufflehead Creek and they often talked about the benefits of living on the outskirts of the small town.

"They want to buy my remaining acres," she said. "They like its location so near the low country with the nutrients from the estuaries. And they already own property abutting mine."

"But you're not going to sell?" he said. "I mean, you just got here. You have your chickens and your plots…"

"I'm not considering selling," she assured him. "But the beauty of the offer is that I wouldn't have to give up my chickens or my house."

She explained all the details as she remembered and understood them. Reed listened intently, nodding occasionally, frowning once in a while. She ended with the generous offer she'd gotten from Palermo.

"Holy cow, Camryn. Twice what you paid?"

"I know. Pretty good profit for living here a few months only."

"Phenomenal. Are you sure they haven't

discovered oil somewhere on your acres? Or a hidden gold mine?"

"I don't think so. They convinced me they just love my dirt."

Reed braced his elbows on the table and leaned forward. "Wow. Almost makes you think you'd be crazy not to…" He paused. "Nope. I'm not giving you any ideas."

He was about to suggest that she sell? She knew what he'd been about to say, and she couldn't disagree with the logic. But his conclusion still left an even bigger ache in her heart. "So you think I should consider it?"

"I think you should do what you want to do, what you think is best for you and your children."

"Nice cop-out answer, Bolden."

"Sorry, but I don't want to influence you."

"That money would easily pay for two college educations," she said.

"And it would give you a lot of options," he said. "You could stay here, move back to Charleston, be near your family again. It's not what I would like to see happen, but being close to your family could be important once you have two kids."

Great. Despite his promise not to influence her, he was freely giving his opinion, and it was sensible. But it was not what she'd been hoping he would say.

"It's not easy being a single mother with two children," he said. "I mean you'll still have me across the field, but I won't be coming over every day like I have been."

She stared at him. "You won't?"

"Cam, I'll always be close, but I've broken ground on my own barn. It'll be finished in the spring."

"Oh. Of course." She stood, carried the empty mugs to the sink. "You've given me a lot to think about."

He put on his jacket, hat and gloves. "It's a big decision. On the one hand..."

No. She wasn't going to allow him to put more sensible thoughts into her head. "Please don't list the pros and cons, Reed," she said. "I can take it from here."

He gave her an odd stare as if he wanted to say more but thought better of it. "Okay, sure. I know you'll do the right thing. But if you want to talk, give me a call."

She went back to the sink, began rinsing the mugs. "Will do," she said. But she'd heard enough. She knew what Reed thought the logical decision would be. She knew what he would advise her to do. She also knew he felt guilty about the way he reacted when she told him she was pregnant. If she took Agri-Crops's offer and she moved back to Charleston, he could forget about the promises he'd made to take care of her.

AFTER LEAVING CAMRYN'S HOUSE, Reed could have wandered anywhere. He wasn't paying attention to putting one foot in front of the other. Luckily he continued to head in the direction of his house across the field.

"What did she think I was going to say?" he said aloud. "If she didn't want my opinion, she shouldn't have told me about the offer. I had to say something, and darn it all, they made her a good deal and she would be silly not to consider it. After all, she's a single lady working twelve hours a day on the farm, not to mention the time spent on her illustrations. Why would she turn down such a great offer to make her life easier?"

As so often happened, his mind raced back to that night along the seawall, under the stars, when all he could concentrate on was Camryn. She'd filled his mind and his heart and caused him to think about a future. Oh, he hadn't been ready to pop any sort of question. They still had to deal with the problem of his rambunctious boys and her overprotected daughter. But once they'd overcome that hurdle, well, he could imagine it. Yes, he could.

And then she'd dropped a couple of bombshells on him. Divorced only a couple of months. Pregnant with her ex-husband's baby. She'd even confessed to panic attacks over bringing a healthy infant into her world.

Her honesty had been too much for him. He was new to this life, as well. He'd only just established himself in Bufflehead Creek with boys that tested his patience constantly. He'd only just begun to establish a practice and a sanctuary for wounded animals. He still had to deal with an ex-wife who questioned his motives and an ex-father-in-law who had made it perfectly clear that he wanted custody of Phillip and Justin.

They were just a bad match, him and Camryn. Or this was bad timing. Sure, she was cute and determined and caring, all qualities Reed admired. She was as much in love with the low country as he was. She loved animals. She was hardworking and ambitious. But she suffered from anxiety about raising her children in an environment of calm and absolute security. Well, darn it, life didn't come with a security net, and Reed didn't need the responsibility of providing her with one.

"You really got yourself into a mess this time, Bolden," he said. "You don't want to live with the extra responsibility but you can't see yourself letting it go." He'd gotten so used to his role as Camryn's champion, to being there for her, watching out for her, checking his cell phone every night before he went to sleep to make sure he hadn't missed a call from her.

That was all okay. He liked being her friend and protector. But did he want his responsibility to Camryn to become full-time? Did he want to entangle himself and his family with hers? Could he see himself adjusting to her ways of raising kids? Did he want another kid, especially one with a father who would probably only complicate the delicate balance he'd have to establish to have a happy marriage and make four kids living under the same roof work?

He answered each question with a decided no. He wasn't happy, hadn't been since that night she'd told him what was happening, which changed everything. In fact after that night, he couldn't remember being so miserable in a long time. But he'd talked himself into making his own sensible decisions about a future with Camryn. If she left, he told himself he would be okay. His life would settle into a routine that suited him and his sons.

"You were right to point out the advantages of her moving back to Charleston," he told himself as he approached the birdcages.

Camryn needs her family. She should be with them, not with some half-baked father of two boys who can't see himself with another kid—ever.

He'd done all he could for her.

He put his gloves on, picked up a trowel and resumed cleaning the bottom of one of the cages. "So why do I have this awful sinking feeling in the pit of my stomach?" he said to the barn owl who was staring at him with bright, knowing eyes. Frowning at the owl, he said, "Yeah, like you have all the answers."

CHAPTER FIFTEEN

TWO DAYS BEFORE CHRISTMAS, Camryn was busy with last-minute details before she and Esther left for Charleston to be with her family. Esther was excited. She would see her father, who'd promised to give Es a special time without his girlfriend and her daughter. And Cam's parents were beyond anxious to see their girls again.

When her cell rang, Camryn stopped putting ribbon on a package and picked up the phone. Brooke. They hadn't talked yet today, and it was already near dinnertime.

"Merry almost-Christmas," Camryn said.

"You too, sister." Brooke asked the normal questions about Camryn's condition. Though Camryn appreciated the concern, she would be glad when the baby was born and people would stop asking her how she was feeling all the time.

"So when do you think you'll get here tomorrow?" Brooke asked. "Mom and Dad are counting the minutes. Frankly, I'm starting to think that you're their favorite."

Camryn laughed. "We'll be there by noon," she said. "I've hired Becky's son, Randy, to feed my chickens and goats, and I want to be here when he comes for the first time."

"You must be a mind reader," Brooke said. "I was just about to ask what arrangements you'd made for the chickens."

"Sure you were."

"Any changes in your relationship with Reed?" Brooke asked.

Camryn had told her sister about the mess she'd made of her confession to Reed. As usual Brooke had sympathized. But she continued to assert that honesty was the best policy. Blasted honesty! Although as Camryn stared at her tummy these days she knew the truth would be obvious now.

"No," Camryn said. "Reed is still a great friend. But the relationship continues to suffer from internal combustion."

"Well, he's not as bright as he thinks he is, that's all," Brooke said.

Camryn smiled. "Yeah. All that education and he doesn't know when a good thing marches right into his life."

"And have you made a decision about selling your land?" Brooke questioned next.

Camryn had made Brooke promise not to tell their parents. She was having enough pressure from Brooke without adding their parents' opinions. Her mother and father would have insisted she move back, probably even saying that the offer from Palermo was a gift from above. She stole a quick look at the business card that still lay on the end table. "No, not yet."

"You'll wait so long that Palermo will rescind the offer," Brooke said.

"Then the decision will have been made, right?" Camryn said. She'd thought long and hard since Palermo's visit about the offer from Agri-Crops. Yes, it was a financial boon. But finding this property had been a life-changing event for Camryn. She loved the low country, the peace and calm, even the work. If she had to decide today, she wouldn't sell. Cottontail Farm was the perfect home for herself and her two children. Even if Reed would never be more to her than he was now. A fulfilling life was more than discovering a great love. Camryn sighed. But a great love certainly had its place in a fulfilling life.

Reed had refrained from giving her more advice on the topic of selling. For that Camryn was grateful. Unfortunately he'd already stopped coming over every day, and she missed his voice on a regular basis more than she appreciated his silence on her decision. The walls of his barn were going up, and he needed to supervise the construction. His veterinary clinic was open and attracting patients. Consequently, his daily visits to Cam had been replaced by phone calls or messages from his sons who stopped by often to play with Esther. Ironic that the children were getting along well now that things weren't so great between the parents.

"Dad said if you need anything…" Justin said the other day.

Camryn had simply smiled at the boy. What she needed most was Dad.

Bringing Camryn's thoughts back to the present, Brooke said, "You know what I think about you returning to Charleston…"

"Yes, I do," Camryn said. "And let's change the subject to you. Any interesting men in your life?"

"Only one, and I'm not having much luck finding him."

Camryn frowned. "Oh, Brooke, you're not still looking for Edward, are you?"

"He's our brother, Cammie. We can't pretend he wasn't born or that he doesn't exist."

"But Brooke, he may not exist," Cam responded. "He obviously doesn't share our birth mother's name or you would have found him. I'm sorry, Brooke, but Edward may not even be alive. Your efforts could be a huge waste of time."

"I told you I located the home where he was sent when our mother gave him up," Brooke said. "It's a start."

"No, Brooke. It's an end. You haven't found any information since. I wish you'd give up this idea of finding Edward and concentrate on your own life." As far as Camryn knew, Brooke hadn't had a promising date in weeks. And Camryn wondered if Brooke's boss at the TV station was aware of how much time she spent spinning her wheels trying to locate Edward. If so, Brooke had better watch out for her future with the broadcast company.

"I'm not going to give up," Brooke said.

"You know that. You and I need to agree to disagree on a couple of things. You're not giving up your farm, and I'm not giving up on Edward. Okay?"

"Fair enough, I guess," Camryn said. "I love you, sis. See you tomorrow."

"Love you, too. Can't wait."

The sisters disconnected. Camryn went back to gift wrapping but stopped again when out of her front window she saw Reed's car pull up to her house. Reed and his sons got out. Each one was carrying a package.

"Merry Christmas," Reed said when she opened the door. "I know you're leaving tomorrow, so this seemed like a good time to bring over our presents."

"Presents!" The excited squeal came from the hallway as Esther bounded into the room. "We have presents for you, too," she said.

Esther took the gifts from Justin and Phillip and sat on the couch. "Mommy, can you find their presents under the tree?"

Reed and Camryn watched as Esther opened her gift from Justin, a squawking, waddling, beautifully feathered mechanical chicken that looked almost real. She immediately exclaimed she loved it.

Her present from Phillip required opening three packages. According to Reed, Phillip had picked out his gift from a catalogue of rare and unusual items. Esther was mesmerized by the three painted bone china eggs that each came with a round pedestal.

"They're from England," Phillip said. And then, in Phillip fashion, he added, "Bet your chickens can't lay eggs that pretty."

Esther set them on the coffee table. "No. These are way prettier."

Justin opened his easel and art set. And Phillip seemed pleased with the video game a mail-order internet site claimed was this season's hot item.

When the kids went into Esther's room to play a game, Reed carried a box to Camryn and set it on the floor. "Don't try to pick it up," he said.

She tapped her toe against the box. It didn't move. "Oh, swell, a crate of bricks. I can really use them to start the border I was going to build around my front garden." She laughed as she tore off the wrapping. Inside was a set of cast-iron skillets and three cast-iron pots with a coating of blue enamel that made each look like a work of art. Perhaps some women wouldn't appreciate such a practical gift, but Camryn couldn't stop smiling. "I can't believe this," Camryn said. "Where did you ever find them?"

"There's a store in Atlanta called Hay Bale. They sell hard-to-find country items. I thought you might like them."

"I love them." She stood and walked over to him, putting her arms around him and giving him a strong hug. "Thank you so much."

Realizing how intimate her gesture must seem, she backed up a step. But not before a sigh came from her lips. She placed her hand over her heart, thinking to muffle the sound pounding in her ears. Definitely not enough time had passed.

Reed raised his hand and let one finger drift slowly down her cheek. "You are welcome, Cam. But I'm pretty sure there's one more thing in that package."

She removed packing material and found a small box at the bottom. She opened it to find a chain and gold pendant with an artist's rendition of the bunny on her property gate in the middle. Camryn choked back a sob. "It looks just like our cottontail."

"I took a few pictures of your gate to give the engraver an idea. I think he came pretty close." After a short pause, which gave Camryn time to steady her emotions, Reed added, "I know you probably haven't decided yet what you're going to do, but I figured either way, you might want a keepsake of the time you spent here."

"Oh, Reed…" Just two words, but she couldn't say more. Besides, those words expressed the depth of her gratitude and her regret at the same time. Reed had been the man who'd filled her dreams, whose kisses had made her knees delightfully weak and who had become her very dear friend. Tonight, when she had time, she would think about how each of these things had led to the sadness she felt now.

She cleared her throat. "I'm almost embarrassed to give you my gift," she said, pulling a box from under the tree. "I'm afraid it's pathetically practical."

"More practical than skillets and pots?" he teased. "I'm sure I'll love it. Everything under my mom's tree with my name on it is shaped like socks, so this looks fascinating."

He seemed to like the new work gloves and heavy wire brushes she'd bought to make cleaning the cages easier. She'd also picked up a few large hanging toys made for birds and a wooden placard that read, "Veterinarians are special. They can't ask their patients what's wrong. They have to know."

"This is going right over my clinic door," he said of the sign. "It's great, Camryn."

She made a pot of coffee and they talked for a while about what their kids had been doing in school, how Reed's parents were, how many new patients he'd seen. All normal things that friends talked about.

"I'll miss you while you're gone," Reed said after he'd called for his boys to come from Esther's room.

"It's only two days," she said, knowing in her heart that two days away would seem like a month.

"Be careful driving up to Charleston," he said. "We're supposed to get a really strong cold front sometime in the next couple of weeks. Even quite a bit of snow. I don't want you to get caught in it."

"I'll be back long before that," she said. "We'll be fine."

"I know. That's what you always say, and I'm finally starting to believe it." He smiled at her belly. "You are fine, Camryn. A fine, strong, beautiful woman."

His words tore at her heart. She wanted to say something equally intimate to him, but knew if she did, she might dissolve into tears.

He ushered his boys out to his car and they drove away.

"Mommy, what's wrong?"

Esther's voice brought Camryn back from the empty place her emotions had taken her. She wiped a tear from under her eye. "Nothing, sweetie. I'm fine." Didn't Reed just say so?

And wouldn't it be wonderful if it were true?

CHAPTER SIXTEEN

CHRISTMAS AT THE MONTGOMERYS' was a relaxing, family time. Linda and Craig Montgomery talked about the new baby at every opportunity, Linda managing to keep Camryn's anxieties at a minimum. And both grandparents doted on Esther, who loved the attention.

Of course, being with the family did not allow Camryn time to talk to Brooke about her quest for Edward. Only on Christmas Eve night, when they were sharing the bedroom they'd grown up in, did Camryn again bring up the potential problems for Brooke if she continued the search.

"You're only going to get hurt, Brooke," she said. "If you never find him, you'll always be unfulfilled. And if you do find him and he's nothing like what you'd hoped for... remember Marlene and what she was like... you'll be devastated."

Brooke started to argue, but Camryn interrupted her. "Yes, I suppose he could be a hero, but what are the odds? With the start he had in life, he'll more likely have bounced from one institution to another."

"I'm not going to give up, Cammie, Edward is a part of us. He's part of our family tree. He could turn out to be a fragile twig or a sturdy branch who could hold us both up. Or we could help him. I've got to know."

"Have you found any information on him?" Camryn asked.

"My lawyer friend wasn't able to find any leads other than a brief stay Edward had in a home in North Carolina. After that, his trail ran cold. But I've hired a private detective who believes he can help."

"And what is this costing?" Camryn asked. "I'm not just talking about money, but also the cost in time away from your focus on your job. Has your station owner said anything to you?"

"Of course not. They love me at WJQC. My position there is as solid as Mount Rushmore. As a matter of fact, I think I'm being considered for a raise and promotion." Brooke paused and took a deep breath. "Don't worry about me, Cam. It's time you thought about your own life and the decision facing you right now."

"I wish you hadn't brought that up," Camryn said. "I'm still no closer to making up my mind. It didn't help that I saw Reed yesterday. We exchanged gifts by the Christmas tree. It could have been romantic, but unfortunately…"

"I'm so sorry, Cam. I wish the relationship had worked out the way you wanted it to. I hope my advice to tell Reed the truth didn't jeopardize your chances with him."

"Of course it did," Camryn insisted. "But Reed would have known I was pregnant soon enough."

Brooke's voice, low and husky, was choked with emotion. "Come home to Charleston, Cam. I can't wait to be an aunt to this new little guy or girl. And Mom and Dad are about to explode with the excitement of having another grandchild."

"Don't bring Mom and Dad into this," Cam said.

"But it's true. We can all help you with the kids. And the love…why those two children would be surrounded by love 24/7. I know that means a lot to you."

"Of course it does, but so does living my own lifestyle, a lifestyle that seems to suit Esther just fine." *A lifestyle that would have been perfect if Reed had been in it full-time.* "We're still close enough to Charleston to come for visits."

"I realize that's true, but I want you close by. I want to know you're a few minutes away, if you need me, or I need you."

Camryn gave her sister a warm smile. "A few miles won't destroy what we have between us."

Brooke shook her head. "My sister, the practical one."

"Someone has to be."

"Something tells me we're not going to solve the Montgomery girls' problems tonight, Cammie. Get some sleep. My little niece or nephew needs it."

"Love you, Brooke."

"Love you, Cammie."

And as it had for so many years, the room settled into a comfortable and enduring peace.

CHRISTMAS IN A motor home, even a large, extravagant one, has its challenges. But Reed's mother wouldn't hear of not hosting her favorite event of the year. Somehow she'd managed to get a six-foot tree, yards of garland and a mountain of presents in the main lounge. The home and nearby trees were vibrant with lights. Even Reed's sister, Penelope, having flown in from New Jersey, was happy to be with family though she had to sleep on a twin bunk bed in the back of the unit.

"Thank goodness you got your home built when you did, Reed," Bertie Bolden exclaimed as she made scrambled eggs on Christmas morning. "I can't imagine all of us squeezing into the camper, but we would have done it. I'm not about to leave anyone out at Christmas."

When a contemplative look crossed her face, Reed said, "What's wrong, Mom? You suddenly seem out of sorts."

"I just wish Camryn and that adorable little girl of hers were here to join us."

Reed still wasn't comfortable with his mother bringing up Camryn, but that didn't stop her from doing so every chance she got. Reed took a sip of coffee. "I'm sure Camryn and Esther are having a wonderful Christmas in Charleston."

Penelope looked up from the floor where she was playing a board game with the boys. Though she didn't say anything, Reed was certain she was eavesdropping on the conversation.

"Can we talk about this later?" he said, giving a secretive nod at Penelope.

"Sure we can, honey," Bertie said. "But I don't understand why you couldn't make it work with that wonderful woman."

Reed sighed. Apparently "later" meant right now. "Mom, I told you, it just wasn't the right timing for either of us. Our kids had problems getting along. Camryn was super busy with all of her businesses. She had—"

"You're busy too, Reed. I see you outside all the time with those rescue animals. And your clinic is starting to draw patients. But being busy is no reason to neglect the most primary needs in your life."

"Mom! Can we please not discuss my *needs* in front of my sons."

Penelope glanced up at him and giggled. "You're in for it now, brother dear. And when Mama's done with you, I want to hear all about this Camryn."

If Penelope weren't so darned cute with

her dark pixie haircut, dimples and long eye-lashes, Reed might have told her to mind her own business. As it was, he just scowled.

"Don't tease, Pen," Bertie said. "I just want to see Reed with a family and hope for a future of happiness."

"I have a family, Mom," Reed said. "And they are all here within arm's reach right now. Frankly, it's more family than I can deal with sometimes."

Bertie transferred the eggs to the micro-wave to keep them warm and began mixing pancake batter. "What happened between the two of you, Reed? You and Camryn were seeing so much of each other. I could tell she really liked you. Did you do something…?"

"No, Mom. Camryn and I still see a lot of each other. We're neighbors after all." Reed had never told his mother about Cam-ryn's problems with anxiety or about her pregnancy. He had promised Cam that the news was hers to reveal whenever she de-cided the time was right. So far Camryn had avoided seeing Bertie when she wasn't wear-ing bulky clothes. But now that his mother's face was the equivalent of a giant question mark, maybe now he should. Once Bertie saw Camryn after she returned, the secret would be obvious anyway.

He took a deep breath. "Look, Mom, there's something you don't know about Camryn."

Bertie wiped her hands on her apron. "She's sick, isn't she? Oh, I thought that might be the problem when you told me she wasn't feeling well. What is it, Reed? Nothing serious, I hope."

Reed spoke to his sons. "Go outside and play a few minutes, okay, boys?"

"But it's cold out there," Phillip protested. "And I'm hungry."

"You won't starve or freeze in the next ten minutes. I'll call you back in before you do."

Reluctantly the boys slipped into their jackets and stocking caps and headed out the door.

Penelope took a seat at the table. "I can stay, can't I?"

"I suppose. You won't cause much interference from a condo in New Jersey."

Bertie set her cooking utensils aside and joined her children at the table. "Stanley," she called to her husband. "Come join us. I have a feeling what Reed is about to tell us is important."

Reed's dad changed from one news channel to another on the TV. "If it is, you'll tell me later, Bertie."

Bertie clasped her hands and stared across the table at her son. "Well?"

"Camryn isn't sick, Mom. She's pregnant."

"Pregnant? Oh, my stars, Reed. Didn't I raise you better than that? Did you take advantage of that sweet girl…"

His frustration mounting, Reed realized the mistake he'd made in blurting out the truth. It wasn't enough that he'd come to the most difficult decision of his life when he chose to break it off with Camryn rather than have a relationship and help raise her child. Now his mother was piling on guilt after she'd jumped to the entirely wrong conclusion.

"I'm not the father!" he exclaimed.

"Well, then who is?" Bertie asked. "I've never seen a man over there…"

"Her ex-husband is the father, the same man who is Esther's father."

Bertie's voice lowered to a near whisper. "Oh, my, that does make for a sticky situation."

"Tell me about it," Reed said. "It happened shortly before Camryn got divorced, and kids meaning what they do to Cam, she set her sights on having this baby even if she no longer stayed with her husband."

"That's admirable, I guess," Bertie said. "A child coming into the world is a blessing no matter the circumstances. Is the ex-husband a decent man?"

"I don't know. I've never met him. But you can see that any hopes I might have had for Camryn and me were complicated enormously when she told me about this."

Bertie nodded thoughtfully. "Yes, I can. But it's not impossible."

"I have no idea how involved this man will be in Camryn's life once the kid is born. I've already had problems with Esther getting along with our two hooligans out there. Add in Camryn's ex and my ex and try to imagine four kids and four parents all making decisions about what's best for two entirely different sets of children. And Camryn and I have very different ideas about how to raise children. It could get really messy, Mom."

"Or it could work just fine with a little compromise," Bertie said.

Reed closed his eyes a moment and considered his next words carefully. "Mom, I appreciate your optimism. I really do. But think about this logically. I've just started up a home and a practice here. Every dime I made when I sold the old practice I've put into developing this piece of property, which, thank goodness, you and Dad gave me."

"I'm not sure how things will go here. I mean, so far, so good, but I could still fall flat. I've got to devote myself to making it work, not just for me, but for Phillip and Justin. I've already got two kids I'm responsible for, and we both know they are a handful…"

"Oh, nonsense, Reed," Bertie said. "I love having the boys around."

"Not all the time!" Reed's father called from his TV chair. "Tell the truth, Bertie."

"At any rate," Reed said, hoping to get the conversation back on track, "I'm just learning to be a full-time father to my own two. I can't take on the responsibility of Camryn's children, either emotionally or financially."

"But does all that really matter?" his mother said. "The important thing is that you like Camryn, right?"

"Of course I like Camryn." He paused. "I like her a lot, but despite what you say, that is not the important thing. My financial situation, her situation with her ex-husband, the success of my practice here in South Carolina, improving the behavior of those two boys…" He sighed heavily. "For heaven's sake, Mom, it's all important!"

A low, muttering sound from across the table made Reed look toward his sister. "I suppose you have something to add to this discussion, as well."

Penelope smiled. "I do know a little about relationships and commitments. That is my game after all."

"Of course you do, dear," Bertie said. "What is your professional opinion? Obviously Reed is missing a wonderful opportunity with Camryn."

"I don't know that, Mom. I've never met her. And even if I had, my opinion of her isn't what matters. I've seen bad marriages get better and good marriages fall apart. But I do know this. No one should pressure Reed about this. This is his life, his decision. Also, Camryn lives here a few hundred yards from Reed. That's not going to change, is it? No one is going anywhere soon, right?"

Reed felt his face flush. Someone might be leaving. He had tried not to think about that for days now. But it was a possibility that still loomed large in his life. What if Camryn pulled stakes and went back to Charleston?

"So you're saying, give it time?" Bertie suggested.

"Exactly. I want to see my brother happily married as much as you do, but no one can make that decision for him. And no one should try to influence him."

Reed let out the breath he'd been holding. "Thanks, Pen."

"But for now let me just say, I'm starving, and there are presents under the tree, and the boys have knocked twice on the camper door. So I think we should let them in and have a little Christmas."

"Excellent idea," Reed said. He opened the door. "Come in, boys. Grandma has made a great breakfast, and we're going to tear this wrapping paper to shreds."

He shook his head as his sons dashed by him. Thank goodness he sounded happy. He wanted the day to be perfect, and he would do his best to make it so. But now he knew that as far as he was concerned, his Christmas was just another day he would question his decision about Camryn, and another day he would wonder about what she was going to do.

CHAPTER SEVENTEEN

REED HADN'T EXAGGERATED when he'd told Camryn that a cold front was moving into South Carolina. A week after she returned from Charleston, the temperature started to drop, and it hadn't stopped yet, another week later. "The Carolina Ice Age" was the term the news channels were using to describe the rare and unpleasant phenomenon. Thank heavens the sun came out for enough time every day for Cam to get to her chicken coops to feed, collect eggs and check the heaters she'd invested in.

The goats, sporting an extra layer of fur provided by Mother Nature, spent most of their time in the barn, sharing stalls with Reed's two horses, who didn't mind wearing the heavy woolen blankets Reed provided. Rooster became almost entirely an indoor dog, only running outside to take care of business and coming right back in. He spent his days curled in front of the fireplace, earning extra attention from Camryn who envied his patience and practicality.

Reed came over daily to feed and care for his horses. Construction on his barn had stopped abruptly when the cold temperatures made working outside not only uncomfortable but dangerous. Usually Reed stopped at the house after his chores, had a cup of coffee with Camryn and reminded her that the "third trimester was an exciting time for her." She could now look forward to the birth of a healthy baby.

Camryn appreciated Reed's encouragement though she still regretted that his interest in the birth wouldn't be a shared event. Even knowing he wasn't going to resume a relationship with her, she cherished her time with Reed. She still hadn't made up her mind about the offer from Agri-Crops, but the longer she delayed making the decision, the more she expected she would stay right where she was. She and Reed would never have the relationship she'd dreamed about, but having him as a friend was a blessing.

Of course the possibility existed that he might meet someone, fall in love and marry. There must be a woman in close proximity that fulfilled his dreams for his future, one who either did not have children or didn't plan to. If that happened, and if Agri-Crops still wanted her land, well, she could always pack up and leave at that point. Living next to Reed and his new bride would be too much for her to adapt to.

On one particularly freezing afternoon, Camryn drove her truck down the lane to meet the school bus. The weathermen had warned listeners to stay inside, and she didn't want Esther to have to endure the weather even for the short walk up to the house.

"What are we going to do tonight, Mommy?" Esther asked when she climbed into the truck. "We've had the paint for the baby's room for a long time. I think we should paint it now. We don't want our baby to think we weren't expecting him."

"Him?" Camryn said. "Are you very sure about that, Essie?"

"No, but I think I can get along with a boy if we have one."

"Good to know." Camryn hadn't asked the gender of the baby, but her instincts told her she was carrying another girl. "It's probably a very wise idea to paint," she said.

"Plus, we can start assembling the crib together and putting away the baby clothes we've purchased." Fighting her irrational superstition, Camryn had refused to make preparations for the baby until she knew the future looked bright. Now, as Reed said, "the third trimester was an exciting time," and she could relax. She hadn't had even the hint of a panic attack in several weeks.

So Camryn and Esther spent this very cold Friday night painting and organizing while Rooster stretched along the threshold of the baby's room, his eyes alert to every movement. Every once in a while Camryn went over to the mutt and scratched his ears. "You are such a good protector," she said. "We are lucky to have you."

"Rooster is the best," Esther said, giving the animal a hug. "Do you think the baby will like him?"

"Well, you like Rooster, right?" Camryn said.

"I love Rooster."

"And you will be the big sister. The baby will probably do everything you do because he or she will think you are the cleverest, smartest sister in the world. So, yes, the baby will love Rooster."

That night Camryn extinguished the fire in the fireplace, bundled Esther into a warm bed and spent some quiet time looking out her living room window. Holding a mug of hot tea, she watched snowflakes swirl to the ground. Ice hung from tree branches, turning her yard into a crystal wonderland, beautiful to look at, yet frightening somehow at the same time.

The cold snap was predicted to abate in the next couple of days. The wonderland would disappear and work could continue, the work of raising chickens and building barns. Camryn shivered when she heard a loud crack outside the window. A tree limb, heavy with ice, snapped from the trunk of an old live oak tree and crashed to the ground.

"Wow, that was close," Camryn said. "I hope we don't have a branch come through our roof."

Thinking she would stay alert for a bit longer, Camryn sat on the sofa and picked up a book. After an hour she drifted off to sleep.

And then, in the middle of the cold dark night, everything in Camryn's world came crashing down just like that tree branch had.

It might have been two o'clock or maybe three. But Camryn was too startled to even look at a clock. She jerked awake when Rooster began growling. At first the dog's sound was a low, menacing grumble. Just a flash of his pointed teeth showed in the dim light from an end table lamp.

"What's wrong, Rooster?" Camryn said. "Is someone outside?"

The dog leaped up from the rug in front of the dead embers in the fireplace. In two bounds of his long, gangly legs he ran into the kitchen, stopping at the locked back door. He stood there, his breath coming in short, ragged gasps, his ears raised, his tail pointed.

Camryn hugged her heavy robe close around her and walked to the back door. At least Rooster had stopped growling, but he was definitely trying to convey a message with a repeated whine that alarmed her. "Do you need to go out?" Camryn asked. "It's so cold out there. Maybe you can hold it until morning."

Rooster jumped at the door. His front legs pressed against the wood panel, his head was equal with the window at the top. His breath fogged the pane of glass. He continued to whine, ending his show of discomfort with another low, raspy growl.

"Okay, okay, I get it," Camryn said, staring out the window and looking all around her yard. "I'll unlock the door for you, but I'm not going out. Just run around quickly, do your thing and come right back in."

She opened the door and Rooster raced outside with a speed and intensity she'd never seen from him before. He didn't stop to sniff. He was a blur of tan-and-gray hair heading straight for the chicken coop. If he'd been on a launch pad, Camryn figured he'd be flying into the stars by now.

"No, Rooster! Come back." She clapped her hands, usually a sure doggy sign that Rooster had better stop what he was doing and alter course immediately. He ignored the signal.

"Blast it all," she said, lifting the heavy collar of her robe and burrowing her head deep inside the soft fleece. She stepped outside, peering into the darkness. The cold stung her cheeks and made her eyes water instantly. In the dark shadows she saw motion. Rooster, yes, but there was more. Several creatures she couldn't identify raced madly through her chicken-feeding ground.

The next noises penetrated the cold as the

confusion and blur of activity continued just yards away. Rooster barked madly and the chickens squawked. Horrible, brain-tingling sounds. And above it all, the terrifying grunts and pants of creatures whose sole purpose was to destroy.

Her heart began to pound. She tried to draw a breath through the icy air, but each attempt to fill her lungs was like a dozen tiny pinpricks in her chest. She tried to holler, but no sound came out. All she could do was run, not toward the house and her open kitchen door, but to the chicken coop and her beloved dog.

There was nothing to grab in the way of protection for her and Rooster. A light dusting of snow covered the ground, obliterating everything but the mayhem. So Camryn waved her arms, drew strength from somewhere deep inside and yelled at last. She screamed, not recognizing the sounds coming from her own throat.

She almost stumbled, and realized, in one agonizing moment that would stay with her forever, that she'd been about to lose her footing over the prone body of Rooster. The night sky provided little light, but she could see the carcasses of many chickens strewn about the yard in pools of blood. And facing her with only more dire intent in their small, hooded eyes were three animals that looked almost like pigs but were rougher, wilder and meaner than anything in a barnyard. What they were doing might have been a matter of survival to them, but they were pure evil to Camryn.

She waved her arms again, tried to cry out but the only sounds she made were those of grief and agony. And the creatures came toward her as if they'd only just realized that new, meatier prey had entered the scene. "Back. Go away!" she screamed. They continued advancing.

"Mommy, where are you?"

Her daughter's voice shook Camryn into awareness. She glanced toward the kitchen door. There, framed in the light, was Esther. And she was coming outside.

"No, Esther, don't come out here!" Camryn cried. She turned toward the house but had no idea if she would get there before Esther became a potential target. "Go inside, now!"

"But Mommy..."

"Don't argue. For God's sake, Es, do as I tell you."

Camryn's warning mingled with her desperate cries. Were all her newfound dreams, and Esther's, too, to end this way, at the mercy of scavenging animals?

And then a loud shotgun blast cracked through the awful stillness of that cold and dark night. The pigs turned away from Camryn and rooted among the bodies of her chickens. Another shotgun blast, and they bounded out of the damaged coop to a nearby field. Each animal had the body of a hen in its jaws.

Esther began crying. Camryn went to her knees and opened her arms for Esther to find shelter there. They both trembled with cold and shock. *Please don't let my daughter see what has happened here*, Camryn prayed into the icy night.

Moments later she felt a comforting hand on her shoulder. Reed stood beside her, his breath quick, harsh gasps through the wind whipping around them. There was a shotgun in the crook of his arm.

"CAMRYN, THEY'RE GONE," Reed said. "The shotgun scared them off."

Only tiny, pitiful sounds came from her

mouth, sounds that made him think her heart had been torn out of her chest. Her arms were so tight around Esther that he wondered how the child could breathe.

"Come with me," he said. "Let me take you and Esther into the house. You'll freeze out here." He reached for her arms to help lift her, but she shrugged him off violently.

She said something, a two-syllable word he didn't understand at first. So he bent down closer to her lips.

"Rooster… Rooster," she said, while shielding Esther's ears with her hands.

"Where is Rooster?" Reed asked.

Her eyes darted to the scene of the chaos. "I think he's…" She couldn't finish the sentence.

"I'll check on him," Reed said. "Let me get you both in the house first."

She nodded, aware that Esther wasn't dressed for this weather. He gripped her upper arms and helped her rise. She kept Esther close to her chest, bundled in the robe that was keeping both of them as warm as possible.

Esther buried her face against her mother's breast. She asked questions with a frightened, trembling voice.

Reed started to walk them back to the house, and suddenly Camryn's knees collapsed. She would have gone down, but he stopped her from falling. Without asking, he took Esther from Camryn's arms and carried her quickly to the door.

When he returned, Camryn was clutching her stomach. "The pain. Oh, Reed, it hurts."

He scooped Camryn into his arms and raced to the house. "You'll be okay, Cam," he kept saying though he had no idea if it was true.

"What were those animals?" she said.

"Wild boars," he answered. "They're not uncommon around here, but they rarely venture into populated areas. I suppose the cold made them come this far in search of food."

She sobbed loudly as Reed carried her over the threshold. Esther was sobbing now, asking relentlessly if her mommy was okay. He got her to a chair and tried to get Camryn to sit, as well.

"No, I can't. Lie down." Her words faltered. He took her to the living room and reclined her on the sofa. "The boars didn't get to you, did they?"

"No, but they were coming. If you hadn't…"

"Shh." He smoothed her wild, windblown hair from her forehead. "But I did." He saw her wince. "Tell me where it hurts."

"It's the baby," she said. "I've hurt the baby."

Next to the sofa, Esther wailed. "What's happened to our baby?"

"We don't know anything yet, sweetie," Reed said. "Probably your baby will be fine." He smiled at her and she calmed. "Go to your room and get some clothes on. You're going over to my house."

"Where is Mommy going?"

"To the hospital," Reed said. "The doctors need to check her out and tell us everything is fine."

"You're a doctor," Esther said.

"Not the kind we need, honey. Now please go and get dressed. I'll call Miss Bertie to come stay with you."

Esther stood defiantly. "I'm not leaving my mommy."

Camryn sucked in a breath, held it a moment. "Do as Reed says, baby. Please."

"Where is your phone?" Reed asked when

Esther had gone to her room. "I forgot to grab mine when I left the house."

She pointed to the coffee table. Reed dialed 911 and requested an ambulance. "They'll be here in a few minutes, Cam. Just lie still, try to take long, slow breaths through your nose."

"I think they're labor pains," she said. "It's too soon, Reed. I can't have the baby tonight."

"We'll let that baby and the doctors decide. I'll stay right here until they arrive."

"No! Outside. You have to see to Rooster. I think they killed him. He did all he could to protect us."

Torn by two responsibilities, Reed decided he might best be able to help if he checked on the dog. The last thing he wanted to do was cause more stress for Camryn, and this was what she wanted. He unlocked the front door so the EMTs could get in the house. "I'll be outside," he said, taking her hand. "Try to relax. I know that seems impossible, but try, okay?"

"Let me know about Rooster."

"Of course. As soon as I reach my mother, drop Esther with her and the boys, and do what I can for Rooster, I'll come to the hospital. You just think about a healthy baby being born in a couple of months."

She smiled through trembling lips. "Thank you."

"That's what I'm here for...whatever you need, even if it means scaring off a pack of wild pigs." He went to the hallway and hollered to Esther. "I'll be outside, sweetie. You stay here with Mommy." Then he went out the back door, grabbed the shotgun from where he'd dropped it in the yard and hoped he could save a dog.

DAWN WAS LIGHTING the morning sky when Reed finally got in his vehicle to drive to the hospital. He wasn't tired. His senses were too alert, his mind too focused on the tasks ahead this day. After making certain the ambulance arrived, he'd bundled up Rooster and carried him to his clinic across the field. No words could express the gratitude Reed had felt when he found a pulse in the dog's neck.

And thank goodness for his mother. She was already at his house when the ambulance driver had dropped Esther off, a favor Reed had shouted to the young medic who'd no doubt defied protocol by taking the short detour. Reed had talked to his mom this morning, and she assured him that all was well, though Esther was worried and fretting.

Reed had worked on Rooster for three hours. The dog had severe lacerations in his neck and abdomen. If he'd lost much more blood there would have been no chance of saving him. Now sedated, Rooster showed all positive signs of coming back from the attack. Reed called the hospital and learned that Camryn was in satisfactory condition and she had not given birth yet. Then he called the feedstore to ask Becky if her son could come and stay at the clinic while he went to the hospital.

So many crucial acts and decisions had been made, and now Reed faced the toughest one…seeing Camryn after hoping all night that she and the baby were fine. The aggressive nature of the boars was rare but not unheard of. When threatened with battle or starvation, almost any animal would do what was necessary to survive.

He would stay at the hospital as long as Camryn wanted him to, but when he left, he would examine the chicken coops for damage. Reed was certain Camryn would ask, and he wanted to be sure of his answer since he'd already noticed the carnage. The screens had been ripped from the wood structures. Chicken carcasses littered the field, including the ones of Esther's beloved Ameraucanas. How would he tell the two women who'd come to mean so much to him that their Easter Egg chickens were gone?

The two women who had come to mean so much to him...the phrase kept repeating in his mind the whole way to the hospital. He wished he'd been there for them sooner before their peaceful paradise had been so cruelly devastated. All he could do now was promise to help them get back on their feet. There was strength and hope in rebuilding. He wished Camryn and Esther would find that to be true.

A pale, delicate woman lay in the hospital bed when Reed entered her room. Yet, despite the ravages of the night, she looked beautiful, calm now, and so sweet and inspiring, a symbol of surviving the worst and coming through with resolve and dignity. Reed went to her bedside, leaned over and kissed her forehead. "I'm so sorry."

CHAPTER EIGHTEEN

CAMRYN RELEASED A LONG, slow breath. Reed did that for her. Made her feel secure, protected. He'd once rescued Esther. Now he'd saved her, brought her back from an all-consuming panic that could have gotten her killed.

She stared up at him, tried to smile her appreciation for him being there during the night, but there were still too many questions. "How is Esther?" she asked.

"She's fine, with my mother and the boys." He looked down at her tummy. "I understand this little one is okay, too. Waiting his chance like a good boy. Or girl."

Camryn nodded. "Yes. The baby has a good, strong heartbeat. But… Rooster?" Part of her didn't want to hear the answer—the part that had let Rooster out the back door without considering his safety. The part that knew she would have to tell Esther if the dog were gone.

"He's in the best place he can be," Reed said. "In the brand-new Bolden Veterinary Clinic."

Camryn hiccuped, felt tears start to sting her eyes. "Then he's not… He's alive?"

"Very much so. He'll have a few battle scars but I think he will recover fully. Right now he's sedated, and when he leaves the clinic he'll probably resent the heck out of having to wear a cone until he heals." He smiled. "We guys hate to admit to a sign of weakness."

Tears fell freely down Camryn's cheeks. "I don't know how to thank you. If you hadn't come when you did…"

"But I did, and I'd like to think I will always come when you need me, Camryn."

She considered his words carefully. He was promising to always be a good neighbor, nothing more. And she was grateful. Truly she was, though she'd allowed herself to dream of more.

He gently touched her belly. "So are you feeling any repercussions from this one after he got a firsthand look at the downside of country life? I can imagine he's been kicking up a storm."

"I love every move he makes," she said. "I definitely put stress on him, started premature labor, but the doctors controlled the pain and contractions. Now we're both back on track with a little over two months to go."

Reed took her hand. "That's wonderful, Cam. How long do you have to stay here?"

"Until tomorrow. I called my sister, and she's coming down this morning to take care of Esther until I go home."

"I would have…"

"Reed, you've done enough. You're already taking care of one Montgomery, the four-legged one. It seems we've been nothing but trouble to you."

He chuckled. "I'd like to say that you Montgomerys are no trouble at all, but I guess we both know that isn't exactly true. But you're worth the effort."

"Reed…" She swallowed, gathered her strength. "What does the damage look like? How bad is it?"

His eyes darkened, and she knew the news was not good.

"I would judge that about half the chickens didn't make it. The boars had pretty well torn the coop apart to get to them. And when the birds starting escaping, there were so many of them. They were pretty easy pickings for raging boars."

"What about the Ameraucanas?"

He shook his head.

"Poor Esther."

Reed patted her hand. "Do you want me to pick you up tomorrow and take you home?"

"That would be wonderful. Yes." Home. She wished she could go home to Cottontail Farm. She wished last night had never happened. But she knew her peaceful paradise had changed forever. "It won't be home for long, however," she said.

He gave her a confused look. "What are you talking about?"

"I spoke to my parents this morning. I'm going to Charleston for the remainder of the pregnancy."

"Are you sure that's necessary?" His eyes rounded with shock. He obviously hadn't expected her to say she was leaving. "We'll take care of you. Between me and Becky, and my mother's cooking… Heck, half the people in Bufflehead Creek will help out."

"I appreciate that," she said. "But I can't impose on my friends any longer. The doctors have said that I need complete bed rest until the baby comes, so that means my care involves much more than just looking after me. There's Esther to consider." She sobbed. "I need my parents now, Reed. This has made me realize how much."

Reed rubbed his jaw where a dark stubble of beard had grown overnight. "I guess I can understand that. But you'll come back when the baby is born." He smiled again, trying to make the most of a situation that had obviously left him surprised and uncertain. "We've got rebuilding to do."

"No rebuilding, Reed. What happened last night has left me broken. I've had to make a decision. If Agri-Crops's offer is still on the table, I'm going to take it. I'm going back to Charleston for good."

"Cam, you need time." He sat on the edge of her bed. "The horror of last night will fade. Your determination will return. I just know it. Don't make a decision until you've had a while to think it through."

"I have thought it through," she said. "My time in Bufflehead Creek has been a dream, really. A wonderful dream in so many ways. But I have to consider my family. I will soon have two children who depend on me.

I have to do the grown-up thing and focus on what's best for them. The lives of my children are where my determination lies now."

His eyes blinked rapidly several times. "But Camryn, your daughter loves it here. You told me so yourself. There's no reason to think that this second child wouldn't be happy here, too."

"Maybe, but the bottom line is I made the decision to move here without consulting with Esther. I know her time on the farm has been good for her. She's been content. But she gave up a lot to move here."

"She's a little girl, Cam. Parents always make the decisions. I certainly didn't consult with my boys before moving here. I told them what life would be like, and my predictions have pretty much proven true."

"But you're not alone. Your parents live a few hundred yards away. But I'm…" She looked away. "I only have Esther and she only has me. And I… I simply can't go on after what happened last night. I jeopardized this baby's future. We almost lost Rooster, and we did lose our chickens."

She tried to smile through the cloud of her despair. She was unspeakably grateful that he was urging her to stay, especially after telling her to consider Agri-Crops's offer just a few weeks ago. He valued her friendship. She would never question it. But she couldn't stay. "I've had a wake-up call, Reed. I have to do the right thing."

"How can you think you're alone?" he said, his voice raised and practically argumentative. "Haven't I been here for you since I moved in? Don't you know that I'm just a phone call away?"

He had unknowingly pinpointed the problem as far as she was concerned. He would always be a phone call away. "You've been wonderful, Reed. So much more than a neighbor and a guy who rents my barn. I thought at one time…" She stopped, took a long, deep breath and placed her hand over her belly. "But everything has changed. Soon your barn will be finished. Your practice will continue to grow. Your boys will require more of your time away from the farm as they develop interests."

She sat up straighter in the bed and gave him an intense stare that she intended to convey both her appreciation and her resolve.

And she hoped that resolve would continue until she had left Cottontail Farm behind.

"I simply can't ask more of you than you've already given," she said. "I need my family, more than I ever thought I would. My parents are willing to make room for us and give this baby the best chance for a healthy beginning." Brushing away a tear that had fallen on her cheek, she said, "This is the right decision."

He nodded, a slow, deliberate sign of understanding but not accepting. "So how long? When do you plan to go to Charleston?"

"Tomorrow. Esther and I will drive back with Brooke. I've spoken to my mother, and she's already begun preparations."

He clenched his hands tightly. "But Cam, you're leaving so much unsettled. You've established businesses here. You have friends. Your market sales increased all through the fall."

She sensed he was grasping at whatever straws were left in his arsenal to change her mind. He was such a good friend, a good man, but he would never be more. Even now, when he seemed confused, upset, even perhaps a bit desperate while coping with her decision, he couldn't offer more. He wouldn't admit how he truly felt about her and take on the responsibility of another family.

"Your farm is how you've increased your income, made a good living for you and Esther," he said. "And you've been succeeding. I hate to see you give it up."

"We won't starve, Reed. Besides my design work at Southern Square Press, I worked for a time at a gallery in downtown Charleston. My boss said I should contact him if I return. I think he will give me my old job back, part-time anyway."

"That's good, I guess." He paused a long, thoughtful moment. "But what about your animals? The goats, the chickens that are left?"

This was the question she had dreaded, another favor she had to ask Reed even though he'd done so much. "I have two choices," she began. "I can ask you to take the goats to your property. The cold weather has passed, and they'll be fine outside. All you would have to do is feed them until I can find them good homes. The chickens should sell easily. Until then, Randy, Becky's son, has agreed to come out and feed them. My second choice is to ask Randy to care for the goats, as well, but he's in community college…well, you know."

"Stop right there," Reed said. "Of course I will take the goats to my place. I'll feed the chickens, too, if needed."

She smiled at him. "It's funny how this all worked out, isn't it, Reed? At the feed-store that first morning, you asked me for a favor. And now it seems that all I've done is ask so much of you."

"Have you ever once heard me complain?"

"No, you haven't, and I guess that makes you a part of the dream I was talking about." She took his hand and squeezed it tight. "Thank you, Reed."

A tremulous sigh escaped his lips, but he pulled himself together. "And the house? What will happen to it after Agri-Crops takes over the land?"

"I'll sell it, I suppose. Once the baby comes, I'll return and clear out my personal belongings."

"So I'll see you then, after several months have passed?" There was a painful finality in his words.

"We can talk on the phone," she said. "I'm

sure I'll call to check on you and the boys… and the goats."

"Yes, and the goats," he said. "I guess you've thought everything out very carefully."

"I hope so. I'm sure there will be road-blocks along the way—" she stopped, sniffed "—some too painful to talk about." *Don't say it, Cam*, she thought. *You have to let this go.*

A nurse came into the room. Reed stood and backed away from the bed. "How are you feeling, Camryn?" the nurse asked.

"Pretty well."

"Good. Your vitals are fine, and the baby's heartbeat is back to normal rhythm. As long as you follow doctor's orders, there's no reason you can't expect a full-term birth."

Camryn nodded. "I will."

"Okay, then. You should be going home tomorrow, as planned. I'll prepare the discharge papers, and the doctor will release you in the morning. Do you have a ride home?"

"She does," Reed said.

One last act of kindness, Cam thought. And then her mind played a horrible trick on her. *What will I do without him?*

Reed picked Esther up at his parents' motor home on his way to meet Brooke at Camryn's house. The child was full of questions. What happened to the chickens? Were her Ameraucanas okay? Where was Rooster?

Camryn had made Reed promise not to discuss the fate of the chickens until she'd had a chance to prepare Esther. But over the phone, she had told her daughter the truth about Rooster. Reed was glad she had. He was able to sit with Esther and explain about the dog's injuries and assure the child that her beloved pet should be okay.

Both Brooke and Reed kept Esther from seeing the ruined chicken coop. For the rest of the afternoon, Reed and Randy did what they could to clean up the yard. When they were finished, the destruction still tore at Reed's heart. And not just because he was sworn to save animals and relieve their suffering. But because the unforgettable event had broken Cam's heart.

The next morning Esther went with Reed to pick up Camryn. Brooke stayed at the house to pack essentials for the trip to Charleston. Esther still didn't know they were leaving that afternoon.

"Rooster is a hero, isn't he, Mom?" Esther said when they were all in the car and driving back to the farm. "He was protecting us."

"Yes, he is a hero," Camryn agreed. "I'm going to ask Miss Becky to bring some extra fine doggie treats from the feedstore so Rooster will know how grateful we are."

"When will he be able to come home?"

Camryn looked to Reed in hopes he would answer this question. He could provide the necessary medical details until she explained that Rooster wouldn't be coming back to Cottontail. When he was well enough, he would come to Charleston, too.

"Rooster was injured pretty badly," Reed said. "But he's a strong, brave dog, and we want him to have the very best care, don't we?"

"Yes, we do," Esther agreed.

"Then I'm going to suggest that he stay in my clinic for a while until he's all better."

"Can I come see him?"

"Maybe not right away," Camryn said. "We want Rooster to stay calm and quiet so he will heal more quickly."

When Reed pulled into Camryn's drive, Brooke came out the door immediately. She helped Camryn get out of the car, gave her an encouraging hug and assisted her in walking to the front door.

Esther followed behind them. "Mommy, why is Auntie Brooke acting like you're sick or something? Didn't you say you were okay?"

"Don't worry, kiddo," Reed said. "Your mommy is not sick, but she has been in the hospital for what we call observation. Your aunt Brooke is just acting like a concerned sister." Reed put his arm around Esther and walked her to the house. "I have a hunch that you will know all about those feelings once you become a big sister yourself."

A calm and compassionate man, Camryn thought. *He always knows what to say.*

"LET'S GET YOU in bed," Brooke said to her sister. "I'll bring you some lunch when you're settled in."

Camryn looked up at Reed with the big blue eyes that had done him in the first time he'd seen her. She smiled, a slight tremulous lifting of her lips that didn't seem much like a smile at all. "Thanks for bringing me home, Reed," she said. She breathed deeply, keeping her gaze locked with his. "That sounds so shallow. I should be thanking you for, well, so many things over the past weeks."

"You have thanked me, Cam, even though that was never once necessary." He took her hand, realizing that he was no longer needed in her life. She had her sister, her daughter, her parents, maybe even her ex-husband, the father of her baby. They would take care of her, and after a few phone calls and one more trip back to her farm, she would get on with her life and Reed Bolden would fade from her memory.

Just as well, Bolden, he said to himself. *You've given her no reason to keep a memory of you fresh and alive and meaningful.* But the fact remained. He simply couldn't offer her more than friendship—the most heartfelt kind—right now. Every time he thought about how much he would miss her, he ended up remembering the awesome responsibilities in his life and the awesome obligations soon to be in hers. Maybe if they'd met at a different time…

Her voice interrupted his thoughts when she called from the bedroom. "Essie, will you come in here, please? I have to talk to you, sweetheart. There are things you need to know."

"Okay, Mommy."

Reed knew the next few minutes were going to be difficult ones. Camryn would have to tell her daughter about one of the terrible aspects of farm life and survival of the fittest. And she would explain that they were leaving with Brooke and going to Charleston, and Esther's life was going to change.

"And so will yours," Reed said to himself as he walked out the front door and left the women to deal with the immediate future. If only things had been different…

Reed stayed busy the rest of the afternoon. He had patients in his clinic, especially Rooster, who needed twenty-four-hour monitoring. Reed was grateful Becky's son didn't have studying to do for Monday classes and could stick around and help. Phillip and Justin came to the recovery room often in the next hours, each time begging to see Rooster. Reed didn't let them closer than the window to the equivalent of his intensive care unit, though the boys complained.

One visitor did get to go inside the recovery area. In the late afternoon, after Brooke's car was packed, Brooke drove her sister and niece to Reed's house. Camryn stayed in the car, but Esther ran into the clinic calling Reed's name.

"Hey, there, kiddo, what's going on?" he said when he met her inside the door.

"I just have to see Rooster," Esther said. "I know he'll be okay, but he needs to know that I love him. I have to tell him."

"Of course you do, honey." Reed placed a hand on Esther's shoulder. "Come on. I'll take you to him."

They walked into the sterile environment of the care unit. Only one cage had an occupant, and Esther found her dog right away. "Hi, Rooster. It's me, Esther. How are you feeling?"

The dog didn't move but the monitors attached to his body showed that he was breathing normally and his heart was beating.

Esther looked up at Reed. "He's not moving, Reed." She hiccuped, camouflaging a sob. "He's not dead, is he?"

"No, Esther, he's fine. But when an animal gets hurt as badly as Rooster did, they tend to sleep a lot. That's good. It's what we veterinarians want them to do. He's not feeling any pain."

"But he doesn't know I'm here."

"I'll bet he does, Esther. Rooster is a smart dog. He can't respond to you, but I'm sure he hears your voice."

Esther poked a finger between the bars of the cage. The tip just reached Rooster's nose and Esther stroked it gently. "You have to get better, Rooster. Mommy said we are going to get you some special treats."

Rooster sniffed loudly. His upper lip quivered and rose.

"Look, Reed," Esther exclaimed. "He's smiling. He did hear me. Rooster loves treats."

"You see?" Reed said. "He knows your voice even when he's sleeping."

Esther nodded. "Will you tell Justin to talk about me a lot when he comes to see Rooster?"

"I will, and Justin will be happy to have long conversations about you."

"And maybe I can call once in a while to see how he's doing? I know how to use the cell phone."

"Call whenever you like, Es."

She nodded. "Okay. I have to go, Rooster. Mommy said I could only stay a minute, and I think it's been longer than that already. We're going to Charleston until Mommy has her baby and then we're coming back here to get you." She leaned into the metal bars and made little kissing sounds. "I love you, Rooster. Don't forget us."

Reed turned away. This was why he became a veterinarian—so he could heal animals and return them to their families or to the people who loved them. And he dang sure was going to return this special dog to this child.

"Okay, Esther, I'll take you to the car. Don't worry about Rooster. I will treat him like the hero he is."

"You're a hero too, Reed," she said when they walked out of the recovery room. "You saved him."

He didn't walk Esther all the way to the car. He stood at the top of his drive and watched her climb inside. Before turning around, Brooke tooted the horn. Camryn raised up from the back seat and waved. Reed didn't want to remember Cam's face the way he saw it now, drained, pale, sad. He wanted to remember the energetic, hardworking pursuer of dreams, the first friend he made in Bufflehead Creek, the best one he'd ever had.

CHAPTER NINETEEN

ON WEDNESDAY AFTERNOON, the fourth day at her parents' house on bed rest, Camryn took a break. She sat outside under an old oak tree in her childhood backyard.

The temperature was unseasonably warm today, sixty degrees, comfortable for the end of January.

Esther would be home from school soon, and the arrival of her daughter every day was the highlight of Camryn's hours. Esther was happy because Cam had arranged for her to go back to her previous school, and Esther remembered some of her old classmates. All that was required was for Camryn's mother to take Essie to school and her father to pick her up.

Life should have been perfect for Camryn. She was being well cared for by a family that loved her. The local obstetrician had given her encouraging news. Esther was doing well except for missing Rooster and Reed's boys. And Camryn had gotten positive feedback from Mr. Palermo of Agri-Crops, who said he was certain the deal they'd talked about in Bufflehead Creek was still good. He needed to check with his superiors and he would get back to her by the end of the week.

Yes, everything was going according to the plan Camryn had made when she left her farm, the plan she had to follow to assure the healthy arrival of the baby she now knew was her second daughter. Unfortunately this plan was not the one Camryn had decided upon for the rest of her life. That plan involved a small town, a farm and a brood of chickens. So now she didn't know what she was going to do with the years ahead of her.

Stay in Charleston, work at the gallery? Live with her parents indefinitely? They had made it clear that they would be happy to have her. Move to her own place and struggle as a single mother with two children?

Mark had come to see her on Monday. He'd been sympathetic enough when she told him about the wild boars, stopping just short of saying he'd "told her so" about the move to the farm. Camryn was certain he would support his daughters financially, but she questioned whether he would have a significant role in their everyday lives. Mark's relationship with Paula was progressing, and she envisioned a wedding ceremony for the two of them. Once that happened, Mark would be a daddy to Paula's daughter, too, a live-in daddy, not one who made time for his two daughters when he could.

Camryn plucked a leafless twig from a low-hanging branch of the tree and began stripping it of bark until she could find the green belly, a sign of spring coming before too long. The tree would soon be vibrant with life, providing shade to the whole family. The tree would have a purpose, so why didn't Camryn feel that she had a purpose, as well?

At the farm, she never once woke in the morning with the thought that she didn't have a purpose in life. On those acres, there was always more to do than there were hours in the day. Now she was living a life of bed rest and an artificial calm that she strived constantly to maintain with cups of tea, naps and sweet romance books.

She no longer breathed the smells of her garden, the ones that soothed her by just being in the air. She no longer gathered warm eggs, gifts from her chickens that proved they were a working family, each creature, large and small, contributing to the tranquil routine of her days.

Oh, my, how desperately she missed… all of it.

"Hi, Mommy. I'm home from school!"

Esther's voice brought Camryn back to her reality in the sweetest, most positive way. She held open her arms and Esther scampered into them.

"Grandma said you were out here," Esther said. "Are you okay? Is our baby okay?"

"Yes, sweetie, we're both fine. I just felt like a bit of sunshine. It's such a beautiful day." She managed to fit Esther on her lap despite her expanding belly. "How was school today?"

"It was okay. We played a game that Justin would have loved. It was a spelling game, and he was the best speller in our class."

This wasn't the first time Esther had mentioned the friend she'd left in Bufflehead Creek. Cam knew she missed him. Oh, the wonderful irony of childhood hurt and forgiveness, as natural as the sun rising.

"Are we going to do anything tonight?" Esther asked, her voice hopeful. It had been

so long since they'd done something sponta-
neous and fun. Even a trip to the ice cream
shop would have been nice, but Camryn
knew that wouldn't happen.

"I think Grandma is going to the supermarket," she said. "I'll bet she'd love to have
you go with her."

"Okay, I'll do that," Esther said, "But first
there's something I'd really like to do."

"What is it?"

"Can I call Reed? I want to ask him how
Rooster is, and he said I could call him
whenever I wanted to."

"Then of course you can," Cam answered.
She took her cell phone from her pocket and
handed it to Esther. At the farm, Camryn
rarely remembered to take her phone when
she went outside. Since returning to Charleston, the phone had become a constant com-
panion. "Reed's number is in my contacts
list," Cam said. "Do you know how to find
it?"

Esther gave her a grown-up look, foreshad-
owing what she would be like as a teenager.
"Of course, Mommy. Everyone knows how
to use a cell phone."

Esther took the phone, stood up and stepped

away from Camryn. She punched in the connection. Cam's heart hammered just knowing who would be on the opposite end of the call.

"No, Reed, this isn't Mommy. It's me, Esther," the child said.

"I'm fine. We're all fine. I just wanted to call to find out how Rooster is."

She paused, listening. When she grinned broadly, Camryn knew the news had to be good. "Wow," Esther said. "He walked around the clinic today? That's really good, isn't it?"

Reed obviously confirmed Esther's evaluation because the grin stayed in place.

"Do you think he misses me?" she said after a moment. "Tell him I miss him, too. And Reed?"

Another pause. "Can I talk to Justin, please?"

When Reed's son got on the line, Esther told him about the spelling game in school. She assured him that he would have won. "And Justin, I want you to watch Rooster all the time, when you're not in school at least. Make sure he's eating and sleeping, and not itching too much. And Justin, you can show him a picture of me. I'll have Mommy take one and send it on the cell phone, okay?"

Camryn swallowed a lump in her throat.

Thank goodness the days didn't drag for a nine-year-old as they did for an adult. But it would still be quite a while before Esther would see Rooster again. Just as soon as possible after the baby was born, Cam would bundle her little family in the car and go back to Bufflehead Creek...to see Rooster, of course.

Esther disconnected and handed the phone back to Camryn. Reed hadn't asked to talk to her? Why should he? All the information she needed concerning her farm she got from Becky's reliable son, Randy. But still, Cam had to work to hide her disappointment.

"Reed told me to tell you hi, Mommy."

"Oh, that's nice."

"You should call him and tell him hi back yourself."

Camryn sighed, slipped the phone into her pocket. "Maybe I will, sweetheart. Soon."

REED SHOVED HIS PHONE into his jeans pocket and continued feeding the birds recently transferred to his care from the Low Country Rehabilitation Center. What was wrong with him? All he could think about while talking to Esther was telling her to put her mother on the line. Just one word from Camryn, just a chance to hear the inflection in her voice, and he would know that she was okay. And then he would be okay, too, and could maybe relieve some of this awful ache in his heart.

What should he have done? Try to stop her from packing up and leaving the farm with her sister? Of course not. Camryn needed care, attention, the best medical advice. Charleston was no doubt the best place for her to be. And besides, what had he offered in place of the choice she made? More of the same? A man who adored her but couldn't commit to making a family with her? A man who'd never been much of a father anyway, and who suddenly agreed to take on the care of four children, each one as different from the other as any kids could be?

Reed was a trial-and-error father who believed in letting his kids make mistakes and suffer the consequences. Camryn was a mother who believed in avoiding consequences of any kind. Safety first, that was Cam's motto. There was no way these two people could form a united front with four different children, especially when two of them had a biological father constantly in the background, criticizing, correcting when the mood struck him to be concerned.

No, Reed had chosen the safest path for himself and his boys. "Get your own house in order," he'd said to himself over the last few days. "Make a good home for your sons. Don't take on any more responsibility when you're barely able to handle the situation you've inherited from a woman who cared more for a South American cattle rancher than she did her own children." Not that Reed would have won any awards for his fathering techniques before, but he was trying now. His priorities were in order, weren't they?

So why was he so miserable? Why did he miss coffee in the mornings in that cozy kitchen? Why did he miss helping a woman who was determined to make a success of her little patch of land and her flock of chickens? Why did he dream every night of holding her, kissing her? Why did he allow himself to contemplate a future with a woman who brought more into his life than he could handle?

Why did he want to jump into his SUV and take the quickest route to Charleston?

His cell phone rang and he took it from his pocket. The word "Camryn" identified the caller. A muscle in his chest clinched. His hands started to sweat. At the same time, the hole in his heart started to fill up with warm, wonderful feelings.

"Camryn. Hi, how's everything going?"

"I'm doing well," she said. "The doctor said bed rest is doing wonders for me."

"Really?" He didn't want to appear skeptical. "I'm sure it's doing wonders for the baby, but how about you? How are you adjusting to being a lady of leisure?"

She chuckled. "Inactivity has its good points and bad. Tell me about your boys, your parents, Rooster, my chickens and goats. Don't leave anything out, Reed. I want to know it all."

She seemed hungry for information about her farm, and he fed her even the minutest details about the place she'd left behind. She asked questions. He answered each one, avoiding mention of the attack by the boars, compensating with news of neighbors and events and the people she'd come to know.

He ended his litany of Bufflehead Creek details with, "It's not the same without you here, Cam."

"I know. It's very different for me, too."

Her voice hitched. He sensed she was on the verge of tears. "Nothing is the same."

His heart soared. "What are you saying? Do you want to come home to Bufflehead Creek? Because if you do, I'll leave right now…"

"I can't," she said. "This baby… In a few weeks…"

"In a few weeks, what, Cam?"

"I don't know. I can't make any decisions now. What happened that night… I'll never forget it."

"And you shouldn't. It's part of the cycle of country life, the good and bad, the almost incomprehensible. There were lessons to be learned that night about being cautious, being careful, and most of all, being accepting of all of life's ups and downs. Nature can be a beautiful and cruel teacher." He paused a moment before adding, "But that doesn't mean we don't live our own lives to the fullest. It's the challenges that make us strong."

"I wanted to hear your voice, Reed," she said. "And I'm glad I called. You always have a way of calming my worst inner turmoil."

"I'm glad you called, Camryn. If it's okay

we'll talk often. You have a responsibility now to have a healthy baby. That's what is important. If I can help you through this, you know I'm willing. I may not always be up to the task, but I will always try." He took a deep breath. "Camryn, I…"

"I know, Reed," she said. "We'll talk soon. Goodbye."

He put his phone back in his pocket and looked toward the house. Both of his boys were coming around the house toward the birdcages. Reed pulled himself together, straightened his spine and smiled. *There has to be a way to work this out*, he thought, as his life erupted into the chaos of being a dad.

JUSTIN REACHED HIS father first. "Hi, Dad. Guess what?"

Oh, great, a guessing game. A dozen or more ghastly ideas popped into Reed's head. *I was in the principal's office today. I threw up in class. I got in a fight on the playground*, etc. Before actually picking one of his choices, Reed considered that just maybe the right answer would be that Justin had gotten an A on his math test today.

"Don't ask him," Phillip said. "Justin had another one of his dumb ideas."

"It's not dumb," Justin said. "It's nice. Don't you ever want to be nice?"

Phillip scowled. "Nope."

"Tell me what the idea is," Reed said. "I won't know if it's dumb or nice if you don't tell me."

Justin grinned. "Okay, here goes. You know how Camryn's chicken coop got all messed up when the boars attacked?"

"Yes, I know that. The pigs rooted through the screen and splintered some of the wood. It's pretty rough."

"Well, my idea is that we should fix it… you, me and Phillip." He eyed his brother. "Phillip has to help."

Reed had already thought about trying to restore the chicken coop. Even if Cam decided to sell the farmhouse, a sturdy coop might make a difference in the price she could ask. And if she didn't sell, then she'd need the coop even more. He figured he'd hire some guys from town to come out and do the work, but Justin's idea was much better.

"That's a wonderful idea," Reed said.

Phillip stomped his foot, kicking up a whirl

of dust. "Well, I don't! I've got enough to do without taking on somebody else's problems."

"Like what?" Reed asked. "Homework and video games?"

Phillip didn't answer. He just glared off in the direction of the destroyed coop.

"Tell you what, boys. I'll go over there in the morning and check out the damage, see what materials we'd need to make it right again. If it looks like we can do the job, I'll run into town and pick up wood and chicken wire."

Justin smiled and gave his brother an I-told-you-so look of triumph. "That would be great, Dad. Then we can fix it this weekend."

"Hmm, it might take a few weekends," Reed said. "But it will be fun, all of us together, working on a project." He looked hard at his oldest boy. "No one gets to sit this one out, pal. You might even discover that you enjoyed doing something for our neighbors."

"Come on, Dad. They're not even our neighbors anymore," Phillip pointed out.

"That's true for now," he said. "But things might change." *If I have anything to say about it.*

CHAPTER TWENTY

ONCE REED DECIDED to fix up the chicken coop, he became a changed man. His mornings started early with rounds to his patients and a trip to Camryn's farm to feed her chickens, who'd been displaced for a couple of days but were now roosting happily in what was left of their coop. Reed gathered the eggs, and when they began to fill up his refrigerator, he took them to town and sold them to the diner. A coffee tin in a top cupboard became the symbolic "Camryn's start-over fund" where Reed tucked the profits from his egg gathering.

Reed didn't know if Camryn would even be interested in starting over, but it didn't matter, because he was starting over with his own life by rebuilding hers. The project at Camryn's turned out to be a bonding experience for the Bolden men. They worked hard, laughed a lot and chased a bunch of chickens around Camryn's yard.

And when they ate some of the eggs, Reed saw a sense of pride in the boy's faces and appetites.

The restoration of the coop was meant to be a surprise. The boys wanted it that way, but Reed took pictures of the progress over the weekends as they hammered and stapled and made a pretty good home for the chicks. The final picture of the finished project brought a feeling of accomplishment to all who'd worked on it, and Reed and his sons, including Phillip, were anxious to show the pictures to Camryn and Esther.

Reed called Camryn several times over the next few weeks. He shared news of his clinic, the town, his parents, his sons, with special emphasis on Rooster, whom he'd become to think of as a member of his own family. When it was time to return the dog to its owners, Reed and his boys would have a hard time letting go.

Sometimes Reed thought Camryn needed cheering up, and he was glad that he could be the one to do that. For a woman who had been busy most of her days, this inactivity had to be difficult. Most times, though, Camryn seemed genuinely happy to hear from him. She asked about Rooster, talked about Esther and her family. The pregnancy was progressing as it should, but the doctor was monitoring her closely.

The one main dark spot on Camryn's horizon seemed to be her relationship with her sister, Brooke. Reed didn't ask why the twins might have had a falling out. He knew their love was strong and abiding, and whatever the problem, they would work it out.

"How is my house?" Camryn asked him during one phone call. "Have you been inside to check things out?"

Since she had sold the acreage to Agri-Crops, he wasn't surprised that she didn't ask about the few acres she'd turned over to a garden. And he was encouraged that she asked about the house. Yes, he'd been inside, several times actually. Each time he went in the door, smelled the scents that reminded him of Camryn and studied the little things on her shelves, he felt close to her. And he missed her even more.

"Everything is great," he told her. "The house looks like you are going to walk in the door any minute. Nothing has changed."

Except maybe for his growing desire that she would do exactly that—walk in the door any minute.

"Some serious farm equipment has been on the property adjacent to the house," he told her. "I'd say Agri-Crops is preparing the soil for a spring planting."

"I would be excited to see what crops they're planning and watch them grow."

"Does that mean you're coming back?" he asked her.

"I don't know, Reed. I can't decide anything until the baby comes and I know she's healthy. I do worry about how I would manage, just the three of us."

She paused. He held his breath. "But I think about it often," she said.

He wondered if what he was feeling for Cam was love. Lyrics from romantic songs and verses of poetry popped into his head with regularity these days. Oddly, her absence seemed to have cleared so many of the doubts from his mind. Talking to her on the phone, hearing her voice, picturing her smile intensified the feeling. Could a man fall hopelessly in love with a woman over the phone? Reed was sure he had.

CAMRYN EXPERIENCED THE same mixed emotions she always felt after talking to Reed. Today he'd made her feel especially homesick by describing little details of the farmhouse she'd left behind. But she was happy that he had been inside her home and sensed that the visits were his way of maintaining a connection between them. Was it enough of a connection? She couldn't say. The one she dreamed of involved a forever life of six people bound together through the hardships, challenges and joys of living together. But if he did not want to assume the role of father to her two children, she knew she would have to sacrifice her own desires for the needs of her daughters.

And so she waited out the long hours and even longer days until Grace Evelyn would enter the world, filling her mother's heart with love and gratitude and liberating her from the exile to which she'd been confined. What would Camryn do then? That was the question that consumed her thoughts and often filled her with dread, because it seemed the peace and tranquility of the life she'd known in Bufflehead Creek would only be a fading memory.

"Are you busy?" Brooke poked her head into Camryn's room a few minutes after Cam had disconnected with Reed.

"Not now," Camryn said. "And as you well know, hardly ever."

"It won't be long now," Brooke said, staring at her sister's cumbersome belly. "My goodness Camryn, you're as big as a house."

"Still three weeks until my due date," Cam said. "Though I wouldn't be surprised if this little girl came early. I've been feeling twinges…"

"I have something to tell you if you won't get upset."

"No, I won't get upset," she said. She could well imagine that everyone in her family was tired of waiting out this birth and coddling to Camryn's needs. Though not one of her family was as tired of the ordeal as Camryn herself was.

"Why would I get upset?" Camryn said. "Unless this is more about our phantom brother and his never-to-be-discovered whereabouts."

Brooke gave her a sheepish look and settled on a comfy rocker their mother had purchased just last week, another gift to ensure that Camryn would stay in Charleston. "Well, it is about Edward."

"Oh, Brooke, you've got to stop this search. Besides the money you've spent trying to track down this man, you've missed days of work, and…"

"My job is fine," Brooke insisted. "And the last I heard, the money I make is mine to spend however I want."

"Of course it is," Camryn said, "but honey, the likelihood is that you'll never find Edward and you'll spend the rest of your life wondering what happened to him."

"Well, we have eliminated some places he isn't. Prison, for one," Brooke said defiantly.

"You're sure of that?"

"Yes. I've done a background check of every Edward imprisoned in the state of South Carolina over the past thirty years. None of their backgrounds match the details, as scant as they are, of our brother."

"Okay, so he hasn't been in prison in South Carolina. That only leaves prisons in forty-nine more states to investigate."

Brooke scowled, prompting Camryn to think she'd gone too far. For some reason, one that Camryn couldn't understand even after hearing her sister provide the motivation for this search, finding this long-lost brother had become the central objective of her sister's life.

"Can't you be on my side for once?" Brooke challenged. "Or at least pretend to understand?" She leaned forward in the chair, commanding Camryn's attention. "He's out there, and he's our flesh and blood. Doesn't that mean anything to you or are you so wrapped up in your own problems and your own little family that you don't even see that I need a family, too?"

Her words were like a bolt of reality, and Camryn suddenly understood why her sister was so obsessed with this quest. Brooke, the career woman, the serial dater, the one who seemed to have it all, didn't have what Camryn was fighting so hard to protect. But Brooke had never professed an interest in having children, or, for that matter, getting married and settling down.

Camryn got out of bed and padded over to her sister. The twinge she'd been experiencing suddenly became a slicing pain. She held her stomach with one hand and reached for her sister with the other. Probably another false alarm, she told herself. "Brooke, you have a family," she said. "You have Mom and Dad, me and Esther, and soon, Grace. We all love you."

A single tear fell down Brooke's cheek, and she swiped at it as if it burned her skin. Crying was so unlike her. "I know that," she said. "And I love you, but if there is more for me out there somewhere, I need to know it. I need my connection to something bigger, because as wonderful as Mom and Dad are, they are not our connection to the past. I'm tired of being the girl who has always had to fabricate a family history just to feel like I belong."

Camryn rested her hand on Brooke's shoulder. "I'm so sorry, honey. You go ahead and do what you have to do. I won't criticize you again."

"Really?"

"Really." She smiled. "At least, I'll try not to. Now what did you want to tell me about Edward when you came in…"

She couldn't get the last word out. A crippling pain started at the top of her abdomen and spread downward, taking her breath. She clutched her belly.

Brooke jumped upfrom the rocker and

walked Camryn back to the bed. "Cammie, what's wrong?"

"Get my suitcase out of the closet," Camryn said. "It's all packed."

Brooke rushed to do as Cam asked.

"How fast will that fancy car of yours go?" Camryn asked as she struggled to the door.

"Pretty darn fast," Brooke assured her. "Are we about to have a baby?"

"I hope not for at least fifteen minutes," Cam said. "It takes that long to get to the hospital."

AFTER HAVING THE usual shower and snack-time arguments with his sons, Reed finally got the boys to bed. Tomorrow was Friday, and he'd promised them a movie in town and all the popcorn they could eat. He'd just settled on his sofa when his cell phone rang.

"Who could that be at this hour?" he said to the wiry bundle of fur curled up in front of his fireplace. "Hope we don't have to go down to the clinic to see a sick friend of yours, Rooster."

The dog whined at hearing his name, and Reed sat up straight when he saw the name on his caller ID.

"Camryn? Is this you?"

"Hi, Reed. It's me, Esther."

"Sweetie, what are you doing up so late? Is something wrong?" He'd risen from the sofa and already starting planning the essentials he would throw in his suitcase if he needed to leave the house immediately.

"I'm up late because I don't have to go to school tomorrow."

"Are you sick, Essie?"

"No. I just called to tell you that Mommy had our baby. Mommy said I could call you."

Relief made Reed weak in his knees, and he sat back down on the couch. "Of course you can, Es. That's wonderful news. Is everyone okay?"

"Yep. I saw Mommy a few minutes ago, and she was holding my new sister."

"How does the baby look to you, Esther?"

"Pink and wrinkly. But Mommy and Grandma say that's normal. Her skin will stretch out soon. And she's really little. That's because she was born three weeks early. Mommy said she was anxious to meet me."

"I'm sure she was. And how does your Mommy feel?"

"Okay, I guess. She keeps smiling at baby

Grace and kissing me more than usual. The doctor said she can go home tomorrow. That's why I don't have to go to school. I get to help out at Grandma's house."

Going home tomorrow. That was good news. Apparently the early birth didn't come with too many complications. "Esther, tell your mother that I will call her in the morning. Will you do that, please?"

"Sure. And will you tell Rooster that we had the baby?"

Reed glanced over at the dog who was scratching at his midsection, unmindful of the change to his family situation. "You bet I will, sweetie. Rooster is going to be one happy dog."

"Okay, thanks. You can tell Justin and Phillip, too."

"I will. Hope to see you soon, Esther."

"Me, too. I have to hang up now."

"Okay. Thanks for calling."

Reed maintained the connection long after he knew Esther had hung up. The phone felt warm to his palm, a reflection of the heat slowly building in his chest. Yes, Rooster would be a happy dog. But Reed was way ahead of him. Mother and baby were doing fine. He grinned, feeling giddy and silly. *What's going on with you, Bolden? You'd think it was your baby cuddled up next to Camryn in Charleston.*

It wasn't, of course. Grace had a father. He was probably in the hospital room with Camryn right now. So why did Reed feel like running around all of Bufflehead Creek handing out cigars?

AT BREAKFAST THE next morning Reed told the boys about Esther's new little sister.

"That's cool," Justin said. "When do we get to see the baby?"

Phillip poured milk on his cereal. "Don't be stupid, Justin," he said. "It's just a baby. We'll see it when they come back."

Reed had avoided telling his sons that Camryn's plans might mean that she and Esther would never come back. Maybe he hadn't told them because he hoped the possibility of her staying in Charleston wasn't an option. Maybe he wasn't ready to accept that Camryn was going to make a life without the Bolden men in it. But now it was time.

"Here's the thing, boys," he began. "Camryn and Esther may not be coming back to Bufflehead Creek."

His spoon poised halfway to his mouth, Justin gaped at him. "What are you talking about? I thought they were just going until the baby was born. Well, now the baby is born."

"Yeah, and we did all that work on the chicken coop," Phillip said. "You mean they won't even see what we did?"

"They have to come back," Justin chimed in. "We have their dog!"

As if he understood every word, Rooster stood up from the rug by the kitchen sink, wandered over to Justin and put his head on the boy's knee.

"All of these are important matters," Reed said. "That's why we're not going to the movies tonight."

"What?" Phillip's voice raised an octave. "Why not? You promised."

"I know I said we would," Reed agreed, "but something more important has come up. Now I think I want us to go to Charleston."

"All of us?" Justin asked.

"Sure. You, Phillip, me and Rooster."

"Just to see a baby?" Phillip said.

"Not just to see a baby," Reed explained. "We haven't seen Camryn or Esther in over two months. I don't know about you guys, but I kind of miss those girls."

"Me, too, Dad," Justin said. "I'd like to go to Charleston. Why don't we make it a surprise? I'll bet ol' Esther won't be able to think of a thing to say."

Reed stared at his older son. "Phillip, what do you say? You can go with us or you can stay with Grandma."

"That's my choice? Go see a baby or stay with Grandma?"

Reed shrugged. "Yep."

"Okay, I'll go. But I'm not changing any diapers."

Reed laughed and ruffled Phillip's hair. "Fair enough. We'll leave as soon as the bus drops you guys off. We'll be in Charleston before it gets dark. I'll make a hotel reservation for us after you leave for school."

He made a mental list. And get someone out here to watch the clinic and feed the animals. Thank goodness his barn was finished, so whoever he hired to watch the place wouldn't have to run to the next property to care for the horses. He'd have to carefully label all the animals' medications and treatment plans. Another plus…his rehab center wasn't too crowded at the moment. He'd wait a few hours and then call the hospital to make certain Camryn and Grace had been discharged. And he'd look up the address for Mr. and Mrs. Craig Montgomery.

Reed hurried about his chores. He experienced almost the same excitement he'd felt when he was a kid and his parents were taking the family on a special vacation. Like then, he was hopeful, unable to focus on everything he had to accomplish in a few hours.

As the day wore on, doubts began to filter into the positive energy in his brain. Would Camryn be happy to see him? After their phone calls, he believed she would be. Would Mark be around? No question—a baby changed everything. Would Mark pressure Camryn to get back together? Would Mark wonder what this man and his two sons were doing at the Montgomerys'?

Did Reed actually know what he was doing there? He knew for sure that he missed Camryn with an ache that wouldn't go away, and he needed desperately to tell her that. He was hopelessly in love with Camryn— with his memories of her, his thoughts of a future with her, his romantic dreams of a life with her. Yes, Reed knew why he was going to Charleston, and it was to try to win Camryn back.

He longed to have her back in his life if she would have him. Even more, he wanted her to *be* his life, with her two kids, dozens of chickens and overprotective nature. Reed didn't want to add any stress to Cam's situation, but he had to tell her how sorry he was for his reaction when she told him she was pregnant. He had to make it up to her. He had to convince her that four children between them didn't scare him nearly as much as being without her did.

So Reed pushed aside any lingering negative thoughts, made his plans and packed some clothes and video games for his kids. Hopefully, in a few hours Camryn would be making plans to leave Charleston.

CHAPTER TWENTY-ONE

By seven o'clock Friday night Camryn was sitting in her four-poster bed in a room with lavender-flowered wallpaper surrounding her and looking down at the baby sleeping in her arms. This room was so comforting and reminiscent of happy days from Camryn's childhood, but still something was missing, something even this new little angel couldn't fill.

Her mother opened the door and stepped into the room. "There's someone here to see you, dear. I told him that you weren't really up for visitors, and since I didn't know him…"

Him? Camryn's heart tightened in her chest. "Who is it, Mama?"

"He says his name is Reed Something-or-other. And he has two boys with him, both of whom immediately ran into the backyard with Esther, and that large, ungainly dog you brought at Christmas, who for the moment is in the backyard also."

Camryn's arms trembled so violently she thought she would wake the baby, but thank goodness Grace slept right through the excitement coursing through Cam's body. She squinted her eyes and imagined Reed in her mother's formal living room. She dared not open her eyes for fear her mother would see her tears.

"I'd like to see him, Mama," she said. "Please send him up."

"We don't know him, Cammie. Your father and I can't just send a stranger up the stairs to your room."

Bless her mother's heart. She said the word "stranger" with that combination of Southern charm and serious caution. "It's okay, Mama. I've told you about Reed. He's my neighbor from Bufflehead Creek and my very good friend. Esther called him yesterday to tell him about Grace being born."

Linda Montgomery nodded. "Oh, yes, you did mention this man. Well, all right, then. I'll allow him to visit for a few minutes. But Camryn, if the children bring that dog inside the house, I'll have to insist they put him in the garage. He doesn't appear too tidy."

Camryn opened her eyes and wiped the

moisture from her lashes. "The dog is Esther's pet, Mama. He's part of our family, but I'll tell Esther to clean him up a bit."

Linda shook her head and turned toward the door. "Well, okay, I'll send Reed up. Do you need a few minutes to ready yourself?"

Camryn grinned. Another Southern characteristic. A woman always needed a few minutes to "ready herself" for a caller. "I look okay, don't I, Mama?"

"Truly, Cammie, you look beautiful," her mother said.

If Linda only knew. This particular gentleman had seen her daughter in all states of grime, including wearing clothes covered with chicken poop. At least today she'd had a shower, and she and Grace were appropriately dressed in new night clothes.

Linda left the room, and Camryn counted the seconds until she heard heavy footsteps on the solid walnut staircase. The sounds of the steps ended as Reed walked across her mother's heavily carpeted hallway. He walked into her room, smiled, and said, "Nice place you've got here."

Camryn figured he'd been uncomfortable around her family's nineteenth-century antiques. Even the house, a classic example of pre–Civil War architecture, was enough to take any person's breath away.

"The Battery is only two blocks away," he added, impressed by the home's storied address.

Camryn smiled. "My parents bought the place forty years ago, when the house still looked like the Yankees had marched right through the middle of it. But my mother had a vision for the place, and the price was right, before people went a little nuts to acquire Charleston property. They've put a lot of work into it."

He walked over to her bed. "It lacks some of the contemporary appeal of my early-twenty-first-century two-bedroom modular, but it will do in a pinch."

He leaned over the side of the bed. "So this is Grace. Well done, Mommy. She's a beauty, and looks just like you."

"Thank you."

"I'd ask to hold her, but I'm scared out of my wits. If she were a newborn foal or a calf, I wouldn't have any qualms at all, but she's so…human, in a tiny, delicate sort of way."

Camryn explained that the baby was healthy though only a few ounces over six pounds.

"I don't even remember when my sons were that little. But I guess I wasn't around all that often."

"You missed a precious time, then," Camryn said. The look of regret she saw in his eyes told her that he agreed.

"So how are you doing?" he asked. "You look, well, beautiful and happy. Maybe a little tired. Did the birth go off without a hitch?"

"Mostly. I started labor in this room, my sister rushed me to the hospital and, five hours later, I met Grace. She was more than two weeks early. I have a hunch she's going to be just like Brooke, never content to wait her turn."

As if she'd heard her name, Brooke burst into the room. Apparently not taking into account that her sister had company, she blurted out, "So, did your creep of an ex show up to see his daughter yet?"

She stopped suddenly, stared at Reed and mumbled an apology.

"No, he didn't," Camryn said. "He's stopping by on Sunday."

"Isn't that nice? Hopefully before Gracie is in toddler clothes."

"Brooke..."

"Sorry. Mama always says we shouldn't show our family's underbelly to guests." She grinned at Reed. "Guess I don't consider you a guest, Doc."

"How are you, Brooke?"

"I'm fine now. But you're lucky you didn't see me yesterday when I was driving Cammie to the hospital and her contractions were already five minutes apart. I thought I was going to be delivering a baby."

"I'm sure you would have done great," Reed said.

"Why are you here, Doc? Curious to get a peek at the second most beautiful baby ever born?"

"Something like that," he said, giving Cam a warm smile.

Brooke smiled at her sister. "Did I interrupt anything?"

"No. I'm just basking in Reed's compliments about Grace."

"Did you know that galumpy dog of yours is running around outside?" Brooke asked. "Mama's watching the back door like a hawk. She wants to divert Rooster into the garage before the kids invite him in for cookies and ice cream."

Camryn gave Reed a questioning stare. "Is he really okay, Reed? We've been so worried about Rooster."

"He's fine, but he does need a good grooming. I haven't been able to spruce him up since he had so many stitches. But a bath is in his near future."

"I think I'll go down and let Rooster know I'm on his side," Brooke said. "You guys need anything, just let me know."

Brooke left the room, and Reed pulled a chair up close to Camryn's bed. "Are you still on bed rest?" he asked.

"No. I can do almost anything now, but Mama remembers the way birthing was in her time, and the mother always took advantage of her 'ordeal' as Mama calls it and took to bed for at least a couple of days. Maybe now that you're here, she'll let me rejoin society."

"Is that what you want, Cam? To rejoin Charleston society?"

"Heavens, no, Reed. I'm sure Charleston society has totally forgotten about me.

I wasn't very successful at playing my role when I was married to a corporate ladder climber."

Reed took her hand and held it in both of his. "I can guarantee you that you haven't been forgotten in Bufflehead Creek," he said. "I've delivered a few dozens of your eggs to the diners in town, and all I hear for my efforts is, 'When is Camryn coming back?'"

"It's nice to be missed."

He held her hand against his cheek. "Oh, you are, more than you know."

"But apparently not by Grace's father. I guess you heard that he hasn't even stopped to see his new daughter."

"I'm so sorry, Cam. I wasn't the world's greatest dad, but that is unforgivable."

"It's okay. In a way I'm glad Mark hasn't shown up. He's only seen Essie four times since we've been here, and truthfully she doesn't seem to miss him."

"Hey, Dad!" The call came from the hall-way.

"What is it, Justin?"

"Can we bring the pictures in now?"

"Sure. Bring them in."

"What pictures are you talking about?"

Reed placed Camryn's hand back on the bed. "You'll see soon enough."

The boys and Esther came into the room. Phillip and Justin took a few tentative steps toward the baby and then held back. "So that's her," Phillip said.

"Say hello to Grace, boys," Camryn said. "And come closer so I can give you a hug."

They accepted Camryn's hug and mumbled greetings to the baby, which Grace slept blissfully through.

Justin thrust some papers into his father's hand. "Here, Dad. Show her how cool it looks."

"What looks cool?" Camryn asked.

She took the papers and gasped in surprise. "This is my chicken coop!"

Justin grinned. "Yep. All fixed up. Except some photos are of the coop before we started our work. We wanted you to see the difference."

"Isn't it cool?" Esther said. "Justin and Phillip did practically all the work themselves."

Camryn gave Reed a knowing glance as she flipped through the pages. "Oh, my gosh. It's beautiful. Are you telling me that you guys did all this?"

"We did," Phillip said. "Took us a bunch of weekends, too!"

For the second time in just a few minutes, tears filled Camryn's eyes. "You know what? I love you guys."

Reed stood. "Okay, kiddos, that's your cue to leave. Go play with Rooster in the garage."

The boys started to leave, but Justin stopped and turned back to Camryn. "We like Rooster. We don't want to give him up."

Esther's mouth dropped open. "Justin, you can't have my dog!"

"Not now, Justin," Reed said. "We'll talk about this later. Rooster is not your dog, remember? Not yet anyway."

"But you said, 'not yet.' What does that mean?"

"Go on, all of you. I've got to talk to Camryn."

When they were alone, Camryn stared up at Reed. "Yeah, what did you mean by that?"

"We've become awfully fond of that dog," Reed said.

She smiled. "He is a great dog, but Esther and I are very fond of him, too."

"That's kind of a problem, Camryn."

Camryn held the pictures up for Grace to see. "This is our chicken coop, sweetie," she said. "And Rooster is our dog. You'll have to meet him later." She finished the statement with a coy look at Reed.

"Don't you think we could share Rooster?" he asked.

"That sounds plausible, but I don't even know yet where Rooster will be living."

Reed grinned. "Oh, I've got that all figured out already."

"You do?"

"He's going to live in a little farmhouse on Cottontail Farm."

"But Reed, I don't know…"

"I do," Reed said. "I wish you'd come back to Bufflehead Creek, Camryn. You and Rooster and Esther and Grace." He leaned closer to her on the bed and gently touched Grace's face. "I've had more than two months to experience life without you, and I've decided I don't like it. I miss our coffees together in the mornings. I miss sharing chores and checking up on what the other is doing. I miss talking about our kids and deciding who's doing what right."

Suddenly Camryn had the craziest notion that what Reed was describing was what she'd dreamed about. Her heart started playing a crazy rhythm. She smiled. "You want me to move back to the farm so you can have coffee and share a dog?"

"That's oversimplifying the situation, Cam. I want you to move back to *me*. And here's where it gets complicated."

She held her breath, imagining what he would say next.

"We each have a house, but neither one is big enough for all six of us. So I figure we've got to maintain both households for a while until we can start building something more permanent on our property. If we don't do that, maybe we can put the kids in one house and you and I in the other. They can call if they need us."

She stared at him a long moment. The light in his eyes gave him away. "Oh, that would be great," she said.

"Right. Like you would live like that for even two minutes. But here's the thing, Cam. I want it all. You, at least four kids, one shaggy dog, a bunch of chickens and every sick turtle and bird with a wounded wing in the low country. And I don't think I can settle for anything less."

Camryn decided that caution was the last feeling she should follow at this moment. He had presented her with a dare, and she was more than willing to accept it. "Reed Bolden, is this a marriage proposal?"

"I guess it is. Give me that baby, would you?"

"I thought you were afraid to hold her."

"I just proposed to you, Cam. What could be more frightening than that?"

He took Grace and gently laid her beside her mother. "Now if it's okay with you, I'd like to give you a two-month-overdue kiss to seal the deal, or at least persuade you to think about it."

"I'm already thinking about it."

He leaned over her, cradled her face in his two hands and kissed her. Gently, then more ungently, then with a passion that seemed to guarantee their future together. When he drew back, Camryn struggled to catch her breath. All of Reed's kisses had been wonderful, but this one, the one that held such promise, she felt all the way to her curled toes.

"When can we go home?" she asked.

"As soon as you're ready, sweetheart. But first I've got to hold that baby until she feels almost as comfortable with me as she does with you. If I'm going to be any manner of daddy to little Grace, then we've got to get to know each other inside out."

He picked up the baby, cradled her in his arms. She squirmed, opened her eyes and gave him a face. "I think she's got gas," he said.

"No, that's a smile," Camryn said. "She's already very advanced for her age, and like her auntie Brooke, she appreciates a handsome man. And she definitely knows a good deal when she hears one."

* * * * *

Don't miss Brooke's story!
It's coming next!
And for other great Heartwarming
romances by Cynthia Thomason,
visit www.Harlequin today!

Get 4 FREE REWARDS!

We'll send you 2 FREE Books
plus 2 FREE Mystery Gifts.

Love Inspired® Suspense books feature Christian characters facing challenges to their faith... and lives.

FREE
Value Over
$20

BETTY NEELS COLLECTION!

Buy 3 and get
1 FREE!

Experience one of the most celebrated and beloved authors in romance! Betty Neels will delight you with her signature brand of storytelling: happy romances, memorable couples and timeless tales of lasting love. These classics have been combined in 2-in-1 books for your reading pleasure!

YES! Please send me the **Betty Neels Collection**. This collection begins with 4 books, 1 of which is FREE! Plus a FREE gift – an elegant simulated Pearl Necklace & Earring Set (approx. retail value of $13.99). I may either return the shipment and owe nothing or keep for the low members-only discount price of $17.97 U.S./$20.25 CDN plus $1.99 U.S./$2.99 CDN for shipping and handling per shipment.* If I decide to continue, I'll receive two more shipments, each about a month apart, each containing four more two-in-one books, one of which will be free, until I own the entire 12-book collection. Each shipment is mine to keep for the same members-only discount price plus shipping and handling. I understand that no purchase is required. I may keep the free book no matter what I decide.

☐ 275 HCN 4623   ☐ 475 HCN 4623

Name (please print)

Address   Apt. #

City   State/Province   Zip/Postal Code

Mail to the **Reader Service**:
IN U.S.A.: P.O. Box 1341, Buffalo, NY. 14240-8531
IN CANADA: P.O. Box 603, Fort Erie, Ontario L2A 5X3

Get 4 FREE REWARDS!

We'll send you 2 FREE Books plus 2 FREE Mystery Gifts.

FREE Value Over **$20**

Both the **Romance** and **Suspense** collections feature compelling novels written by many of today's best-selling authors.